Maude headed for the front door. "I'm sort of looking forward to operating a travel agency, you know? Though I don't quite understand how we're going to get customers if we don't advertise."

Pete Swain stood on the front porch, accompanied by a dark-eyed young woman and four children. They all looked uncomfortable in their traveling clothes, and each had a suitcase.

"We want to visit Loretta's aunt Fran in Louisville," Pete said. "She died six years ago, so it'll have to be before that. How much for the round trip?"

THE WHISPERS

Book One
of
The Gates of Time

Dan Parkinson

A Del Rey® Book
THE BALLANTINE PUBLISHING GROUP • NEW YORK

A Del Rey® Book
Published by The Ballantine Publishing Group

This book is a creation of Siegel & Siegel Ltd.

http://www.randomhouse.com

Library of Congress Catalog Card Number: 97-94628

ISBN 0-345-41380-6

Manufactured in the United States of America

First Edition: April 1998

10 9 8 7 6 5 4 3 2 1

Cherish today the memories
of yesterday, and make today
the memories of tomorrow.
Memories are the harvest of both past and future.

This book is for Wilma Jean.

∞

Whether time travel is possible is not the question. We know that velocity alters duration. The technology to manipulate time is within our reach, and has been for decades. Unfortunately, it is neither economically practical nor politically expedient to pursue the research that might produce discoveries in this field.

—M.A. DRURY, *Discoverance*

∞

∞

If it happens, it can.
—Murphy's Corollary

∞

Author's Note

Most of what we think we know is rationalization of preconceived notions. We favor accepted truths over actual truth. We wrap ourselves in perfected fabrics of fact and view with suspicion those erratic intuitions that do not match the weave.

Bound by our time, we accept the bonds of common knowledge. We smother our insights, shun inspiration, and clip the wings of ideas. Given wild, free minds, we tie hobbles upon them. We break them if we can, put them in harness, force them to the beaten path, and replace reason with limitation. We make them mundane. The thoughts we admit are ordered thoughts, confined to predetermined purpose. Inexorably, systematically, we create our "selves" in our own stubborn image.

We ignore what we cannot verify and defend our positions with elaborate logic based on the smug certainty that where we think we started was truly where we were. Thus each premise, right or wrong, rests securely upon the sturdy footing of the mistake that preceded it.

That which conforms to our illusions we fortify with formidable structures of proof, while what fails to fit we reshape until it does. With all the resources at our command, we deceive ourselves, avoiding the ultimate test of each of those "basic" truths we so revere: Is it actual, or only what is accepted? We prefer the fine cloak of common knowledge to the uncharming rags of wisdom.

Faced with the unknown, we look away. It is not there, we

tell ourselves. There is no unknown, because there is nothing more to know. We find comfort in a universe of things, knowing that each thing in its time and place has three reliable dimensions—no more, no less—and therefore will always fit nicely within our accepted disciplines.

But consider: In a universe perceived as two dimensions, there would be no up and no down. A third dimension would be inconceivable because it would occur outside the directions of the compass. To perceive it would require a complete reassessment of universal perceptions.

Paradigms would fall.

Such might be the ultimate test of common knowledge and of each truth within it—is it actual, or only perceived?

For example, did yesterday really come before today, or have we misinterpreted the phenomenon of hindsight?

We make light of such questions because we fear them. We have reason to fear them. To freely question the nature of the universe is to meet oneself face-to-face.

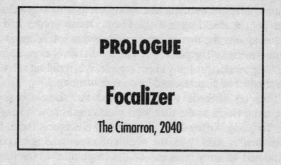

PROLOGUE

Focalizer

The Cimarron, 2040

The siege was nearing its end. Even the boy watching from the willow copse could see that. The latest barrage had lasted through the day, round after shattering round thudding into the limestone shelves and blasted slopes of the Revivalist stronghold. Each impact blossomed in a flowing ball of bright fire and sent gouts of sundered stone aloft to rain as debris on the darkened earth below.

It was methodical demolition. It was a slaughter. The Revivalists were dug in, deeply entrenched in the caprock and stocked with provisions. But they had no weapons capable of reaching their tormentors. For the batteries of the Royal Artillery, spread along the flats beyond the river, it was target practice.

It was a land engagement, of course, and strictly conventional. Few viable authorities had survived the Paper Revolts of three decades before, but one that remained was the Edict of Enroachment. It was the final vestige of international order, but behind its skeletal facade was the combined power of all the once-mighty military regimes of the western hemisphere. Worldwide economic chaos had led to worldwide social ruin. The mission of the Protectorate Authority for Common Trust was to fend off the final plunge into barbarism—to hold the line for civilization until things worked themselves out, somehow.

Built on the ruins of NATO and empowered by the Edict of

Encroachment, PACT straddled two oceans with a structure as tenuous as spiderweb. But like the spider, its sting was lethal. It was both a shield against the fanatic Asian hordes and an arbiter among the myriad small regimes that had arisen in the Euro-American Theater. PACT did not dictate or even address the internal affairs of any client regime. But it did set rules for the conduct of disputes, and its decrees were final.

Thus no airborne weapons ranged the skies above the Cimarron Basin as the man who proclaimed himself King of the Tri-State, Arthur Rex, disciplined his subjects there. But none were needed. With the wealth of a heartland at his command and an army built around the capabilities of the Royce AATV, King Arthur had all the weapons he needed.

The Revivalist rebellion had been a brief, hot spark. Now it was being snuffed.

Squadrons of sleek, steel cavalry waited, in driving ranks flanking the artillery batteries, as the shape of Long Mesa was methodically altered by barrages. The AATVs waited like panthers, ready to sweep across the river and complete the job when the artillery had finished its demolition. With each thunderous volley, the stone cap of the mesa seemed to erupt in flying debris, and new clouds of whitish dust drifted on the wind, flowing up the valley.

The boy's hiding place was downriver, a spread of willows and wild plum thickets at the very edge of the river. Shallow waters snaked along a dry sand bed just beyond, pooling here and there. Crouched in the thicket, the boy had watched through the afternoon as the king's forces pounded away at the crumbling mesa rim. While the sun was high, he had seen the AATVs scurrying around the base of the mesa. Like great, sleek animals of steel and fire, the roving vehicles had toyed with retreating Revivalists, concentrating them for the kill. By the time the artillery was assembled on the flats, the AATVs were alone in the field. All the surviving Revivalists had retreated into their burrows and bunkers under the cap of Long Mesa.

The laser-aimed guns of the artillery were deadly. Four times the boy had seen great slabs of the flat-topped hill break loose and slide downward, converging at the bottom in huge clouds of dust and debris. The gray-white clouds tumbled, rolled in the wind, and surged away like giant fogs, drifting up the valley. And as each cleared, restoring visibility, the lasers danced and the guns of the Royal Artillery spoke again. Again and again.

After the third strike there had been a brief lull when figures moved atop the shattered mesa. A standard was raised, white fabric fluttering at its peak. The boy knew what that meant. The Revivalists wanted to surrender.

He squinted, shading his eyes. The mesa top was a long way off, and the people up there were tiny creatures at this distance. There were seven or eight of them in sight, or maybe more. He couldn't be sure. But one among them caught and held his attention. A dark-haired man, the one who had raised the staff. The boy rubbed his eyes, trying to see better. The man was ragged and thin, with darkness on his cheeks where unshaven whiskers grew. His hair was unkempt, blowing in the breeze like the tatters of clothing he wore. He looked terribly alone up there, as if apart from those around him. And yet, somehow, he looked strong—strong and determined.

The boy squinted, trying to see him better. Then suddenly he was gone. A flicker of motion, as if the very air around him had somehow shifted, and he was gone. Around the white-flagged staff, others gazed around in wonder . . . and again the guns of the Royal Artillery roared.

The lull had been only momentary. From the artillery flats seeking lasers homed on the tiny figures above, and the guns thundered. Projectiles screamed overhead, and the cap of the mesa erupted again in gouts of smoke and fire.

When the dust and smoke rolled away there was no flag up on the hill, nor any movement there. The boy hid his face in his hands, muffling his sobs. He was frightened and hungry, lost and confused and terrified. He was ten years old.

Long minutes crept by as the guns continued to speak.

Now the west rim cast a long shadow across the flats, reaching toward the artillery field. The bombarded mesa across the river bled stark in red sundown. The shelling had become sporadic. The gunners were tired. Evening was coming on and it was a long forty miles from these wild Cimarron breaks to their comfortable barracks in Camelot. For a long time now there had been no sign of life on the mesa.

As the evening sun rode the horizon, the barrage ended. The last thunders rolled away, their echoes trailing up the valley, and in the silence the boy heard powerful engines purring to life. The lines of AATVs began to move. Easily, lazily they crept to the bluff above the riverbed, plunged down it in little clouds of dust, then crawled across the sand, three squadrons in formation. The nearest machine splashed across a surface runnel not more than fifty yards from where the boy lay hidden.

Red sundown gleaming on their cowls, the king's machines nosed up the river's east bluff, climbing like huge, dark beetles, and found their footing on level ground. The purr of massed engines became a whine and then a howl. The beetles grew legs and became racers, streaming away, converging in a half moon toward the base of the ruined mesa.

Horrified and fascinated, the boy watched. These were the King's Cavalry, the royal hounds gathering to the kill.

The sun was huge as it sank below the western rim. The crushed, blasted mesa stood silent in creeping shadows as the AATVs assembled below it, tipping and clambering among the rubble at its base. Up at the caprock, great holes had been gouged out and nothing moved except the wind of evening.

The central squadron began its climb, turreted noses sniffing toward the demolished stronghold. Then the watching boy gasped and raised his head higher. Sharp young eyes had seen movement up there—furtive, ghostlike movement, gray on gray in the shadows of the shelf.

The AATVs were halfway up the mesa's shoulder when things—squat, round shapes—began appearing on a ledge below the caprock shelf, forming a line at the very edge. There was a twinkle, as of a torch being ignited. Then brief flickers appeared all along the line.

One of the round things plunged over the edge, careening downward toward the advancing engines. Then another, and another. For a moment the tableau on the mesa's face seemed frozen—the AATVs advancing, noses high and arrogant, as a ragged line of rolling objects hurtled toward them. One of the objects struck an AATV and bright flame billowed, engulfing the vehicle. Then the one next to it was hit, and the fifth in line, and the third. All along the advancing front, AATVs exploded into brilliant flame. Soaring balls of fire climbed above them in the evening dusk.

Some of the objects missed the crawlers, rolling past them to shatter and flame in the rubble below, among and around the waiting ranks of the reserve squadrons. And now, as the seconds elapsed, the wafting breeze brought the roar of explosions and the shrieks of men—men in the AATVs, screaming as they died.

George Wilson's Revivalists had kept a secret in reserve—one last weapon to hurl at King Arthur's forces.

Stunned silence hung across the valley for long moments. Several of the AATVs on the hill, some of them trailing fire from their shells, were turning to flee. But then the Arthurians responded. Guns thumped and roared on the flats, and fury erupted on the mesa. Round after massive round smashed home, as scarlet lasers traced the erupting air. A giant sliver of limestone caprock tilted outward and smashed down, shearing away the ledge below. A fleeing AATV bounced skyward atop a gout of smoke and debris. Another flipped aside and fell dead on its back. Two more took direct hits as gunners across the river fired ahead of their laser traces.

Then a projectile entered the little cave below the sheared caprock, and the entire mesa shook and danced as internal explosions sundered it.

The boy clamped his hands over his ringing ears, but still the thunder went on as the fury of King Arthur's artillery unfolded anew. They would not stop this time. They would not quit until the entire mesa was blasted rubble.

Somehow, it had grown dark. The boy had lost all track of time. As if in a trance, he watched the horror unfold across the river. He almost didn't hear the scuffling sounds behind him, but suddenly he became aware that he was not alone. Someone else had entered the thicket. He heard branches parting, sobs of labored breath, and suddenly someone plunged through the punishing vines and fell, almost upon him. His startled eyes looked into the pleading, tear-streaked eyes of a smudged and bleeding face.

It was a woman—a ragged, tattered woman weak from exhaustion. She tried to move away, then just lay there on the sand, staring at him in the gloom. Dark blood seeped from a cut above her ear, matting the moon-pale hair on that side. But it wasn't her head she touched with a fluttering hand. It was her belly.

On impulse the boy drew a scrap of cloth from the pouch at his belt and laid it across the woman's injured head. She put her hand over it, pressing it in place, then raised herself on her free elbow.

She stared at him. "Why, you're only a child," she said. "What are you doing here?"

He didn't know how to answer her. He wasn't sure what he was doing here. "Watching," he said finally.

She glanced aside, toward the artillery out on the flats. "You . . . you aren't with them?"

"No," he said. "I've been hiding from them."

The roar of bombardment continued in the distance, but under it now came another sound, much closer—the low purring of powerful engines.

"Scouts," the woman breathed. "They'll comb the area. They don't intend to leave anyone."

"Why?" the boy asked. "Why are they fighting?"

She tilted her head. "How could you not know? Where are you from?"

"Someti—somewhere else," he said.

She lowered her eyes. She was very tired. "There is a man," she said, "a man who says he is king. But he must be stopped. Because of what he has done . . . and what he will do if someone doesn't stop him."

"What will he do?"

She hesitated, then looked up at him again. "He might live forever. He intends to try."

The boy thought about it and shrugged slightly. "You are a Revivalist," he said.

She was startled. "Then you do know. You know about Revivalists."

"I know they lost," he said.

"They . . . lost?"

"I heard that. At another time."

She seemed to sag, as in defeat. The whine of searching AATVs was closer now. By rising moonlight the boy could see long, dark shapes moving down the valley, coming toward them. Beams of bright light swept here and there.

"We have lost," the woman whispered. "Georgie . . . my Georgie . . . he said it was futile. But still he tried . . . as long as there was hope. He knew what Arthur would do. He knew better than anyone."

"Where is he?"

"He was up there," she whispered. "He tried to raise the white flag, to save the last of them."

The machine noises were closer. Abruptly the woman sat upright and pulled a leather pouch from beneath her torn blouse. Opening it, she lifted out a small, shiny cone of some lustrous material. She held it out, and the boy took it. It was surprisingly heavy. "Do you know what this is?" she asked.

A hesitant recognition lit the boy's eyes, but only for a moment. The thing was familiar somehow, but when he tried to remember, the memories evaporated. "No," he said.

"Georgie called it a focalizer," she said. "There are only two of these. Arthur has the other."

He started to hand the thing back, but she refused it. "You've hidden from them," she said. "Maybe you can hide again. Don't let them have that. If you can't keep it, then bury it. Just don't let them get it."

A beam of light sliced through the willows overhead. She put a trembling hand on the boy's shoulder. "I trust you," she said. Again her free hand went to her belly, tenderly. But it was only a reflex, and only for a moment. With fierce determination she focused on the boy. "Now, stay down."

Before he could react she leapt to her feet, dodged through

the willows, and was gone, out across the open riverbed. Almost on top of the boy a searching AATV hesitated, kicked up sand, and swerved, going after her. Bright light shot out, searching.

For a moment, an eerie silence descended upon the land, as if everything had slowed abruptly, then stopped. Oddly, it was like the sound of a Royal Artillery shell, screaming overhead— a screaming, rising whine as it approached, then an instant's suspension before the pitch lowered and the shell passed, going away. This was no sound, though. Only a perception. But it seemed as if everything—everything around—had shrilled, slowed, and paused for a heartbeat. Then the world was as it had been. Lights flashed and engines thrummed as mechanical coursers veered to follow where the woman had gone.

The boy didn't wait to see what must follow. Crouching low, hugging the bright thing to his breast, he scurried away, crawling, dodging and darting, fleeing the searchers the woman had diverted.

For hours he traveled, seeking distance from all the horrors he had seen. By late moonlight he paused to drink from the river, then turned westward, up into the rising breaks. In the hills above the valley he hid again and watched AATVs passing below—a parade of machinery followed by marching men with the guns of the Royal Artillery among them. When the army had passed by, foragers and ambulances bringing up the rear, he angled downward. Dust of passage obscured him as he intercepted the line of march and joined it.

By first light he plodded along beside a shell transport, and when a curve in the road hid him from view, he climbed aboard and hid himself in shadows among the artifacts of war. Through a slit in the forward hull he watched the rolling plains and greening fields creep past. The remains of a little old town were silent as the army passed through. A weathered, battered sign said the place had once been called Satanta.

More miles passed, then ahead rose the towers of Arthur's mighty fortress of Camelot.

When Arthur's troops returned from the Cimarron, the boy was with them, unseen. He waited until the motor pool was quiet and the soldiers dispersed, then crept from his hiding place, hugging the bright cone he carried.

The Whispers told him where to go, then, and what to do.

Beyond the motor pool and the arsenals was a wide parade ground, almost deserted in the high, hot noonday sun. Past it, great skeletons of steel rose toward the sky. A new tower was going up there—a tower that would dwarf the other towers of Camelot. The stone structure rose a hundred feet high amid the platforms and braces, stone without feature except for a single, wide portal at ground level. The top of the great, encasing wall was jagged, incomplete, and its slant revealed a central shaft within the tower that seemed to descend into darkness.

"Deep Hole," a voice said, and the boy whirled around. A man stood behind him—a tall, calm-looking man with dark wind-whipped hair and piercing dark eyes. The man's slight smile was a reassurance. "Hello, Edwin," he said. "I'm Adam."

Around them, shadows shifted and Whisper voices chattered in that way that wasn't quite real sound. Adam's smile deepened, became ironic. "Don't upset yourselves," he said, not to the boy. "I know why he's here, but he's far too early."

Ignoring Whisper protests, Adam held out a hand. "I'll help you," he told Edwin. "Take my hand."

As their fingers touched, the world around Edwin seemed to spin, to grow dark and murky. For a moment he felt dizzy. Then the world righted itself, but it wasn't the same as before. The parade ground now was paved with slate and red tile, and where there had been iron rigging now stood a tall, forbidding tower, complete and ominous. The single opening at ground level was a wide portal with bright, steel doors standing open. The only other features in the structure were a ring of wide windows at the very top, just under the bronze roof peak. Off to the right, a squadron of armed men in bright livery was marching away, toward a distant gate. No one else was in sight.

"Come with me," Adam said.

Hugging his bright metallic cone, Edwin followed the man across the paved yard and through the open portal.

A silent, powered lift carried them to the highest level, and they stepped out into a huge room with windows all around. The only feature in the room was a big, elaborate chair of shining steel, mounted high above a grated shaft in the floor. Above the chair hung a vastly complex apparatus of wires and circuits, with a shiny cone at its base. The cone was just like the one the boy held.

As the lift door closed, motors hummed softly and Adam glanced around. "They're coming," he said. "Hide behind the throne, Edwin. Climb onto the braces there and stay out of sight."

Edwin headed for the "throne," glancing back only once. Adam was not there. He was nowhere to be seen. But as the boy flattened himself among the braces on the chair's back, the Whispers were with him again.

"Ood ut taw we let lew," their soundless voices said. "We'll tell you what to do."

The lift opened and a big, strong-looking man in regal garments stepped out. Three other men followed him, gaping around at the vast chamber before them.

The first man strode partway across the pristine floor, then turned. "Welcome, gentlemen," he said in a voice that was an amused growl. "This meeting of the Trilate Council is adjourned." Without warning, concealed zen-guns flared. The three men slumped where they stood, their eyes wide with shock and disbelief.

"Now," silent Whisper voices told the boy behind the throne, and he knew what to do. It took only a moment, then the world spun again and Edwin Limmer found himself kneeling among construction rubble at the base of the unfinished tower. Adam was there, lifting him to his feet.

"It is done," the man said. "Let's slip out the postern gate." He handed the boy a package, without explanation, but by its feel and its weight Edwin knew what it was. It was a little lustrous cone, like the one he had carried before. But he knew, too, that this was another one. He stowed it under his cloak.

In the hills beyond Camelot, Adam left him. Edwin didn't really know where he was going, but a place hung in his mind—a place among rolling hills where cottonwoods lined a little stream. He angled southward, somehow knowing it was the right direction to go.

There was a place he knew, and he would find it. He had never been there, that he could remember, but he knew where it was. In an abrupt little valley on the high plains, there would be a wandering stream. At a place where the stream curved, there would be a grove of cottonwood trees. Above and beyond the trees, three out-thrust points of limestone caprock, like ships' prows, were a landmark.

He knew exactly where it was. He would go there, and he would dig a hole there and bury the thing under his wrap.

Wide, rolling plains swam to life around him as the first light of dawn brightened the eastern sky. The plains were vast and illusory. They seemed to go on and on in all directions, farther than the eye could see. The boy seemed to be alone in a vast, flat world where the only vertical features were random dark stalks rising here and there, head-high little totems that only emphasized the vast nothingness around him.

Yet he did not feel alone. The Whispers were with him. They were a presence and many presences. It seemed he had known them all . . . that each nuance of presence was familiar to him, if only he could remember. And yet the traces of memory were like smoke in his hands. When he searched—really searched—there was nothing there.

How could one remember things that had not happened yet . . . and would never happen now because they were so long ago?

Still, the Whispers were there. Sometimes, if he listened just right, he could hear their voices, as he did now. "D'm rifnoc," one of them—or maybe more than one—said. "Sisse'h-dopiah." The voice was soundless, but still a voice.

"Why?" he asked them, speaking to the wind. "Why must I find that place where the stream is?"

For a time there was no response, then the soundless voices came again, this time in words he could understand. Slowly they spoke, and awkwardly, as if laboring to put the syllables into place one by one.

"It is the right place," they told him.

"But why?"

The voices hesitated, as if uncertain how to answer. Vaguely, somehow, he understood their dilemma. How could the knowledge of one age be imparted to another? Once, he realized, he had known what they knew. But that was another when. Then the voices were back.

"It is your place, Edwin," they said. "It is where you were born . . . ten years from now."

∞

Dimensions are the directions within which measurements are made. Time is a dimension. It is the direction within which duration occurs, just as height occurs between up and down. Duration varies, but time does not. Time was, is and will be changeless. Like the other dimensions, time is the arena for the changes and varieties that occur within it.

Time does not move. It always stands still.

—Notes on temporality,
The Waystop Users' Manual

∞

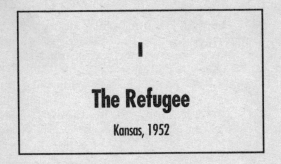

I

The Refugee

Kansas, 1952

In western Kansas one seldom hears the wind. Its sound blends with the sweeping, rolling distances that confuse the eye and diminish everything on them. Like horizons beyond comprehension, where miles and wheat fields lose themselves in hazed immensity, the constant wind is omnipresent. The senses grow immune to it and it is no longer heard at all. It is just there. Only when the wind demands attention, as in the howling of blizzards or the wild gusts of summer storm, is it noticed—then, and when it ceases momentarily and ears unaccustomed are subjected to the sudden sound of silence.

Stars beyond counting glittered in moonless, black-crystal sky, their silvery light enough to brighten the rustling sea of ripening wheat below and reflect on the chromework of the 1949 Hudson half hidden there. The wind muffled the sounds of "Red Sails in the Sunset" on the car radio and the sporadic conversation of adolescent male voices.

"God!" one of them protested. "Change that station! I'm gettin' seasick!"

"Where's Del Rio?" another said. "Find Del Rio! They always got somethin'."

"Yeah. A gallon of holy water and instructions on how to baptize yourself. Lemme see that thing!"

The Hudson rocked softly as occupants changed places, and the radio spat a fast sequence of garbles and statics. Then, *". . . singing roll a bowl a ball a penny a pitch!"*

14

"Dammit, Harold, that's not Del Rio! Tombo, show this fart how to work your radio!"

"One time they advertised bull-taming kits," a third voice said. "A strong rope an' a sharp knife. Change your bull's mind from ass to grass." The radio gargled again, then blared, *"On top of Old Smokey-ey-ey . . . !"*

"That's Del Rio," Harold decided. "Where's that bottle, Corky?"

"I don't know why I'm sittin' out here with you turds," Corky whined. "I'd a hell of a lot rather be checkin' out Mary Beth right now."

"Then why aren't you?"

"Ruthie's got better boobs."

"Well, you're not with her, either! Shit, Corky! Pass the damn bottle!"

"Tombo, you got lousy taste in drinkin' liquor," Harold rasped. "Sloe gin, for God's sake!"

"I thought it was regular gin." Tombo growled. "Get off my ass about it! Anyhow, I need to go home. Dad's takin' Mom to Amarillo tomorrow and I got to keep Lucas."

"You're skippin' school to baby-sit?"

"Yeah. It's Aunt June's birthday." The Hudson rocked as its front tires scuffed the sandy soil. "I think the Bullet has a loose steering rod. You guys know anything about steering rods?"

"I know more about boobs," Corky said. "I guess we could go to the Pit and see if there's any girls there."

"This time of night? Shit, it's nearly two o'clock. Everything's closed. Anything out loose now would give you crabs."

"Two o'clock? Christ, my folks'll kill me. Tomorrow's a school day."

"Not for me," Tombo said. "All I got to do is baby-sit Lucas."

"Crap. Anyhow, what the hell you know about crabs, pissant?"

"I know as much about crabs as you know about boobs!"

Static rattled on the radio, then cleared. *". . . if I stand starry-eyed, that's the danger in paradise . . ."*

"Oh, shit!" Harold wailed. "They're playin' our song!"

"Whose song?" Tombo sounded interested. "Yours and Ruthie's?"

"Mine an' Betty's. Christ, I think I'll die! Betty has thrown me over for a couple of other guys!"

"Your song oughtta be 'The Third Man Theme.'"

"I thought you were horny over Mary Beth," Harold said.

"Well, I am! But Ruthie's got better boobs."

"Somewhere in space," the radio sang, *"I hang suspended . . ."*

"Hell," Corky mourned, "I may never love again. Who's got the bottle?"

"Listen to that!" Tombo said.

"What?"

"The wind's quit."

In the silence they listened, realizing the immensity of Great Plains stillness. Gone was the constant, soft murmur of ever-present wind. Beyond the Hudson's open windows, tall wheat stood motionless, its waves stilled. Even the tinny blare of the radio seemed muted. For just an instant, the world seemed to wind down and stop. And in the stillness there was a distinct *pop*, like a cork being pulled.

"What was that?" Heads poked out of the Hudson, peering around.

"Somebody popped a fart," Harold swore. "Geez. Corky!"

"It wasn't in here," Tombo decided. "It was outside. Is somebody outside?"

"I don't see anybody."

As quickly as it had stilled, the wind came again, dancing across the dark miles. "I gotta get home," Tombo said. "It's late." The Hudson's starter whined, and its engine responded. Tombo pulled the light switch and froze as headlight beams flooded the area ahead. Directly in front of the car, leaning on the hood, was a man—a very old man, weaving on unsteady legs, squinting at them through the windshield. For a moment he stood there, like an apparition from another world. Then he fell from sight.

For a long moment there was only silence and the uncaring wind. Then: "My God! Who was that?"

"Tombo, you asshole, you ran over an old man!"

"I didn't run over anybody! We aren't even moving!"

"Hell, I saw him fall! What the shit's that old fart doing in front of the car? Christ, you *must* have hit him. Didn't you see him fall?"

"How could I hit him? The car isn't moving!"

Doors opened and the three piled out, crowding forward, peering around the hood, over the fenders. On the ground a foot from the front bumper, the old man was on hands and knees, trying to push himself upright. Strong young hands gripped his arms and hauled him up. Tombo peered into his eyes by car light. "Hey, mister, are you all right? God, Harold, he doesn't weigh hardly anything! Mister, are you okay?"

"Turn him loose," Corky said. "See if he can stand up by himself. There . . . woop! Catch him! Jeez, mister, don't fall down again. You aren't hurt, are you?"

Suspended between strong hands, the old man shook his head slowly. "We kngath, yeiko mya," he rasped.

"What?"

"Tish, oh!" the ancient one said, scowling as if the words hurt him. "Yeko . . . okay! I'm okay! Tunim a eemig." He shook his head fiercely, like a dog shaking fleas. "Damn chronophasia," he muttered.

The boys looked at one another, mystified. "He talks funny," Harold said. "Like he's about half foreign or somethin'."

"He doesn't look foreign," Corky said.

"How can you tell? God, he must be a hundred years old!"

Tombo squatted by the left headlight, looking mystified. "This must be his billfold," he muttered. "I guess he dropped it. But I can't find a name or anything. Just pictures of Deanna Durbin and Buster Crabbe. He isn't broke, though. God! There's better'n three hundred dollars here."

"They said they found him in a wheat field," Matthew Hawthorn told B.J. Connors. "His name is Ermil Day. That's about all I could get out of Tombo. So I called you."

Connors seemed to fill the bedroom door—a square, massive man with thoughtful eyes. The worn silver badge on the breast of his always-neat shirt glinted softly in the morning sunlight slanting through Venetian blinds. Matthew peered around him, at the old man asleep on the couch. A few feet away, Tombo Hawthorn snored loudly in his own rumpled bed. The youngster looked like death warmed over, and the room reeked of regurgitation. Irma Hawthorn had tidied her son a bit, but he still looked pale and shamed, even in sleep,

"Sicker'n a dog." Matthew smiled faintly. "Reminds me of how I was the day I signed up for the draft. Thought sure I'd be off fightin' Japs first thing."

"Nobody's fighting Japs now!" Irma snapped.

"No, but there's plenty of Chinese commies in Korea, love."

"Sloe gin!" B.J. rumbled. "Wonder the kid ain't still pukin'. Why would anybody leave sloe gin where kids could get at it?" At a high-pitched, angry shout from the next room, he glanced around. "The baby okay?"

"Lucas is fine." Irma sighed. "I just got him dressed and fed him breakfast."

B.J. turned away from the door, and Matthew retreated to give the big man space in the narrow hall. "Looks like nobody's hurt," B.J. said. "Anything missing?"

"No, but dammit, B.J., you better do something . . ."

"About what?"

"We can't have that old man in our house. We don't even know him."

"He prob'ly just wandered off. Old people do that sometimes. Maybe somebody passin' through lost him."

"Well, we can't keep him. We were supposed to leave for Amarillo an hour ago. Tombo's supposed to look after things."

In the tight, overfurnished little living room, B.J. paused at a reading table. "This all of his stuff?"

"All I could find. He wasn't any help. Old codger sleeps like he was dead. How old you suppose he is?"

"I don't know. Older'n anybody I ever saw." B.J. sorted the little pile of belongings carefully. A dime-store wallet, three keys on a twist of baling wire, an Esterbrook pen, a rusty Barlow knife, a folded handkerchief, and some pocket change. The wallet looked brand-new. Its celluloid holders were unscuffed and contained cardboard-print likenesses of Deanna Durbin and Buster Crabbe. In the pocket of it were three one-hundred-dollar bills, a fifty, two tens, a five, and a one-dollar bill.

The bills were fairly new but not uncirculated. B.J. put the wallet down and inspected the keys. Two were Ford keys—door and ignition. The third was a vault key from the Citizens State Bank.

"I guess I can have the old gentleman removed from your premises, when he wakes up." B.J. shrugged. "But if you want anything more than that, you'll have to charge him with something."

"Hell, he's trespassing!"

"Not if Tombo invited him in, he isn't. All he's doing is sleeping. Come on, Matt. That geezer's no trespasser. He's just an old man that got lost. He belongs around here somewhere."

Irma Hawthorn appeared in the hallway. "Matthew, hadn't we better call somebody, let them know we're not coming?"

"They're expecting us at Amarillo," Matthew explained to B.J. "It's Aunt June's birthday."

"Well, you better leave somebody in charge here, then. That boy of yours won't be in shape for anything today." The big man glanced at Matthew. "Sloe gin," he muttered. "Why would anybody keep sloe gin? I'd rather drink kerosene."

"I'll stay and look after the boys, if you want," a soft, rasping voice behind Irma offered. The old man stood there, sleepy-eyed but apparently unharmed. His Hawaiian-print shirt and khaki pants hung on him like tent cloth, but he stood straight. His eyes were clear and his voice level. As Irma turned and gasped, he bowed slightly. "Hello, my name is Ed Limmer. I appreciate your hospitality."

"Limmer?" Matthew blinked. "Tombo said your name was Day. Ermil Day, he told me."

"Not his fault," the old man apologized. "He heard it in reverse. That's probably how I said it. Chronophasia's a nuisance, but I'm over it now."

"And you'd keep the kids while we go to Amarillo? Why?"

"I owe Tombo a favor," the old man said simply. "He'll be okay in a few hours. Meantime, I'll look after things here."

B.J. squinted at the codger. He seemed healthy enough and in control of his faculties. He was just . . . old. "Where you from, Mr. Limmer?"

"Horton County," the old man told him. "I'm here on business, but I kind of got lost."

"Told you, Matt." B.J. nodded. "Sounds to me like that solves your problem. "Mr. Day . . . I mean, Mr. Limmer . . . is your baby-sitter."

"We don't know him!" Irma protested.

"Hate to disappoint Aunt June, though," Matt countered.

"Don't worry about it." B.J. nodded. "I'll keep an eye on the place till you get back."

"I need to go to the bank," Limmer said. "But tomorrow will do. By the way, what day is this?"

"It's the twenty-sixth of May," B.J. said. "Monday."

"What year?"

"Why, 1952, of course." They all looked at him suspiciously. "You don't remember what year it is?"

"One year's like another." Limmer shrugged. "I've seen a lot of years. After a while they all look alike."

From the hallway a child's voice called, "Momma? Momma, where's Teddy? I want my bear!"

"That Lucas!" Irma started for the sound. "He's being cranky."

Limmer headed her off. "I'll tend to him," he said. "I know about cranky."

"Don't you have any other clothes?" Irma frowned at the old man's rumpled khaki trousers, Hawaiian shirt, and baseball cap.

"I seem to be missing my luggage." He shrugged.

"Well, you can afford a change of clothes. While you're in my house, I'll have you presentable."

Monday evening, the Hawthorns returned from Amarillo and Edwin Limmer showered, shaved, and went to sleep. He was exhausted. But he had two loyal friends. "I guess Mr. Limmer knows about everything there is," Tombo told his parents. "Did you know the next war we're in will be in Vietnam?"

Little Lucas had his own opinion of the old man. The two-year-old had adopted him totally, even preferring him to his teddy bear.

Tuesday morning, Limmer listened patiently to Irma's complaints about Matt's aunt June and accepted breakfast as payment for his services. Tombo left for school, but when Limmer started to leave the house Lucas clung to the old man. "More story!" the child insisted. "Wanna know 'bout King Arthur!"

"Later, Tadpole," Limmer promised. "Got things to do first."

"How 'bout treasure?"

The old man's eyes grew thoughtful, then he nodded. "You'll have your treasure, boy. All in good time."

B.J. Connors gave Limmer a ride downtown, quizzing him patiently but learning nothing of any use. Limmer might be old, he decided, but he wasn't going to tell anybody anything he didn't want known.

Half the old man's answers were nonsensical, the rest simply puzzling—like claiming to be ninety-eight years old. Nobody B.J. knew was ninety-eight years old, unless it was that fellow down at Cushing who claimed to be Frank James. Still, when Limmer said he was born in the year 2050—a nonsense answer, obviously—it *did* work out to ninety-eight years. It was just the wrong direction.

On Kansas Avenue, Limmer spent an hour shopping. Then, clad in JCPenney's best—Arrow shirt, Hall suit, and white buck shoes—and smelling of Old Spice and starch, he went to the bank.

He wasn't surprised that his signature matched the signature on the vault contract. The Whispers were erratic sometimes, but they were meticulous. A bank vault ready and waiting—with a lease dating back three years—was no more notable a thing than a lurid Hawaiian floral shirt or a dime-store wallet with pictures of Deanna Durbin and Buster Crabbe.

Alone in a cubicle, Ed Limmer looked at his legacy from ninety-eight years of retrosync—a valid Kansas title to a 1949

Ford automobile, a current tax receipt for the same car, a little star-shaped medallion, and a roll of quarters in a paper sleeve.

The "medallion," of course, was a playback, and when he pressed its hidden control it beeped at him. And the quarters weren't quarters. Unwrapped, they looked more like machine washers of blued steel. CWs, he thought with a smile. Compact repositories of data. He inserted the first wafer in the playback and activated it.

". . . herbicides for the control of field bluestem," a bored, nasal voice told him, "should not be used after your first shoots appear. Winter wheat is susceptible to some of these compounds. But Zingo-Three is effective right on into spring. This is Walter Wall, your county agent, with the morning report for Thursday, May 30, 1952." The voice became sepulchral—pronouncements from the bottom of a stock tank. "Beef futures on the Chicago market closed up one-eighth, cutters and packers up a quarter, spring lambs off an eighth . . ." it droned on and on.

Then the playback beeped an attention signal, and the recorded voice sounded almost alive. "An item of particular interest," it said, "soybean futures more than tripled yesterday in active buying after Cargill's announcement of process facilities at Wichita and Des Moines, for paint base and industrial fibers. Speculators on the floor of the Chicago exchange drove prices as high as seven-forty before closing at seven-nineteen. In Kansas City, short-term futures on cured milo are . . ."

There was more, but Limmer had what he needed. Thursday, May 30, 1952, was two days away. So Wednesday, the day of the soybean rush, would be tomorrow.

The bank had his car, in paid-up storage at Erickson's Garage. Limmer obtained a release on it, then crossed the lobby to where a bald man sat at a fastidious desk. L.Q. Price wasn't in charge of the Citizens Bank, but he was in charge of everything from custodial supervision to customer services, and that included investment counselling.

"How many soybeans will three hundred dollars buy?" Limmer asked him.

"Eh?"

"I want to invest in soybean futures," the old man explained.
"I want an open account, beginning with three hundred dollars.
And I'm placing an immediate order for soybeans. That means
right now. I want to buy today and sell at the close of tomorrow's
market."

"That's pretty unusual." Price gaped at him.

"I'm old." Limmer shrugged. "I don't have time to fool with
long futures."

Price hesitated only a moment. He had long since learned
the futility of arguing with determined old people. The ancient
confronting him was probably crazy as a loon, but he had cash
in hand, and it was his money. "This . . . ah . . . soybean order,
do you want to buy on margin? A three-day life policy will
only cost you . . . ah . . . four dollars."

"Sure," Limmer said. "Buy me all you can get. Just do it
now. And on that open account, I'll want it in two names—
myself as executor, and Lucas Hawthorn, a juvenile, as
beneficiary."

"Lucas . . . isn't that Matthew's youngest?"

"The same. Lucas and I are partners. Now order us some
soybeans, please. And show me where to sign. I have other
things to do. I have to find a place to stay and learn to drive a
car. And I need to find a reliable lawyer."

Price shook his head and did as he was told. They'd never
believe this over at the Blue Goose.

While Price was making his calls, a boy entered the bank,
looked around, then came to the desk and handed Price a
folded note. Price glanced at it and handed it to Limmer.
"Looks like somebody's taking care of you," he said.

The note had a street address and the scrawled message
"Clean room and good meals, you tend the yard."

"That's Faye Jones's address," Price told him. "She cooks
good, probably needs a boarder."

The boy was hovering nearby. He was a sturdy, dark-haired
lad of maybe ten. As Limmer read the message, the boy said,
"I can show you the way."

"Well, thank you, Adam." Price nodded. "But Mr. Limmer might have other plans."

"He still needs a place to stay." Adam shrugged.

Limmer squinted at the boy. "How do you know that? Who said I should board with Mrs. Jones?"

"My mom thought you could use some help." The boy shuffled his feet, embarrassed. "Mrs. Jones makes Christmas candy and gives piano lessons."

"Word spreads in a little town." Price grinned. "But if Maggie Wills says you need a room, you probably do."

"I'll look into it," Limmer decided. "Thank you, Adam. And thank your mother for me. I'll find my way."

"Yes, sir." The boy fidgeted for a moment, then turned and left.

"Kids." Price chuckled. "They don't miss much."

When his business was done, Edwin Limmer stood and shook the banker's hand. "See you tomorrow," he said. "Maybe we'll buy some more futures then."

Price hesitated, then asked, "Mr. Limmer . . . ah, forgive me for asking, but do you have some kind of inside information?"

"Sure." The old man grinned. "I listen to Walter Wall on the radio."

∞

Around and around and around he goes, and where he stops, God only knows.

—Children's rhyme, ca. 2080

∞

II

The Anomaly Man

West-Central Kansas, The Present

Lucas Hawthorn came awake abruptly, with an eerie feeling that something profound had changed. He had dreamed of hearing voices, but the words ringing in his head didn't mean anything and didn't seem to have come through his ears. Still, he was sure someone had spoken to him. "What?" he slurred. "Didn' hear you, hon."

There was no response, and Lucas opened his eyes. Thin morning light outlined the little slats in the window's shutters. It was early—too early to be awake. Yet he was, and something wasn't right. "What did you say?" he prompted, more awake now. There was an odd feeling about the room, as if there were a lot of people around him. But he didn't see anyone.

Behind him, Maude snored softly. Lucas yawned, stretched, and looked around. Then he sat up. Something was definitely strange here. He glanced around the dawn-lit room. Nothing seemed out of place. It was their bedroom, just as it was every morning. But something seemed odd. And a lingering odor made his nose twitch—a new, live scent as if someone who didn't live here had just passed by.

Like an echo, clear and close but not quite real sound, the odd voice came again. "Funny doog," it said.

"What?" Turning this way and that, Lucas peered about the room, then nudged Maude with ungentle fingers. "Did you say that?"

"Mmfff . . . ," she muttered, pulling the covers higher around her head.

"Maude! Wake up!"

She stirred beside him and opened her eyes. "Wha'?"

"What did you just say?"

"I didn' say anything." She covered her head again, then gasped and peered out from under the blanket. "Who's here?" she muttered. "Somebody's here, Lucas." She sat up, clutching the covers around her, and they both peered around at the empty room.

Except for the fact that he couldn't exactly see anybody, Lucas would have sworn that their bedroom was full of busy people. He squinted, his eyes flicking here and there. All around was the *sense* of presences, but he couldn't quite see them. Each hint of shadow was gone before his eyes could find it. But still they were here. With a growl he clenched big fists, edging toward the bedside table. "What is this?" he muttered. They seemed to be all around—a dozen or more figures, moving here and there, looking closely at walls and ceiling, measuring the window frames, making notes on little pads. Lucas had the feeling he had awakened into a dream—a nightmare.

Beside him, Maude whispered, "What are they doing? Remodeling?"

With a grunt, Lucas pivoted to the bedside table and pulled the drawer open. The S&W wasn't there. "What the hell is going on?" he muttered. After pushing the covers back, he swung his legs over the side of the bed, then jerked them back as someone not quite visible raised an imperious hand.

"Tnemom asudge," a soundless voice ordered. Then: "Ayko."

"Lucas? . . ." Maude's voice was a frightened whimper. Lucas bounded out of bed and turned full around, a defender in rumpled pajamas. He felt—sensed somehow—that people he couldn't quite see were scampering aside, out of his way.

Abruptly the bedroom door opened and a man stepped in. This was no specter but a sturdy, middle-aged man wearing odd-looking old coveralls and a St. Louis Cardinals baseball

cap. "You're awake," the man said, without formality. "Sorry
to bother you. These delegates needed to verify dimensions."

"Leave my dimensions alone!" Maude shrilled. Lucas
swung around, barely glimpsing a furtive shadow that scampered back as Maude swung a businesslike fist at it. The
shadow had a measuring tape.

"Sorry," the man in the doorway said. "That's just Peedy.
His specialty is mammalian evolution."

Lucas and Maude gawked at the man, who had started past
Lucas, toward the east window. The man paused, then touched
a finger to his baseball cap in casual salute. There seemed to be
a gap between his hand and his wrist, as if he were wearing an
invisible watch. "Guess you're a little confused," he said.
"Didn't introduce myself. Name's Limmer. Edwin Limmer.
You won't remember, Lucas, but I met you a long time ago."

"Limmer?" Lucas blinked at him, sleepy-eyed. "I know that
name, all right, but you're not him. You can't be. He's dead."

"Not so you'd notice." The man smiled. "It's a common
misconception. I used to be a lot older. But I'm the same Ed
Limmer. Look in your old trust portfolio. Does three hundred
dollars' worth of soybean futures ring any bells?"

"That's ridiculous! Get out of my house!"

"Can't," the man said. "I came with this group to inspect the
place. Have you forgotten the reciprocal service clause?"

"How do you know about that? Nobody knows about that."

"Well, I do. It says that in return for your beneficiary
status, I claim access to and limited use of your domicile at
an unspecified future time. Well, the time is now and I'm
specifying it."

"That's a sealed document! It's in my safe! It's . . . it was
written more than forty years ago."

"I know. By A.J. Thornton, attorney-at-law. I dictated it.
Now, about your house here. What's the total square footage?"

"Uh . . . about eighteen hundred," Lucas said. Then he
bristled. "What are you doing in our bedroom?"

"Measuring," Limmer said. "We'll just be a moment. Where
do you keep your coffee?"

"In the kitchen." Maude pointed. "Left cabinet over the counter. Lucas, don't just stand there! Call the police!"

"I'll call the police," Lucas said. "Get the hell out of our bedroom!"

"Okay." Limmer nodded. "I think we're through here. That wall will have to be reinforced, naturally. We'll be doing structural modification on the other side of it. Studs on sixteen-inch centers, I suppose?"

"Of course they are. The building code requires . . . what do you mean, *we*?"

"Us." Limmer gestured vaguely. "You and me and them. Oh, that's right, you can't see them too well. There's a knack to it. They're Whispers. They're just passing through." He glanced past Lucas. Something less than shadow was hovering by the bed where Maude sat. "Peedy, behave yourself! Remember you're a professional!" The hint of shadow flitted away and Limmer spread his hands apologetically. "Too much time on his hands," he explained. "Whispers get like that. You folks get dressed and I'll go put some coffee on, then we can talk. George is in the kitchen, seeing what he can find to eat. He's pretty well starved, after four days up on that hill."

Lucas blinked, trying to think of something to say.

"Call the police, Lucas!" Maude wailed.

"Call them yourself." Lucas growled. "I'm going to . . . where the hell *is* that thing?" He looked into the table drawer again, then stooped to peer under the bed.

"Your gun?" Limmer asked. "It's over there on the dresser. Do you want it?"

"Hell, yes, I want it! You . . . people are in my house!"

Limmer shrugged, retrieved the revolver, and handed it to Lucas. It was still loaded. Rims of shells glinted at the rear of the cylinder. Lucas checked it, nodded, and pointed it at Limmer. "Get out of my house!" he ordered.

"Let's have coffee first," Limmer suggested. He looked around approvingly. "This place'll do just fine, with some modifications. Do either of you have any experience with electronics? Or maybe crowd control? That might be helpful."

"What the bald-headed hell is going on here?" Lucas demanded. "I'll shoot . . ."

Somewhere beyond the open bedroom door, cooking utensils cascaded to the floor with a resounding crash. Limmer stepped to the door and looked beyond, down the hall. "I'd better go see about George," he said. "I'll be in the kitchen. We'll talk there." With a reassuring smile he touched his baseball cap again, in salute, then disappeared down the hall.

Maude had the bedside phone and was tapping busily at buttons. "Want something done, do it yourself," she muttered. Then: "Lucas, the line's dead. I can't call out."

"Ertal we ees," a voice that was no voice seemed to say, then the room hollowed out, as rooms do when crowds leave.

Lucas closed the door firmly. "Let's get dressed," he suggested. "Then maybe we'll get to the bottom of this."

"You're really him, then? I mean, *that* Ed Limmer?"

"The very same." Limmer shrugged. "Don't worry. You'll get used to it. Technology is always perplexing to those who haven't lived when it was developed. I was born in the future, and I've been in the past. Now I'm on my way back."

"And a . . . a way station?" Lucas squinted over his coffee. The more Edwin Limmer explained—if that was what he was doing—the more confused the Hawthorns became. "You want to use our house for a depot?"

"Not exactly." Edwin Limmer shrugged. "More like a booster station on a pipeline. We could be looking at quite a bit of traffic before long. Handy, the business you're in. The Whispers had a part in that, I guess. You can handle everything as general contractor."

"We only have one extra bathroom," Maude said. "I suppose we could put up two or three people for a day or so with the kids away, but . . ."

"I'm talking about hundreds of people." Limmer shook his head. "But once we're set up they'll be no trouble. They'll just be passing through. You won't even notice them, except for the relegation pips. And that brings me to my point. We're counting on you folks to tend the generator and keep the conduits open."

"Where are they going then, those people?" Maude asked.

"Back in time," Limmer said, as if explaining a trip around the block. "They're time travelers."

"Sure they are," Maude muttered. Cautiously she edged away, to where the kitchen telephone hung over the bar. Her eyes flicked back and forth between the kitchen table, where her husband and the crazy man sat sipping hot coffee, and the pantry shelf where a gaunt, tattered young man with scratches and smudges all over him was wolfing down a pint of cottage cheese. He had already eaten two apples and all the leftover pizza. Cautiously Maude reached for the phone.

"That one won't work either," Limmer told her. "But don't worry. It's only temporary. Toojay had to rewire the circuit to move the box away from the dining room wall. What do you think? Could you folks handle things here for a while?"

"Handle things?"

"Tend the generator. Keep the conduit open. Operate the station."

"What's in it for us?" Lucas frowned.

"What do you want? Money? You'll be paid, of course. I'll cover all expenses, plus a nice retainer and fee for the use of your property. That and found."

"What's found?"

"Well, you'll have more or less free use of the ... ah ... apparatus, when the Whispers aren't using it. There really isn't that much damage that you can do."

"You said tend the generator and keep the whatever open. What do we do, oil and clean, or something?"

"Nothing so primitive." Limmer smiled. "I'll teach you what to do. I'll need to stay on for a while anyway, to get you started."

"No way," Maude snapped.

"What about him?" Lucas indicated the hungry young man, who had now polished off the cottage cheese and was rummaging through the refrigerator. That one hadn't said a word, but when he glanced at them his eyes were distant and haunted.

"George is the technician," Limmer explained. "The Whispers picked him up forty-four years from now. Under rather trying circumstances, I might add. But he'll be all right. He'll install the mechanisms. We'll clear everything out of that dining room there. It's about the right size. That will be the booster stage."

Maude took a deep breath, stepped to the back porch door, and glanced around at her husband. "I'm going to the Johnsons', Lucas," she said. "I'll call the police from there." She turned the knob on the door, then paused, puzzled. "This is locked. So's the other one. How did you people get in here?"

"We came in while the wall was open." Limmer shrugged. "Those stacks of sheet metal wouldn't go through the door."

"What sheet metal? What wall?"

"Oh, you don't know about that, of course. It didn't happen until this afternoon. You can't even order the metal before nine. That's when the supply shops open. By the way, you'll need some welding gear, too, and protective clothing for the four of us. It gets hot in here when the focalizer is first tuned. But don't worry. Booster fields don't burn."

Maude stared at him, the way a box-trained cat might stare at the dunes of the Sahara. It was just too much to contemplate.

"Now hang on," Lucas growled, struggling to get the drift of it. "Just supposing you did jump back in time, through a hole in the wall that we open because you say to. Then if you aren't here to tell us what to do, there won't be a hole for you to have come through in the first place . . . before you told us. And if there isn't going to be a hole in the wall—because you aren't here now telling us there will be, so there isn't any way for you to get here later so you can . . . so you can be here earlier to make later happen . . . I mean, before it does . . . if it doesn't . . ." He trailed off into muttering confusion.

Edwin Limmer nodded his approval. "You're getting the hang of it," he said. "Anachronisms are always a problem. But in this case it doesn't matter. The wall will be open when we arrive, but we're already here so we won't really need it to get here. You see? That's called an empty loop—an anachronism that allows something to happen but no longer matters before it happens because it is already going to happen. Some of them, when the Whispers are from, think that's how the universe began. They call it an accomplished improbability. It cancels itself out."

"Oh," Lucas said.

"I'll go get the police myself," Maude decided.

"Hold it, hon." Lucas raised a hand. "The man mentioned money. I guess we ought to hear him out."

"Oh, that," Limmer said. "Yes, we'll pay you money. As much as you want. It's only money. But I think you'll want something a little more tangible than that for your services. The currency collapse is only a few years away. After that Federal Reserve scrip isn't worth shit. Of course, it already isn't, but when the IRS stops accepting it, nobody will pretend anymore. That's what starts the paper revolts. Inflation, multiple taxation, all the usual government lunacy, then they'll change the design plates and that's what sets it off. I favor commodity futures myself, but you might want to look at venture enterprise."

"Like what?" Lucas glared at him.

"Well, water pumps and hang gliders have a bright future. Also road and bridge consortiums and some real estate. That's tricky, though. Claims and titles get pretty uncertain when court systems collapse. How about travel? That's a good industry. There's always somebody wanting to be somewhere else. Just don't honor credit or cash. Keep it on a barter basis. Tradable goods only. That's pretty depression-proof."

"My aunt Irene and her husband had a travel agency," Maude said scornfully. "They went bust."

"They didn't have a temporal field to play with." Limmer smiled. "Anywhen has a lot more appeal than anywhere."

"We can't run a business here," Lucas argued. "This whole district is zoned residential-only."

"Then don't put up a sign." Limmer shrugged. "Keep it discreet. Letters of recommendation only. Just think! Package tours to the Cenozoic. Organized dinosaur-watching! Or how about reserved seats to watch Rome burn?"

Over by the refrigerator, George Wilson was peeling an

orange. "Be careful," he said quietly. "You're talking major anachronisms here, if you plan to let tourists loose in the past."

"There'll have to be some defined limits," Limmer agreed. "But I think the idea would sell. Just a select group at first. Show them what can be done. Then let them talk it over and think about it. People will always travel if you give them time."

"Leo Whitehead's always talking about how nice Colorado used to be," Lucas said thoughtfully.

"The Brents would love to see Custer's last stand," Maude offered, taken by it all. "They fight all the time about who won."

"Like a look at last year's county ballots myself," Lucas added. "If that water authority vote wasn't rigged, there's no fenceposts in Kansas."

"Then it's settled." Limmer beamed. "George can get to work on the conversion chamber. And we need to order some materials."

"Who pays for it?" Lucas demanded.

"You do." Limmer gestured. "I told you, it's only money. We'll use the Limmer Trust reserve. Good as gold. Built on commodity futures in the past. In the meantime, for petty cash, that bag in the hall is full of U.S. federal currency. Help yourself."

"What is it? Counterfeit?" Lucas glared at him threateningly.

"Absolutely not! Why counterfeit money when there's so much of it just lying around in warehouses and shipping depots?"

"There is?"

"Sure. Always been that way. Back when I was old it was bootleggers and gun-runners. Nowadays it's dope dealers and headbrokers. And there are always lawyers and politicians with cash to stash. You don't think they use banks, do you?"

Across the kitchen, George Wilson frowned, opened a stained vinyl pouch at his waist, and drew out a shining object the size of a milk carton. It was cone-shaped and glinted with a deep luster like melded metals in glass. "There are so many of these now, coming upstream," he said, sadly. "When Magda left Long Mesa, there were only three." He set the thing on the kitchen table. "Arthur had one, and we had the others at Long Mesa. Magda took one with her. I never knew what happened to the third one."

"Magda?" Maude groped, searching for some clue as to what he was talking about.

"His wife," Limmer said quietly.

Wilson turned toward the hall. "I'd like to rest a bit before I go to work," he said. "I feel like I've been through a war."

"You have," Limmer said.

"What war?" Maude stared at the smoke-darkened, sweat-stained man who had just decimated her refrigerator's contents. "Guest bedroom is second on the left. What war? Where? Or . . . I mean, when?"

Wilson nodded tiredly and trudged away, looking for a bed.

"Arthur's Cimarron Siege," Limmer said. "George was with the Revivalists. And he's worried about his wife. She was there, too. That's a little over forty years from now. I'll be involved in that one, too, I guess."

"You were?" Lucas managed.

"Will. It hasn't happened yet, but I'll be there. Or so they tell me. I was only ten years old the first time I made that trip, and I was just in passage. You can't see much from retrosync, especially that close to a major anachronism."

George Wilson reappeared at the hall entrance. "Okay if I use the shower?"

Maude barely heard him. She was staring at Limmer. "So you've actually *been* to the future?"

"That's what I said." Limmer shrugged. "I was born there, but I never saw much of it. I passed through, but I haven't actually been where I seem to be going. I'm not a Whisper, you know. I'm sort of a stowaway. I've been out of time most of my life. Now I'm going back."

"To the future?"

"Back to the future, just like the movies." Limmer grimaced. "My future's the same as yours, except that I was born there. Everybody's headed for the future, except the Whispers. They've already been there. It's where they started. They just picked me up along the way."

"You mean you're an anach—ana—a whatzit yourself?" Lucas gaped at Limmer.

"Anachronism," Limmer said slowly. "No, not exactly. But my base mode is retrosync, so I guess that makes me an anomaly. Step right up, folks." He sneered. "See the world's only living stopwatch. Spent ninety years going the wrong direction and now working his way back to where he started." He sighed, shaking his head. "It's all King Arthur's fault. I'll get that son of a bitch—beg pardon, ma'am—if it takes the rest of my life, which is exactly what it will do."

"It . . . you will?" Maude felt dazed, trying to make sense out of so many things that didn't.

Limmer's ironic smile disappeared and his eyes narrowed. "Damn right I will," he swore. "I know I will, because I already did, even though I haven't done it yet. I was—will be—the paradox in Arthur's Anachronism. And it's all because of him. That bastard! May he bounce forever within the stroke of twelve! I only wish I could be there to see it."

Lucas and Maude shook their heads convulsively, as if besieged by gnats. As one, they turned toward the other stranger. The quiet, somber man in the tattered, smoke-darkened clothing still stood in the hall entry. Though no longer ravenous, he looked exhausted, bleak, and somehow tragic.

"Don't ask me to explain it," George Wilson said, dismissing their stares. His tired, disinterested eyes lingered on Limmer, then shifted to the shining focalizer on the table. "I invented the damn thing, but I'm not proud of it. And I've never understood this juggling of redundancies. That gets into probability equations. It's all aftermath to me. I'm just a technician."

∞

Stretch a point and it makes a line. Spread a line and it's a square. Extend a square and you have a cube. Each action adds a dimension. Now, what you have just done three times, do it again. See? You're getting the hang of it. It's about time.

—EDWIN LIMMER

∞

III

Waystop

The Present

Never in his life had Lucas Hawthorn seen so much cash money, all in one place. It was like something in a TV movie, or behind glass at Coushatta. The package was like a large valise, and it was filled to the scuppers with neat little bundles of currency, mostly twenties and hundreds. It reminded him of the vault in the Heights Bank—part of which he had built—on the Sunday after the grand opening of Heights Mall. There had been some nervous people that day, until the cash was counted and transferred to the depository in Wichita.

"There's plenty more where this came from," Edwin Limmer said carelessly. "This particular trove was stashed in a twin Cessna that took off last night for Kansas City and never made it. Wind shear, probably. It went down east of Great Bend and the FAA has its wreckage sealed off. Two or three Colombian cartel clowns may wind up as 'unspecified disposal' when the inventory reports get out, but they'd blow each other away anyhow. They usually do. Let's get busy."

At Limmer's direction, Lucas got busy on a telephone that worked again, and Maude accessed Lucas's office files on the PC. By noon a makeup crew of surprised construction workers was hacking happily at a section of the Hawthorn house's east wall, opening a hole as high as a door and twice as wide. Double 2 × 10s were shimmed in to make a header for what would never again be just an exterior kitchen wall.

Just beyond, a hundred square feet of carefully tended

Bermuda sod and a flower bed were being bladed away for a loading pad, while a heavy truck and a squat, gasoline-powered forklift waited to unload rusty little bales of sixteen-gauge steel sheet in 24 × 30-inch plates. One of Lucas's own trucks, with its Hawthorn Constructors decals, sat on the paved patio, loaded with building materials and tools.

Hawthorn Constructors' best ramrod, Pete Swain, had been called away from his breakfast to be foreman on this job, and though he was thoroughly puzzled by the whole thing, he asked no questions. It wasn't the first time Lucas Hawthorne had mystified a crew with some harebrained notion, like the solar panel skylights over his sauna or the redwood-shake vestibule he'd added to Maude's greenhouse. Nor was it the first time Lucas had undertaken a job without preapproved financing or building permits.

Pete was used to it.

Eastwood being the secluded and sedate subdivision that it was, the work had not attracted the little crowds of curious bystanders that such a project might have drawn a few miles away in Derby, or over in Wichita. The Hawthorns' twelve-acre lot was bordered by spirea and spruce, with dwarf elms lining the curved drive. It was private property in a neighborhood that valued its privacy.

Nine years as a carpenter, eight as a struggling homebuilder, and five as a general contractor had earned Lucas Hawthorn this piece of heaven on earth, and its location was to his and Maude's liking. Their early years among the cheek-to-jowl crackerboxes off South Pawnee had given them a taste for reclusiveness. Their house was small by neighborhood standards, but its design was their own and the location was ideal—or had been until that day, when a friendly anomaly, a time-machine architect, and a flock of inquisitive shadows introduced them to the fourth physical dimension.

Like most people, the Hawthorns tended to become erratic when they had time on their hands. They were confused, dazed, and overwhelmed by it all, but the money was good. A few calls had set it all in motion, and there was no backing out now. The Whispers had decreed that 1712 Beech Street was to be a time-travel station, and that was that.

"It was pretty cut and dried," Edwin Limmer explained early on. "T2 retrosync, the way the Whispers travel it, is like a conduit. It doesn't run east or west or up or down. It doesn't go any direction in tridimensionality. It is a dimension of its own. T2 runs from then to whenever, theoretically in multiple dimensions. And its route from any past through any future is directly through now. That's the T1 Connection."

He had explained patiently—several times—that T2 is "real" time, the realm of the dimension itself, while T1 is time as life perceives it . . . an apparent continuum in which events follow one after another.

"T2 has no physical dimensions of its own," he said. "How wide is high? T2 *is* a dimension. But there are perceptual dimensions. The path the Whispers found through time—the 'conduit'—exists within dimension. For practical purposes, the conduit is only about two hundred yards wide. It doesn't have walls, of course, but it is confined for practical use. The Whispers think it might have no limit at all. But they haven't figured out how to go sideways yet. So the basic problem is where and when."

"When?" Lucas squinted at him.

"Right," Limmer said. "Of course the when is everywhen. So that leaves where. The conduit *is* T2—or all we can reach of it. Like an elevator in a big building. From inside, you can't see the building. Only the elevator. T2 is real time, so it is everywhere. Which means the conduit interfaces with all physical dimensions on the planet simultaneously. But we're limited to perception, which is where T1 comes in. T2 has no constant locus except what gravitation dictates. But T1 just flits around, here and there. And Arthur's Anachronism caught it at various points and sort of welded it to the tangible planes. Ergo, made-to-order loci for permanent boosters within T1. That pissant Arthur not only screwed up the continuum, he pinned down T1 while he was at it."

"Oh," Lucas said.

"At any rate," Limmer summarized, "this is one of those places. That's why you got the deal you did on this property."

"We bought this tract eighteen years ago!" Lucas squinted at the bland, ironic face across from him. "At a tax sale!"

"I know." Limmer nodded. "If you'll recall, it was the Limmer Trust that alerted you to it. The Whispers saw ahead what would be required behind and arranged for you to have the opportunity to choose to build here later. They only have about two hundred by three thousand feet of surface plane to work with here, and voilà! Here's a house with an architect in residence. Lucky, huh?"

"Builder," Lucas corrected him. "I'm not an architect. Architects are in charge of screwing up specifications. Builders straighten them out. My God, have you people manipulated my whole life?"

"Every choice has been your own." Limmer shrugged. "Wish I could say as much for mine." He glanced at the band of nothingness on his wrist, then said something to it in words that sounded like no language Lucas had ever heard. "Lujeks naw reew," the anomaly said. "Sver rof."

Nearby, Maude perched on a bar stool, counting rerouted Colombian drug money. She shook her head and muttered to herself, "Crazy. Everybody here is crazy except me, and I'm not sure about me. What do we do with this money, Lucas?"

"Put it in your escrow account, a little at a time," Limmer suggested. "It's building finance. The Limmer Trust will capitalize the project on completion."

A squat, rumbling forklift climbed ramp timbers and trundled through her kitchen, carrying bales of rusty steel plates into what had been the dining room. Compound gears whined and hummed over the racket of a gasoline engine like a lawnmower with a shot muffler. The driver nodded his hard-hatted head, flashing a smile from between bulging earmuffs. "Day, miz," he said. The machine's clatter echoed from the walls. Maude covered her ears with fists full of money.

"We just spread these out on the floor?" Lucas asked.

"Right." Limmer pointed. "Edge to edge, wall to wall. They'll polarize to the focalizer, then you can braze them."

"There isn't a real, first-class brass man this side of Atchison," Lucas objected. "Can't we just spot-weld the seams?"

"Don't even think about it," Limmer warned. "Dimensional magnetics isn't like boilerplate. Did you order that acid?"

"Left, dammit, Hong!" Lucas shouted at the forklift operator. "Pete, didn't you give these yayhoos a floor plan?"

"What?"

"I said turn left!" Lucas whapped a hard hand against the forklift's tailplate to get the driver's attention. "I don't want that stuff in the bedroom." Why in hell, he asked himself, doesn't Sam Doherty invest in a couple of electric forklifts? Everybody else uses them.

Hong halted his machine and pulled off his earmuffs. "What?"

"Did you call me, Lucas?" Pete Swain poked his head into the kitchen, as the lift operator removed his earmuffs.

"Take it in there." Lucas pointed. "Ye gods. Left!"

"Right." The driver grinned, replacing his earmuffs.

"He covers his ears to operate a machine," Edwin Limmer mused.

"OSHA regulations." Lucas growled. "Some genius decided motorized equipment had to have backup whistles, in case somebody couldn't hear the motors, and some other genius decided equipment operators had to have ear protection because of all the noise."

"Ah, the good old days." Limmer nodded. "A screwy time."

"And it goes on and on," Lucas jeered. "Never mind, Pete. I was just directing traffic."

Just beyond the gaping hole in the east wall, drills sang and cutting torches sprayed showers of sparks. They were shaping segments for the "bell tower" that would house the focalizer.

Lucas had asked repeatedly about the "generator" that would drive all this and had gotten no clear answer except "Don't worry about it. George will set it up when he finishes his nap." It remained one of many mysteries, right along with why his materials order had included a Bausch & Lomb double-prism photo lens, a pair of six-inch circular supermagnets, four cases of tennis balls—and, most puzzling of all, a hideously expensive astronomical telescope with electronic gimbals. It had been flown in from Denver by special charter and was now mounted on the roof. Its connection to the interior was a thick monofilament cable that would lead to the magnetic "generator." The lower coupling was a foot-thick double coil of light-transmitting monofilament and reverse-coiled copper wire.

When asked about a power source, Limmer only shrugged and said, "You're looking at it. The Whispers have a nine-syllable name for it, but basically it's slowed light. Light converted to gravity by magnetic inducement. It reverses the basic energy conversion of the universe, which converts gravity to light. We use the product of the Nordstrom Singularity to reverse a lensful of sunlight. It isn't a new idea. The Nazis were playing with it at Telemark."

Lucas scowled, searching his mental collection of trivia. "Singularity . . . you mean like a black hole in space?"

"Exactly. Though 'black hole' is a misnomer. 'Gravity funnel' is more apt. The Nordstrom Singularity is the nearest of those with direct outflow in this system. A gravitational singularity is like a storm drain. Gravity draws energy into it, and that energy has to emerge somewhere. What do you think stars are, Lucas? Beads in the sky?"

"You mean this thing of yours is powered by starlight?"

"Sunshine. The star we use is Sol. We'll convert the photons back to gravities, through magnetic interstice. The residual slow light will be our field medium for the focalizer. Sol will do the powering, and we'll use Polaris as our triangulator."

It was nearly noon when the gate signal sounded and Maude went to the front window. "Oh, Lord," she breathed. "It's Mandy. With Ray and the hoodlums."

"Shit," Lucas muttered. "What are they doing here?" With a sour glance at the front hallway, he headed outside. Edwin Limmer followed.

"Let me get this straight." Ray Brink frowned, gaping at the hole in Maude Hawthorn's kitchen where an Oriental man on a short-rise forklift was trundling in with another load of sheet metal, heading for what used to be a gracious and seldom-used dining room. "You're going to have a tunnel through your dining room?"

"Not a tunnel," Maude said. "A conduit. To transport people from whenever to back then. It's about time."

"From whenever to . . . back then," Ray repeated slowly. "Yeah, sure. I guess I better ask Lucas."

Mandy Brink had wandered dazedly around the demolished kitchen. Now she sank into a chair and stared at her sister. "Maude, are you all right?"

"I really don't know," Maude assured her. "It's all a bit confusing."

"What is?"

"Time travel," Maude said. "It's a lot to digest, I know, but it all does seem to make sense. I mean, chronometrics and temporal logistics—the dimensionality thing and all. It's hard to keep track of, though. Like when where is really when and how when is where where ought to be."

"What?"

"No, when. What isn't really a problem. Most whats are pretty three-dimensional."

Mandy blinked and tried to look sympathetic. "Let's do this a step at a time," she suggested. "What are we doing here? Exactly *what* isn't a problem?"

"Not at all." Maude nodded. "*What* is a waystop for time travelers."

"What is?"

"This is." Maude spread her hands, indicating everything in sight. "At least, it will be. The Whispers are waiting for it."

"Who?"

"Whispers. They're people who aren't here yet. They won't be for hundreds of years. But they're just passing through, anyway. They're in ret . . . retrosync. Most of them aren't interested in now . . . except that pervert Peedy. Watch out for him. He has a tit fixation and a tape measure."

Leland and Leslie Brink, hulking teenagers who might have been carbon copies of their father had they been wearing real clothes, hustled aside at the dining room entrance as the forklift passed again. They looked at the forklift, at each other, and at the women. They looked, to Maude, like a matched pair of large, sullen monkeys in violent T-shirts, training pants, and canvas boots. They watched the forklift exit through the hole in the wall, then turned their attention back to the dining room. In there, crewmen were covering the floor with steel plates.

"Weird," the twins muttered in unison.

One of them poked around the kitchen, opening cabinets and drawers, while the other headed for the refrigerator. "Bummer," this second one said. His heavy buttocks crowded the huge, short pants he wore. "Geezer goods, man. Oh, hey, man, check it out! Root beer!"

Outside, Ray Brink accosted Lucas Hawthorn. With a look like a vulture inspecting road kill, he asked, "Where are you getting the money for this, Lucas? I don't see the percentage in destroying your house."

"Hello, Ray." Lucas's glare was the look of a wolf whose den has been fouled. "Nice to see you, too."

"I assume you have a reason," Ray persisted. "Is this some new fad in architectural design?" Spotting Limmer, he turned. "And who is this?" He raised his brows to look down his nose in fine courtroom style. "I'm Ray Brink. I'm Lucas's brother-in-law and business partner."

"Stockholder," Lucas muttered under his breath. "You're not my partner, asshole."

"Edwin Limmer." Limmer took and shook Brink's reluctant hand, arching a brow at him.

"Do I know you?" Brink asked. "Name's familiar."

"Are you in futures?"

"Of course not. Way too risky. Bonds and venture capital. Service industry. Only way to go. Futures are for clowns. What business are you in?"

"Futures," Limmer said.

"Mr. Limmer is my client here," Lucas explained. "It's his project."

"His project? But it's your house . . . isn't it?"

"Damn right it is," Lucas rumbled. "And what I do here is my own friggin'. . ."

Limmer silenced him with a glance, arched a brow again, then looked Brink up and down as if measuring him. "It's a joint venture," he said. "Something that might interest you, in fact. Do you enjoy travel?"

Men were coming from the patio, carrying a tripod of welded I-beams with a calibrated swivel mounted in its arch. Pete Swain helped them lug the thing through the hole, then turned to Lucas. "It's according to spec, whatever it is. We'll have to drill for lug bolts in there."

A faint grin had appeared on Lucas's dour face at Limmer's mention of travel. "Okay," he said, "we'll all clear out while you set it up." He leaned in through the hole and called to Maude, "Let's have lunch out back, hon. It's going to be noisy in there for a little while."

Without ceremony he hustled Ray Brink away, around the corner of the house. Maude shooed Mandy and the hoodlums out after them and followed with an armload of eats.

Edwin Limmer gazed after them thoughtfully. "A century or so," he said to no one but himself and his wrist. "Just a brief excursion, to test the focalizer."

With the unsuspecting Brinks' imminent vacation in mind, he went to awaken George Wilson. It was time to mount the focalizer and align the generator. The device itself lay ready on the kitchen counter—a thick sleeve of alternating copper coils around a Bausch & Lomb lens complex, all encased in a "cage" of electronic circuitry cannibalized from the Hawthorns' microwave oven, a Panasonic keyboard, and two television receivers.

"Forage and innovation," Limmer mused. "Right out of the manual."

∞

Now occurs everywhere, simultaneously. But it doesn't have to be experienced the moment it happens. Every now there ever was is still exactly when it was, when it was now. Then, in terms of perception, is nothing more than all the nows that are no longer now. Thus the difference between now and then is when.

—*The Waystop Users' Manual*

∞

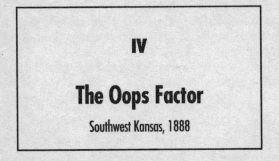

IV

The Oops Factor

Southwest Kansas, 1888

It was John Two Elk who found the sky seed. More precisely, though, the seed found John Two Elk. It bounced off his head a few miles south of Wichita and changed his world forever.

Two Elk had been a famous man in his time. The eagle feather on his old hat was a gift from the great White Bear, and the rusted Colt revolver in his threadbare soogan had once belonged to Captain Jack Hines. Two Elk had seen five territories and three wars, and his likeness had appeared in the *Boston Globe*. Satank had called him "Little Brother." Yellowhair had relied upon his skills, and Hickock had traded moccasins with him.

But all that was long ago. The vast plains and flint hills that had been the domain of the Kiowa were now all cut up and labeled, interlaced with white men's roads and white men's rails and white men's fences. The vast, clean expanses now were blemished—cluttered with the festering little communities that were white men's abodes.

Once he had been Two Elk, and everyone from the Shahi'ena to the roving Kwahadi had known his fame. Now he was just Injun John, because the white men were too lazy to learn the name Tsa'Vapiti.

Now John Two Elk was a wanderer, a roving bone-gatherer. The young eagle had become an old buzzard, doing what he could to keep his belly from growling. The other, greater hungers that haunted him could be drowned now and then in a whiskey jug. On this day he was on his way up from the bone-fields along Hay Creek, his old cart piled tree-high with bleached buffalo bones to trade at the stockyards. Two days out and two days back, gathering and hauling great stacks of clattering bones.

He had awakened in the first blush of dawn and was just arranging scrub twigs over tinder to make a little fire when something popped directly above him, then bounced off his head.

It was a round thing the size of a woman's fist, as yellow as new willow leaves, and covered with short, bristly fur. Around its surface curved a narrow, undulating path of bare, pale skin like a part in drawn hair. Black symbols were painted neatly on a furry surface, and with a gnarled finger he traced them. Wilson 2, they said.

Two Elk held the thing up before his eyes, turning it this way and that. It seemed to be perfectly round. He squeezed it and felt a firm resilience. He threw it to the ground, and it bounced grandly. "Egg?" he wondered. But what kind of egg had bright, greenish-yellow wool? Maybe it was a seed of some kind. He touched it with his tongue, and the taste was not the taste of food. It was lighter than its size indicated, and he shook it. It seemed to be hollow, but nothing rattled inside.

He considered gutting it with his knife but decided against that. To cut it might spoil it, whatever it was. He climbed a low rise and gazed all around. Whatever the thing might be, he saw no others like it. With a grunt, he wrapped it in a scrap of cloth and put it away in his pack. Maybe someone at Dodge would know what it was.

His old horse was grazing peaceably in a nearby ravine. Two Elk returned to his fireset, retrieved his tinder, and put it away. He didn't need a fire today. There was no coffee to brew, and the tough, jerked meat that was his breakfast required no cooking. With a sigh he snugged his pack and brought Horse up to the cart. When she was hitched and harnessed he tossed his pack into the tail of the two-wheel contrivance and set off, angling east of north. Horse plodded along placidly, towing the cart, following him without a lead. Like him, she had nothing better to do.

Two Elk had gone a hundred yards when a raucous noise erupted behind him. It was a low, throaty growl that went on and on. For an instant Two Elk froze, then cursed and ducked aside as Horse raced past him, her ears back, scrawny haunches giving power to her panic. In her wake it rained buffalo bones.

Two Elk's goods only went about thirty yards. The left wheel of the cart bounded over a jutting stone, crashed down into the wind-scour beyond it, and broke into two pieces. Two Elk shouted and Horse swung her head around. Bound in fouled traces, she pawed, trembled, and looked past him. Behind, the mechanical growl continued.

Two Elk turned, blinked, and stared. There, just where he had come from, a thing moved across the grass—a squat, ugly thing with posts standing over it and a voice like grumbling gravel. The thing was coming toward him. Two Elk gawked at the pair of big, iron teeth protruding ahead of it, at the fat gray wheels on which it rolled, and at the man riding it. The man wore faded blue from neck to booted feet. His ears were hidden by black muffs and he had a turtle shell on his head.

As the apparition approached, Two Elk squatted and unrolled his soogan. He found Captain Jack's old revolver and brought it out. He didn't know whether it would fire or not. He wasn't even sure it was still loaded. But he pointed it at the man on the machine.

The man's dark, slitted eyes widened. He did hasty things to his machine, and it turned sideways and stopped. The man's turtle-shell hat went one way and his ear covers another as he rolled from his perch and dived for cover behind his machine.

For a long moment there was silence, then Two Elk's finger twitched nervously. The old revolver roared and bucked. White smoke blossomed at its snout, and a bullet whanged against the machine's frame and screamed off into the distance.

"Holy mother!" the man behind the iron thing shrilled. "Quit shooting! What the hell's going on here?"

Waystop
The Present

"Oops," George Wilson said.

"Oops?" Edwin Limmer repeated. "What do you mean, 'Oops'?"

"I mean that delivery was out of sync," Wilson said, tracing circuitry on the exposed control card of his jerry-rigged generator. "Who's been playing with this panel?"

Limmer frowned, glancing around. The Hawthorn house had been a scene of chaos since the beginning of its conversion to a waystop. But it had been a comfortable, controlled chaos. Since the arrival of the Brinks, however, chaos had become shambles. The Brink twins were maybe sixteen or seventeen years old—a matched pair of bizarre creatures with all the human qualities of warthogs—but they behaved as if they were ten. Spoiled beyond redemption was his evaluation of them. The only thing worse was their father, an officious oaf with a courtroom voice and the wit of an ant.

Limmer felt sympathy for Mandy Brink. Maude Hawthorn's sister was a strikingly beautiful young woman, and somewhere behind her patient, withdrawn attitude he sensed a very real, unique spirit. But whatever spirit was there had been buried, it seemed. Ray Brink was a domineering man, and not one to tolerate second opinions in his domain.

From the moment the Brinks had arrived, the place had seemed full of Brinks. But just at the moment, they were elsewhere.

"You mean you lost your tennis ball?" Limmer asked. "Where is it?"

"Oh, it's where it's supposed to be." Wilson turned to the mercury-level gauge on the focalizer. "It just isn't *when* it's supposed to be. It should have been, and it was for a few minutes. But it bounced."

"Tennis balls do that," Limmer pointed out.

"I mean temporally. The wake is there, then it ends and appears again in another time. The exact coordinates are . . . never mind. It isn't where I sent it anymore."

"So what happened?"

"It's these vectors. They're off. Delivery placement was perfect in three dimensions. The ball arrived well within the conduit. But tempronic coordination is off by three point one-seven syncs. That's a span of plus or minus eight years in T2."

"That isn't much."

"It's enough to cause a skip. It's like a pebble in a pond. If it strikes at the proper angle it penetrates and stays. But at an acute angle it 'skips' off the surface and goes on. Skip-tracing is no problem normally, but in this case we seem to have hit a wobble. In the late spring of 1887, Earth shifted a little on its axis. It does that now and then. The ball hit that wobble."

"So it's lost?"

"For the moment, yes. That skip effect repeats itself. It isn't when or where it should be. My guess is that it skipped farther back and maybe half a quad east."

"Well, it'll turn up." Limmer shrugged. "It's only a tennis ball. The way you said 'Oops,' I thought we had a problem. Sometimes I think the most fearsome word in scientific vocabulary is oops."

"It is," Wilson agreed. "There are no small errors in quantum physics, you know. I can't figure how this setting got off-true."

Limmer looked around carefully, then knelt to inspect a tiny puddle of liquid on the floor under the generator. He touched it with a finger, tasted his finger, and scowled. It was root beer. "The hoodlums," he growled. "Leland and Leslie."

"There," Wilson said. "It's reset. Set up another tennis ball, will you?"

Limmer got another ball from the open carton. The fuzzy yellow sphere smelled like fresh polyurethane and its brand was vivid on its garish wool: WILSON 2. "Why not Spalding?" he asked. "Back when I was old, the kids all used Spaldings."

"They're all the same." Wilson shrugged. "I just prefer Wilsons. I like the name." He paused in what he was doing and looked around, his dark eyes intense and brooding. "Is there any word of Magda?"

"None yet." Limmer spread his hands. "The Whispers are searching, but . . . "

Wilson turned away abruptly, like a man clinging to a steely resolve. He's grieving, Limmer thought. He's afraid his wife is dead.

"She's alive, George," the anomaly said. "Somewhere, somewhen, she survived. The Whispers would know if she hadn't."

"Yes, of course they would." Wilson's voice was low and tight. "They know a lot more than we do, certainly. But they don't know it all."

Limmer turned the tennis ball in his hand. He had wondered about Wilson. The man was, after all, the original inventor of the technology the Whispers had expanded. The initial principles had combined in that mind to make time travel practical. What was still in there, beyond the hardware he had developed? "George, is it possible that there are other times . . . other kinds of time . . . than we know about? Or that the Whispers don't know how to reach?"

"How would I know? I've always thought so. Anything's possible. Identifying a fourth dimension doesn't mean there isn't a fifth beyond it. Or within it or around it. Why?"

"I don't know." Limmer shrugged. "They—the Whispers— they don't know where Magda went. Not yet. But they did find something. They found a man's footprints where hers stopped. No track or trail, just footprints there in the sand. They've found several puzzling things like that. And some-when along the line they've come across someone who—well, who doesn't exist as far as they can tell. And a name. Adam."

Wilson turned again, his eyes narrowing. "Adam?"

"Yes. Does that mean something?"

Wilson squinted, deep in thought, then sighed. "No." He shrugged. "Just a coincidence. God! Where could she be? Did you know we were expecting a baby?"

"Magda was pregnant . . . at the Cimarron?"

"Two months." With a reflexive shake of his head, George Wilson returned to his work. "I'm ready to test," he said.

Limmer set the tennis ball on the steel-plated dining room floor, more or less in the center. Location here wasn't critical. The reflector base offered only one dimension in use—up.

The steel plates gleamed darkly. Every trace of rust had vanished at first activation of the focalizer, along with everything else on the surface of the steel. The plates appeared polished now, and their surfaces flowed with patterns of iridescence.

Wilson double-checked his circuits, then touched a relay. Twelve feet away a tiny hole high in the north wall emitted a little puff of smoke, and the Bausch & Lomb lenses within their copper sleeve glowed faintly. With a sharp *pop*, the tennis ball on the floor vanished.

George Wilson checked his calibrations. "Perfect," he said. "Now if you can just keep those juvenile monsters away from this, it will function indefinitely."

"I have an idea about that. You used Nordstrom as a gravity?"

"Of course. With Polaris for vector." Wilson indicated the little hole in the north wall. "You know the triangulation. The pole star complex is constant in its relationship to this hemisphere, at least for a few hundred more years. The Nordstrom Singularity is equatorial to earth, and it's the most reliable black hole we know of. It's huge, stable, and past flux. The vacuum cleaner of the universe. With proper care, this triangulation won't have to be adjusted again for a while."

"With proper care."

"Right. Just keep those monsters away from it."

"I'm working on that," Limmer assured him.

Pete Swain had paused at the open wall, watching curiously. He hadn't the foggiest idea what was being done here, but that didn't matter. Pete took the professional view that his job was to get the work done, not to understand its purpose. The abrupt disappearance of the tennis ball had shaken him a bit, but he thrust it from his mind. Since the show seemed to be over, he stepped through into the kitchen. "Mr. Hawthorn said to tell you he has a brassiere coming out first thing tomorrow," he told Limmer.

"Brazier." Limmer nodded. "Not brassiere. But that's fine. Those plates aren't going to shift now. The magnetic field bonds them."

Swain nodded, not understanding any of it. He peered around the interior. "Have you seen Hong?"

"Who?"

"Larry Hong. The Chinaman. The metals supply boys are loading up, and they want their forklift. We can't find it."

"It was here a few minutes ago." Limmer spread his hands. "Look around. It can't be too far away."

At the focalizer, George Wilson had turned to listen to them. Now he frowned, inspected his circuits, and did calculations on a pocket computer. He squinted at the results, cocked his head, and repeated the calculations. The answer was the same. The "wake" readings in retrosync were far too big for a tennis ball.

"Oops," he said.

"I can see at least a dozen building code violations from right here," Ray Brink advised sagely. "Not to mention what you're doing to your aesthetics. You're ruining the value of this property."

"It's my house," Lucas pointed out, trying to keep his temper in check. Maude's shyster brother-in-law had always been a prime asshole, in Lucas's opinion, but now the jerk was really on a roll.

"Of course it's your house, Lucas." Ray gave him the thin smile of a wise adult tolerating a rebellious child. "But there are limits. I can't let you destroy the place. How are you going to entertain in a house that looks like a microchip factory?"

"Entertain?" Lucas glared at the lawyer. "You mean like sing and dance for visitors? Cut the crap, Ray."

"Like it or not"—Brink shrugged—"you are a prominent businessman in this community. You have certain social responsibilities. Important people socialize, Lucas. Why, I could promise a half-dozen councilmen, a sheriff, and at least one state senator for your guest list if you'd just give a party . . ."

"If you want politicians entertained, Ray, you sing and dance for them yourself. I'm not interested."

Brink looked immensely pained. "We all tolerate your eccentricities, Lucas, but don't you think this foolishness carries it too far? Look at this mess! You don't even know who these people are."

From the wide hallway at the end of the "dining room," the place did look like a shop of some kind. With its floor covered in metallic tiles and the "bell tower" standing near the north wall above the maze of exposed electronics that was George Wilson's "generator," with a gaping hole in one exterior wall and the surrounding surfaces draped in dark vinyl, it was no longer a dining room at all. It looked more like a stage setting for a low-budget production of *Bimbos from Outer Space*.

Across the room, Edwin Limmer and George Wilson were in conference, tinkering with the electronics. Limmer glanced around, muttered something, and turned back to his work.

"I know exactly who they are," Lucas snapped, glaring at his brother-in-law. "That's George Wilson over there, and the man you met when you came in is Edwin Limmer. You've heard me talk about him for years."

"That's what I mean." Ray returned the glare. "The only Edwin Limmer I ever heard of is the old man who set up your trust, back when you were a baby. Some kind of a soybean prophet. He's only a legend. If he were still alive—even if there ever was such a person—he'd be maybe a hundred and forty or fifty years old. You're being conned, Lucas. I can't believe you're letting these people do this to you, but it's definitely time to put a stop to it. I'm going to have to bring in the authorities, for your own benefit."

"You really would, wouldn't you?" Lucas growled. A tennis ball flicked past his nose and bounced off a wall, followed by another. The balls happily caromed this way and that. Leslie and Leland had found the boxes of balls and were playing war games with them.

"It's for your own good, Lucas." Ray sighed. "I'm just glad I caught this before it was too late to undo the damage. Imagine what this—this little project of yours could do to your insurance rating, not to mention your credibility in the community."

More tennis balls joined the melee, and big, dirty L.A. Gears thudded on the metal floor as Leland and Leslie charged past in huge abandon. "Delinquents," Lucas muttered, his neck darkening as he tried to control his temper. For the thousandth time he told himself that his wife's sister must have been in the throes of terminal PMS when she moved in with this arrogant twit and his offspring.

The house was relatively quiet now. Most of the construction was proceeding outside, where a team was covering the gaping hole in the east wall with polyethylene sheeting while the rest searched the grounds for a missing forklift.

Edwin Limmer wandered across from the "bell tower" and Ray accosted him. "I don't know exactly what your game is, mister," he said pompously, "but it stops here. I'm an officer of the court."

"Good for you." Limmer smiled. "Do you know anything about contour farming?"

"Contour . . . of course not!"

"Shame." Limmer shrugged. "A thing like that would have been very useful in this area a hundred years ago. Plenty of surface water, but the settlers didn't know how to use it. I don't suppose you can use survey equipment, either?"

"I'm warning you, Limmer—or whatever your name is . . ."

"Lawyer, huh?" Limmer looked him up and down. "Do you have any useful skills?"

"He's a handicapped golfer," Mandy offered from the kitchen.

Brink shot a glare at his wife. "Shut up, Mandy," he growled. "It's three-handicap, not *handicapped*, for Christ's sake. Just stay out of this."

Maude bristled. "Chill out, Ray," she snapped, but Mandy tugged at her sleeve. "I just do that to aggravate him," she whispered. "Ray wouldn't know a joke if it fit him."

"Fit . . . you mean, *bit* him?"

Mandy nodded. "He's serious about golfing. I have a ball with that. I tees."

Maude shook her head. "Like taunting a surly bear," she said.

"I know," Mandy admitted. "I'm threading on thin grass."

"I guess you could wrestle a plow," Limmer told Ray. "If your belly didn't get in the way. Any experience with horses?"

"I don't know whether you're a swindler or a lunatic, Limmer! But we'll let the court sort that out."

"Fine," Limmer agreed. "I guess you want to see what we're really doing, then?"

"You bet I do!"

Limmer glanced at Lucas, who nodded slightly. Limmer smiled a cat's smile. "I suppose we'd better show you all of it, then. Mrs. Brink?" He turned. "Would you like the tour, too?"

"You boys go ahead," Maude said quickly. "Mandy can wait here with me."

"All right." With a furtive gesture to Lucas to move out of range, Limmer glanced around the room. The twins had been chasing tennis balls, but now they were wrestling on the steel floor, squabbling over the remains of a two-liter bottle of root beer. "Just a moment," he said to Ray. He walked across to where George Wilson waited. "Hit it," he said.

"One horse's ass, two juvenile delinquents, and a mess of tennis balls," Wilson muttered. "I hope the past was ready for this." He touched his relay.

"Have a nice time." Edwin Limmer waved as Ray Brink, his sons, and more than a dozen yellow tennis balls popped out of existence.

Mandy muffled a startled cry, and Maude clutched her shoulder. "It's all right," she said. "They've just gone on a trip."

"A . . . a trip?"

"Right. Back in time. You can go, too, if you want to. But just this once, sis, make your own decision, without Ray telling you what you want."

"It's true, then?" Mandy stared at her sister, wide-eyed. "What you said about time travel?"

"I guess it is. I believe it. Do you want to go with them? Mr.

Wilson can send you, too, if you like. It's somewhere—somewhen, rather—in the past century."

Mandy blinked thoughtfully. "Ray and the boys, they're—they're still here? I mean, right here where we are but at a different time?"

Edwin Limmer had approached and leaned casually on the kitchen counter. "Not exactly here," he said. "Timelines don't coincide with the same piece of real estate from one day to the next. The earth rotates, you know. But the geographic location isn't too far away. Couple of hundred miles, at most. We didn't shift any loci."

"Can you—I mean, how will you find them to bring them back?"

"Oh, that shouldn't be a problem. Contratemporal motion leaves whorls, just like a fingerprint. Using the same TEF to retrieve, we can find them when we want them and bring them back. As long as they don't somehow smear the track, and they'd have to have four-dimensional perception to do that. We could snap them back right now, but they'd only have experienced a few minutes of relocation. Selective retrieval doesn't work well in short bursts."

"But . . . the past! They might be in danger there!"

"No more than here," Lucas growled. "If that husband of yours doesn't learn some manners, somebody's going to beat hell out of him one of these days. I might do it myself."

"They're having an adventure," Limmer said. "Be a shame to cut it too short. Give them a while. We can bring them back any time, from any time."

"Unless we hit a wobble," George Wilson added from across the room.

"What does that mean?"

"Nothing to worry about." Limmer shook his head. "It's a technical thing. But we have selective retrieval, to a point. For instance, we could leave them there a couple of weeks, and pick them up a few hours from now, if you want."

"Oh." Mandy thought about it. "Does that mean you can

leave them there a day or two and retrieve them maybe next month sometime?"

"No sweat." Limmer shrugged.

"Then there's really no hurry, I guess." Mandy rubbed her chin thoughtfully. "No, I don't want to go. I think I'd enjoy a little on-my-ownness."

"Thought you would," Maude approved. "I know smelling the roses isn't part of 'The World According to Ray,' but you could use a vacation, sis—a little reprieve from Brinkdom."

Limmer went off to look outside, where people were still searching for a missing forklift and its operator. The women glanced after him, then at each other. Mandy had caught it, too—the strange sense of distance . . . of otherness. It was as if he understood everything and said nothing about anything except the subject at hand. In demeanor he was a quiet, sardonic man with decent manners and a reassuring presence. But his eyes were as remote and cold as northern skies.

"Who is he, Maude?" Mandy whispered. "I mean, really?"

"I'm not sure," Maude said. "But he's been around a long time. Maybe several long times."

∞

Time is nature's way of keeping everything from happening all at once.

—EDWIN LIMMER

∞

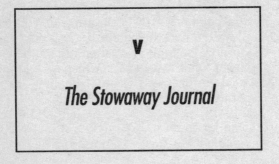

The Stowaway Journal

December 11, 1989

To: Whoever might happen to find and read this, wherever and whenever I lose it. In the event that it is never found, please feel free to disregard this testimony in its entirety, since you won't know about it anyway. And it won't matter. I do this for my own sake, knowing that I will remember less and less as my time elapses.

My name is Edwin Limmer. I was born sixty-one years from now in a cabin on the high Llano—about fifteen years after King Arthur consolidated the four rivers territory as his personal realm. You don't know about that, of course, because it hasn't happened yet.

I was a backward child. That is, without a doubt, the ultimate in understatement. The fact is, I was— and am, and will be—*the* backward child. The Whispers are fairly certain that I'm the only one there ever was or will be, anywhen.

I have lived—so far—a total of 135 years. I was ninety-eight in elapsed duration when I finally got out of the T2 retrosync conduit. That was thirty-seven years ago. I am sixty-one now, and next year I'll be sixty. That's because of a fundamental fact of temporal physics, which the Whispers have named just for me. They call it Limmerism—the law of synchronic displacement. Paraphrased, it means you can take a person out of backward, but you can't take backward out of the person.

I was in my sixteenth year when my mother was born. I never knew her, but the Whispers told me. I will be sixteen again—if I don't die first—in the same year in which I was sixteen before, 2034. That was—and will be—a year or so before Camelot began. The kingdom of Arthur Rex will cover the old Panhandle Free Zone, which used to be parts of the states of Kansas, Oklahoma, Texas, and New Mexico, and maybe some of Colorado. At that time King Arthur was—and will be—still just Arthur Meeks, resident monomaniac at ITR, and plotting treachery in the wake of the Three Brothers War.

You don't know about that war, because it hasn't happened yet. It wasn't much of a war, really. There were—or will be—so many little wars in that period that it might not have been noticed, except that nobody ever really believed that California would form an alliance with Mexico to invade Texas. Mexico, of course, wanted the heartland grain belt and a lock on commodities in world trade. California was just being California. Cultural realignment was the trendy thing at the time.

But that's all long ago, in the time I'm going back to. I have grown independently wealthy on commodity futures, thanks to the crib notes the Whispers provided for me. I have also provided for the financial security of some others, for reasons I don't always understand. But all of that is extraneous activity. My entire purpose in life these days seems to be to accumulate duration . . . just keep going, while I become younger among those growing older. Maybe they'll tell me someday just what the hell I'm doing here.

September 9, 1991

A revelation! The Whispers have a purpose in mind for me. I guess they always did but just didn't bother to tell me about it. It has to do with a phenomenon they call "overloop." Something from the Paradox Equations. If events of the past are dependent on some future occurrence, then the past must stimulate that occurrence so that it will occur.

In temporal terms, overloop is to a closed loop as the securing knot on a boat's mooring line, made fast to a davit, is to a knot with nothing in it. A closed loop cancels itself out. For all its ins and outs, a knot is just bent rope. An overloop, on the other hand, is what keeps the boat of circumstance from drifting off on the playful tides of temporal inertia.

I'm not clear on what part I will play, but somewhere ahead it seems I will come full circle. I will coincide with the situation that caused me—King Arthur's immortality scheme. And there is something I must do when that occurs. Something vital. I guess I'll know it when I see it.

May 14, 1994

So far as I know, I am the only one who got sucked into the temporal singularity that occurred when Arthur threw his immortality switch. I see by my earlier entries that I have already made that clear, but I repeat it in light of the coincidence that binds me to Arthur Meeks—or Arthur Rex, as he designated himself about the time I was twelve.

I won't dwell here on the fact that Arthur Rex is—or was or will be—an unredeemed son of a bitch, a world-class lout, and a psychotic tyrant. By the time it matters, everybody will already know that. But for reasons I am only beginning to suspect, I was caught in the maelstrom when the time-storm came. What happened afterward was all before I was born.

If it hadn't been for the Whispers, I wouldn't have made it.

Retrosync isn't a place. It's a condition. As duration progressed and I got older—while out in regular time the world got younger—I made my essential transitions from age to age in a way no one ever had before. I was living backward, relative to everyone in "real time," and I had only a company of sympathetic but distracted long-time travelers to help me along. The Whispers are people. They change diapers just like anybody else. But they aren't people of any time you—or even I—can truly understand. They come from so far in the future that all this is ancient history to them even as they pass through it.

Some of them are mildly interested in the doings of these ages of ours, but they all have greater things in mind. They are on their way to when it all began, and what their scouts have found there—or, more accurately, then—is better suited to their imaginations than to ours.

They didn't want me, but they accepted me when I was thrust upon them, and they took care of me in my formative times. They saw to my needs, gave me the knowledge and understandings I could deal with, and as soon as I was weaned they began trying to get rid of me.

It wasn't easy. Because of Arthur's Anachronism, my natural chronological direction was from tomorrow to yesterday, and temporal inertia is a powerful force. In total duration, it took them ninety-eight years—from 2050 to 1952—to finally get me going forward in time. And then I began to unwind.

The Whispers were patient, though. They have plenty of time on their hands—every tick of it that has ever elapsed or will elapse for the next few thousand years. I was still a squalling infant when they first tried to thrust me into mainstream. It didn't work, but they kept trying.

Time's flow isn't a straight, narrow trench. It is a wide, curling stream of temporal twists and weaves as wild as storm winds, as constrained as a choreographed, elliptical dance. The retrosync conduit within it is the same thing but in reverse. It is all flowing in the same direction ultimately, but all along the way there are rogue currents—eddies and backwashes that the Whispers can identify because they know how.

It was the backwashes of retrosync that gave them opportunities to get rid of me. It was the insistent central flow that made it difficult.

It happened over and over. They'd set me adrift on an eddy and I'd bob along for a while, parallel to the flow of T2—which is how they see real time. But then the eddy would reverse itself and there I was, right back where I started in retrosync, full circle. Sometimes it was a different bunch of Whispers who fished me out and started again. There was wave after wave of them, coming back from the future, passing through. It was more like a migration than an expedition. But usually I wound up with the same team, whether they liked it or not. They were an offshoot group, a project team of specialists led—if they have leaders—by Teal Fordeen. They roved back and forth in the conduit, doing whatever it is they did.

Their habitat is a "closed loop" called L-383. In time conduit a loop is like a loop in a string—only with more dimensions. You can "roll" the loop anywhere you want along the string, because it's part of the string. But it's still a loop.

Each time I washed back into retrosync, no matter who found me, I was eventually shunted back to that same loop, and they picked up where they had left off—taking care of me and trying to get rid of me.

I can't blame them. Nowhere in the book does it say that Whispers are supposed to be nursemaids for contratemporized persons. They saved my life, and look what they got for it. Me.

October 3, 1994

More and more, I encounter times and circumstances I have encountered before—on those excursions into maintime when the Whispers were kicking me out of retrosync. I haven't actually met myself in these periods, and I'm not sure I would know it if I did. But *déjà vu* is becoming a way of life.

There were a lot of those excursions on the way back to where I began unwinding. It happened over and over again. There'd be a backwash in the temporal currents, and they would stick me into it. The device they used was a modification of the T1 booster they use for their own excursions into mainstream time—an intense magnetic field that approximates gravitic effect. I came to know the tingle and thrust of enhanced gravitation like I knew the sound of wind.

They would sort of gather there, Teal and Elzy Pyar and sweet, cranky little Toocie Toonine and the rest of them, wishing me well and hoping I'd never come back. But when the eddy reversed itself and threw me back, it usually deposited me just upstream from where they had put me in. So here I would come, right back past them—them or others like them—and I'd hear all those quiet Whisper voices saying "Tish'o!" as I passed. Of course, being still contratemporal to them, I was hearing it backward.

May 2, 1995

I suppose I have been fortunate in my preparation. Most of my ninety-eight years as a stowaway
among Whispers, I spent in reverse eddies parallel
to—and effectively present in—real time. Thus, I
am fully bitemporal and at ease in either mode. I
can say without hesitation that I understand you a
hell of a lot better than you understand me.

The Whispers are like a parade in retrograde. In
my life I've known only a few of them singularly.
There was—is? will be?—Ayel Kaydee, who is
always looking for gates, and Zeem Sixten, who
came back from a long time ago to tell me what I
should do earlier, and that crazy Peedy with his
obsession about mammalian evolution . . . others,
too, but not many. Mostly they are just passing
through, observing as they go. Knowing them is like
trying to know a forest. You lose track of the individual trees.

But some I know, and some I remember—harmless, curious people out on a great adventure.

It hasn't been easy. There have been tragedies.
Somewhere—or somewhen—there are Whispers
lost in time, while their friends search for them.
The "Lost Loop" is a mystery to them. It is beyond
their technology. Somewhere in the future, too—
though in their durational past—is a shocking
episode, the massacre of more than ninety WHIS
researchers in a time and place where such a thing
was inconceivable.

And then there was the massive anachronism
they encountered at 2050—a time-storm of enormous proportions. It was the result of time-
tampering by a lunatic named Arthur.

It was Zeem Sixten who told me about Arthur
and set me on my career. The Whisper migration—
that growing, enthusiastic exodus to a past time
when unpredictable frontiers beckon, that tide of

people that was my life in my retrosync years—requires in-stream acceleration points at intervals along the time conduit. The first of these, relative to their starting point in the far future, will be quite a few decades downstream (to them) from Arthur's Anachronism. Getting around that deviation costs them precious momentum, and they need to recover it. They require temporal booster points.

Zeem Sixten offered me the job, and I accepted it. The duration of my life so far is twice the normal life span of ordinary humans, but never within it have I been able to know the pleasures that such years should bring. A man needs company. A man needs the presence of others of his kind. A man needs friends, and a mate. But in all of this absurd back-and-forth life King Arthur gave me, there is only myself. There are no other stowaways—no other temporal reversees.

I have sampled life in tantalizing little tastes far longer than most men live, but I have never known duration of purpose. Throughout retrosync I was an occasional visitor at the gates of real life. And now that I am in mainstream, I swim always in reverse. The liaisons I've found were brief and bittersweet. Friendships must be terminated at intervals. Love cannot even be allowed, when each passing day increases the age difference by two.

I needed something to do, and a reason to do it. Zeem Sixten gave me those things.

Arthur's legacy to me is everlasting loneliness and an emptiness of soul. The only brightness through most of it has been the cold anger of knowing what Arthur did—fifty-five years from now. Zeem Sixten gave me a job—or a series of jobs—and he gave me the knowledge that I will

have a chance to repay Arthur in full . . . when I've
lived long enough.

February 12, 1996
I know the geographic location of the site now,
and the temporal location will coincide with it soon.
There is a committee of Whispers in residence
around it, doing the preliminary fieldwork while
they wait for my arrival. The place is the home of
someone I once knew, forty years ago, when I was
very old and he was still a baby. Such coincidence
reminds me that there is very little that is coinci-
dental when one deals with Whispers.

They will provide a technician to build and install
a temporal effect focalizer—apparently another
refugee from King Arthur's disaster. I gather from
Zeem Sixten that George Wilson and I have some
interests in common.

In return for services, the Whispers offer me a
precious thing: poetic justice. I am an anomaly. I
was Arthur's fault, and I am the one who will show
him the true meaning of redundancy . . . back there
in the future.

Maybe I was already going to do that. It seems to
me I have sensed a destiny like that, a few years ago
when I was older. But it is hard to be sure. The
"unwinding" process from T2 retrosync back to
origin—even the Whispers have no clear explanation of it—is increasingly confusing to me as I go
along. The past muddies. Often I have the feeling
that I am becoming too young to remember things I
once knew. But I *will* have my shot at Arthur. I will
be the overloop that snares him—some time in the
future.

Arthur. That bastard. What is it about humanity
that makes us tolerate pitiless bullies, that makes
so many of us hail them as our leaders? How many

have there been like Arthur? How many more will there be? Among the Whispers, I have encountered no such beasts. Maybe there aren't any. But the Whispers come from a long time off. When will the riddance of Arthurs begin?

Still, this one at least will pay the price of his crimes. He will discover the truth of the adage: Be careful what you wish for, because you might get it. By his own actions he inconvenienced the Whispers and at the same time apparently achieved his fondest wish ... but not in exactly the way he wished. I don't know much about that. I suspect even the Whispers aren't quite sure exactly what happened—or will happen. But I do know I'll be part of it.

I owe the Whispers. They accepted me, cared for me, and did their best for me. I have seen how they provided for my future, and I suspect they even left a nice surprise in my past. I hope so, but there is only one way to find out.

[Undated Entry] *Observations and notations*

The time has coincided with the place, and I have met George Wilson. He was—or, rather, will be—lead duck in the flock for the Institute for Temporal Research. The head honcho. The main man, scientifically. Surprising for one so young. But he was—will be—recruited directly from the Tolafsson Foundation's think tanks by the ITR. He will prove to be a true prodigy in applied angle-field manipulation. The temporal effect focalizer, using selective celestial gravitation as its energy source, will be his personal brainchild.

And when Arthur confiscates the device for his own use, it will be George Wilson from whom he will steal it.

No wonder Wilson will lead the Revivalists in their revolution against Camelot. Who will ever

have had a better reason to despise the tyrant—
except, of course, myself? Though of course that
will be before my time. I won't be born until ten
years after Wilson's revolution ends.

The Whispers say that what I have never had,
George Wilson had and lost. His Magda, his beloved
wife, will be among the missing at the Cimarron.
Apparently even the Whispers have not found her.

∞

Time is a state of indefinite, continuous duration in which events succeed one another. It is inexorable and seems inescapable. Since human awareness began, time has been regarded variously as a taskmaster, a grim reaper, a grindstone, a runaway train, a malevolent tyrant, a shackle and a ticking bomb. In a real sense, humanity has founded its collective psyche on the certainty that time is a thing.

Only with the advent of bitemporal experience did it become clear that time is no object.

—P.F. FOSTER, *Time and the Human Condition*

∞

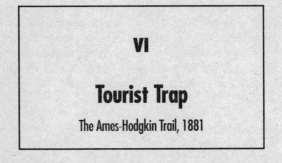

VI

Tourist Trap

The Ames-Hodgkin Trail, 1881

Out of hazed distance they crawled, a moving, meandering body of beasts flanked by dusty riders on dusty, plodding mounts—a herd in transit, up from the Strip and bound for the rails, shrouded by the dust of its own passage.

Bill Holly rode long point, bringing Rocking A's cows north to the waiting pens. Though his shoulders sagged with exhaustion, his sun-creased eyes were clear in the shadow of his battered hat. A double bonus rode on this job, and for good reason. Since winter cut there had been talk of bunch-cutters and ambushers. Somebody didn't want Rocking A to reach market, and everybody knew it. Still, two weeks up the trail, not a single critter had been lost, and trail's end was almost in sight. Only one more river to cross.

Cloudbanks stood in the west like a great, blue-gray mountain range, and there were thunderheads atop them—ominous, mushroom caps of cloud where little lightnings danced. It would be raining now up in the caprock. But the Cimarron was just ahead, with clear trail beyond all the way up to Wichita. Once across the mile-wide valley ahead, it would be lazy work the rest of the way . . . barring trouble.

Cresting a long swell, Holly reined Stargazer to the left, then halted. Ahead, hundreds of little gray mounds dotted the short-grass prairie like beestings on a honey-robber's back. Here and there, every fifty yards or so, furry foot-tall rodents stood guard atop the mounds, little sentinels protecting their domain.

"Varmints," Holly muttered. "If it ain't one thing, it's six!"

The prairie dog town had always been there, as far back as anyone could remember. But in recent seasons it had grown. Once the mounded digs had pretty much petered out about Mule Creek. But now they were everywhere ahead, extending for miles . . . a vast city of burrows and humps where a stray cow could break a leg or a good horse ruin itself in the blink of an eye.

"Ain't no other way about it," Bill Holly told himself and his horse. "We just got to go around." Shading his eyes, he stood in his stirrups and surveyed the distances. Westward, a mile or so, the prairie dog digs thinned. It would add hours to the trail, circling the herd off that way, but the alternative was unacceptable. Prairie dog towns were sure trouble for any four-legged critter bigger than a wolf or badger, and a man who'd take cows or horses into a dog town was loco. Holly had seen cattle driven into a prairie dog town. He had seen good beef stumble and fall as the burrows trapped their legs, had heard their bones snap, and he had seen the animals around them panic and stampede.

Many an unwary drover had lost his profits trying to cross a dog town.

The herd was still a good ways back, and Holly stepped down to stretch his legs. He walked around Stargazer, inspecting the day mount's underpinnings, then loosened his cinches to let the horse have a breather. After unslinging a saddle canteen, he poured water into his hat and let the horse drink. When it was done, he took a few swallows for himself and replaced the canteen.

He was rightly proud of himself for this drive. Five hundred and fourteen head of prime steers, all the way up from Supply, and not a one lost so far. God and the elements had cooperated for once. Water in every stream, no storms and no interruptions. The herd wasn't even truly trail-broke, for lack of aggravation, but Holly didn't mind that at all. The sky overhead was clear, the wind gentle, and there wasn't anything between him and Wichita now except a prairie dog town and one more river.

Beyond were a couple of days of short-grass and the holding pens of Wichita.

Man might almost relax, with things going so easy, he thought. At the notion he frowned, shaded his eyes, and looked all around. There was still the talk of stampeders, and even if there weren't, experience had taught Bill Holly that there is no such thing as a trouble-free drive.

Still, there had been no sign of troublemakers so far, and there wasn't a thing in sight that could cause them grief now. Even the dog town was only an inconvenience. They would just go around it.

He relaxed again, a grin spreading across his dusty, whiskered face. "Like fallin' off a log," he muttered.

The herd was within hailing distance now, and he waved. Back at point, T.J. Hastings returned the salute. With a lazy gesture, Holly pointed westward. In the distance, Hastings waved again and danced his cow pony to the left, crowding the lead steer. The critter shook its head and veered westward, and Holly could see riders on that side moving up to correct the turn.

"Right as rain," Holly told himself and his horse. "Just like a turn needs to be. Ought to be set to music, it's that pretty."

As if choreographed, the herd angled westward from its original path and Holly nodded his approval. "Let's take 'em home, boys," he mused. "Be there come payday, sure enough."

He turned toward his mount, and something popped. A bright, greenish-yellow thing thumped on the hard ground and bounded upward, striking Stargazer squarely on the nose. The horse whuffed, went white-eyed, and lunged to the side, tugging at its reins.

"What th' hell? . . ." Holly was almost jerked off his feet. The yellow thing fell, bounced again, and then there were more of them—little fuzzy globes of bright yellow, bouncing and popping all around. One of them bounced off Holly's shoulder and he whirled, reaching for his Colt.

Stargazer whinnied, tried to rear, and Holly fought him down. With a leap, he bounded into his saddle . . . and from there to the ground, flat on his back, as the saddle flipped downward on loose cinches.

The next thing Bill Holly saw was a frenzied Stargazer, saddle askew, racing belly-down toward the herd of cows. In the dust of the mount's departure a fuzzy little yellow globe hopped onto Holly's chest and bobbled there. He grabbed it, flung it away, and sent a shot after it. It seemed to explode on first bounce, thirty feet away, and the echoes of his .45 rolled away into the distance.

Scrambling to his knees, he whirled, his gun leveled. Three people stood there in a tight knot, gawking at him. The two in short pants—they looked like a pair of grotesque apes in weird, ill-fitting suits—screamed and hit the ground, flailing as if they would bury themselves. The third, a duded gent with a thing like a melted cravat dangling from his pristine collar, stared at Holly with eyes the size of dollars. "Wait!" he shrilled. "I'm an officer of the court!"

Holly looked past the strangers. In the distance, Stargazer was thundering down on the herd . . . and the herd responded. Faced with the sudden specter of a berserk horse charging toward them, five hundred and fourteen prime cow-critters did what cattle do best. They bawled, milled, and stampeded, scattering astonished riders in all directions as they headed for Texas.

Bill Holly stood open-mouthed, his six-gun dangling from limp fingers. "Jesus H. Christ," he whispered.

The stranger in the melted cravat turned this way and that, blinking in bewilderment. "Where is this?" he wondered vacantly. "Where . . . where'd Lucas's house go?"

Still ignoring him, Bill Holly squatted on his haunches and picked up one of the little yellow spheres. It was fuzzy, like a starched squirrel might be. It had its name printed on it in black letters. Its name was Wilson. He shook his head, stood again, and gazed with haunted eyes at the distant melee of his departing herd. "My cows," he muttered. "My cows are gone."

The stranger approached him hesitantly and offered him a little white rectangle of bleached cardboard. "Possibly I can be of assistance," he said. "Brink's the name. Raymond J. Brink, attorney-at-law."

As if returning from a long trip, Bill Holly turned slowly to focus on the stranger. Eyes as hard as blue granite in a tanned-leather face drilled through the lawyer. "I ain't that pleased to meet you, stampeder," he growled. "Right now I'm tryin' to decide whether to stomp the hell out of you, shoot you, or take you into Wichita and hang you. Where'd you come from? What in God's name did you do to my cows?" He thrust the yellow sphere into the man's face. "And what the devil is this thing?"

"Tennis ball." Brink blinked. "Just take it easy now, sir. I don't know anything about your . . . your cows. What I want to know is where's the Hawthorn house? Where'd everybody go?"

"Who?"

"Everybody!"

"Ever'body I know is yonder, chasin' my cows. Maybe I'd best just shoot you." Holly raised his gun, then hesitated as the two large juveniles got up from the dirt and started wailing. "Daddy!" they warbled almost in unison. "I don't like it here!" one whined. "The root beer is spilled!" the other chimed in.

"Shut up!" Ray Brink shrilled. "Amanda, can't you . . . oh, she isn't here, is she?"

Running hooves drummed the hard ground and T.J. Hastings hauled up in a cloud of dust. "What happened, Boss?" he drawled. "Who's these?"

"Stampeders," Holly told him. "Where's my horse?"

"Dave's bringin' him in. What spooked him like that?"

"These did." Holly held up his fuzzy sphere. "Tennis balls. How about the herd?"

"Take us till evenin' to gather 'em, I reckon." Hastings was shooting hostile glances at the Brinks. "We gonna hang these scutters or shoot 'em?"

The pair of juveniles gawked around as if they had never seen cow country before, and their mouths dropped open as T.J. Hastings sidled his mount toward them and a big six-gun appeared in his hand. "I'll do the honors," he drawled. "No sense wastin' rope."

"Now just hold on!" Ray Brink demanded. Hastings brought his gun around and the two juveniles bolted, running like big, ugly clowns, their soiled canvas boots thudding on the hard ground. Their oversized short pants flapped around their legs, the crotches catching them about the knees and threatening to bind and throw them.

Hastings stared after them, then laughed aloud. He had never seen such a ludicrous sight. He leveled his .45 and triggered a shot. Beyond the fleeing pair, a prairie dog mound exploded in a cloud of dust and sand. He fired again, over the heads of the fleeing pair. "Git!" he yelled.

In a moment the two were into the prairie dog town, darting and hopping to avoid burrows while tan rodents scurried for cover all around them.

"They'll keep," Hastings growled. "How 'bout this one, Bill? Want me to shoot him?"

"I ain't decided just yet," Holly decided. "But right now, why don't you and the boys see if there's anything useful he can do. We'll pick up those kids after we gather the herd. Right now, let's get our cows back."

Wichita, Kansas
The Present

"Tesla almost understood," George Wilson explained, wandering through cluttered aisles lined with memorabilia, forgotten treasures, and junk, while a fascinated Lucas Hawthorn followed behind him. "That crazy old refugee. He realized that electricity and magnetism are related phenomena. He observed that where either one exists, the other is there, too."

"Mirror-image forces," Lucas intoned, trying to keep up with the rambling dissertation. The two of them—the phlegmatic building contractor and the man from the future—might have seemed slightly out of place in Mary Beth's Mementos, but only because they were the only men in the place. Wilson was looking for something, and Lucas hadn't the slightest idea what it was. "I'll know it when I see it" was all the technician had told him. And so had begun their tour of antique shops and junk stores along Wichita's North Market strip.

"That's how he saw it," Wilson agreed, kneeling to study the hinges on a Bulldog coalburner with a tag dating it to about 1890. "He just didn't look far enough."

Tagging after him, Lucas had paused to peer into an old, leather-bound trunk. Trinkets of a bygone age lay on a shelf above—a straight razor, a wooden stereopticon, some yellowed linen napkins, a dented railroad watch, two pairs of antique eyeglasses ... "Look at this." Lucas pointed. "This looks like it might have been a—"

"A tennis ball," Wilson agreed. He read the display card on the shelf. The trunk and its contents had been recovered from an old hotel near the stockyards, when it was torn down in the 1950s. There was no indication whose property the things might have been.

"One of yours, maybe?"

"Wouldn't be surprised." Wilson shrugged. "What goes around comes around." He gazed to his right, his eyes lighting on a corner ahead where a Wurlitzer juke box and a Magnavox console radio were on display. He headed for them, with Lucas tagging after him.

"What do you mean, 'didn't look far enough'?" Lucas pressed.

"You mean Tesla? He was a genius, you know. But he was limited by his time. He was working in an entirely new field. Nobody really knew what electricity was, or magnetism, either. They don't yet, for that matter. But he saw the significance of their relationship. He saw them as basic forces, somehow joined. As you said, mirror-image forces. He didn't have any evidence to indicate that they weren't what they seemed."

"They weren't?"

"Of course not. They aren't forces at all. They're just effects. Like light isn't a force, just an effect generated by a source. What we see is daylight. What makes it is the sun. And we know now that the sun—like every star—is the emergence into real space of the gravitational effluent of black holes."

"Then electricity and magnetism are twin effects?"

"You're not bad, for a primitive." Wilson nodded. "That's right. Both electricity and magnetism are effects of gravity, which *is* a basic force. The clue is that its effects are multi-dimensional. Every electrical field has a corresponding magnetic field existing at right angles to it. And vice versa."

"Gravity," Lucas mused.

Wilson nodded. "Gravity. The force that rules the planes and creates the dimensions. That's what powers T1. Once you understand that, time is relative."

"So Tesla didn't understand the gravity of the situation?" Lucas ventured.

Wilson was fiddling with the face-panel controls on a large, antique radio. Now the technician glanced around at the contractor ironically. "You sound just like Edwin Limmer," he said. Straightening, he slapped the hardwood top of the Magnavox radio. "This'll do," he said. "Twelve vacuum tubes, oscillators, and mechanical tuning plates. All hardware and amperage, no electronics. Buy it."

Maude and Mandy were hanging curtains in the strange-looking area that had once been Maude's formal dining room. It was no longer a construction site, but neither was it a typical household space. The gleaming metal plates covering the room's floor were now a bright tile pattern, bonded by neat brass seams. The "bell tower" by the north wall was disguised as a mirrored cabinet, and the temporal effect focalizer at its crest seemed nothing more than a peculiar trophy resting atop a shelf. Where the huge hole had been in the exterior wall of the kitchen area was now a solid-seeming brick fascia wall decorated with copper cookware and a large, ornate clock.

Pete Swain's craftsmen had done good work. Any building inspector would be satisfied that the alteration done here was nothing more than interior redecorating to suit the tastes of a pair of somewhat eccentric homeowners.

"Victorian England," Mandy said, stretching on tiptoe to

adjust the spaces between curtain loops. "I'd like to see Piccadilly Circus when it stank."

"Probably still does," Maude observed. "I'd like to see Louis Fourteenth in his Sun Palace myself. Or maybe Vesuvius erupting. That should be fun."

"You're weird, Maude," Mandy noted. "Why don't we compromise and visit the Forbidden City in Peking? We could make it during the Boxer Rebellions, if that kind of thing turns you on."

"You make me sound like a monster." Maude shrugged. "We could take tea with Martha Washington, if that suits you better."

"Terminally dull." Mandy shook her head. "I'd rather watch the first Olympic games."

"I know," Maude said. "All those undressed young Greeks. Probably unwashed, too."

"So was Martha Washington."

"Do you miss Ray and the boys yet?"

"Like a hole in the head." Mandy cocked a pretty brow. "How does that look?"

"Like chintz in a fortress. But it'll do."

The doorbell sounded, and Maude stepped back to survey their work. "I'll see who that is. Any ideas about these other walls?"

"Anything beats landscape plastic," Mandy assured her.

Maude headed for the front door. "I'm sort of looking forward to operating a travel agency, you know? Though I don't quite understand how we're going to get customers if we don't advertise."

Pete Swain stood on the front porch, accompanied by a dark-eyed young woman and four children. They all looked uncomfortable in their traveling clothes, and each had a suitcase.

"We want to visit Loretta's aunt Fran in Louisville," Pete said. "She died six years ago, so it'll have to be before that. How much for the round trip?"

∞

The ascension of Arthur Rex to the steel throne in 2035 ended an era of realignment which some have compared to the Renaissance period of ancient Europe. It also marked the end of the Three Brothers War, the Federated Free Zones and the ITR project.

In many respects, Arthur was a remarkable man. Through treachery, brutality, and sheer force of will, he destroyed both ITR and the Panhandle Free Zone, then reassembled the fragments to create his Camelot. Once crowned by his own hand, he turned his attention to the assembly of wealth and the question of how to live forever.

—*The Chronicles of Camelot*

∞

VII

Camelot

2046

Lindy Rae Koch, who for five months had been Lady Sedgewick, was in residence at Camelot when the squire brought the message from the kitchens. Lindy Rae had, in fact, never been in residence anywhere else but Camelot since her court wedding to Lord Sedgewick the past spring. Lord Ronnie had wanted to take her home to Wichita, but the king had intervened. Lord Sedgewick was needed on the western frontier, where the mountain campaigns were in full swing.

Ronnie had been away three months now, and his messages were curt and quite military. Lindy Rae was disappointed that he seemed to take so well to the business of soldiering. It had not seemed his style during their brief courtship. She had envisioned him rather as lord administrator of towns and lands, exacting king's decrees and collecting king's taxes and coming home to her each evening.

Lady Sedgewick, who was just eighteen, was lonely. As a member of the kitchen staff through her flowering, she had often been tired but never lonely. Then Ronnie had found her and claimed her. She was aristocracy now, and life was different. There were no confidantes among her peers.

Thus when the squire—a dismal old man with a perpetual leer—appeared at her door with a sealed message from the kitchens, she thanked him warmly and smiled prettily enough to trouble his dreams for weeks. In her sitting alcove she read the letter.

"Lindy," it began, and she knew it was personal and secret because no one in the kitchens would have openly called a lady by her pet name. "Do you remember the foundling two years ago?" the message read. "Well, there is another now, younger but of amazing similarity. Please come if you can." It was signed "L."

She had not seen Lucy these five months, except at a distance, but the freckled girl had been her best friend. Lindy and Lucy, she recalled—the Ls of Vat Three.

Another foundling! They had shared a great secret, two years earlier. A mystery and a challenge. They had been working in the cereal pantry, just the two of them, and suddenly there had been a child there with them, a little boy. The waif wore clean, simple clothing and had seemed dazed. He swayed, looking around, and almost fell.

It was a marvel how he came to be there. No children were allowed inside the castle walls except those who worked there—and, of course, the children of the great personages who resided there—and he was none of these. Yet there he was, deep in the vast complex of the kitchens, in the cereal pantry.

But the true mystery came when he recovered his balance and a smile brightened his face, showing dimples on both cheeks as he looked from one to the other of the girls. The smile broadened with recognition. "Lucy," he said. "Lindy."

Lindy knew, and Lucy likewise swore, that they had never seen the child before. But still he knew them, and they had not the heart to turn him over to the guards. So two fifteen-year-old girls had entered into a conspiracy. Behind crates in the pantry they made him a bed and set him a pot, and they took turns each day seeing to his feeding, while they schemed to smuggle him out of Camelot Keep and place him with some peasant family.

But the plan never matured. The little boy disappeared. On the third day he was simply gone. They never saw him again, nor heard any faintest rumor of him. Lindy still was puzzled by his disappearance, just as she was puzzled that he had been there at all.

He had been six years old, he said, and his name was Edwin. There was a second name, but she didn't remember it. They had tried to coax more from him, but it had been a muddle. He spoke of living somewhere else, but he could neither name nor describe the place. The impression had been of a broad, bright place where nothing really was very clear and nothing remained the same from moment to moment. And he went out from there sometimes—there were people who helped him to go out—but he always seemed to go right back.

The day Edwin disappeared was the day of inventory, and the girls had been terrified that he might be found. They had both seen what happened to miscreants in Camelot. Twice in Lindy's memory the kitchen staff had been assembled to march out and witness an execution. Both times the victims had been wretches accused of stealing from the king's larders. Lindy had never forgotten the sound and stink of the zen-guns, or the many colors of fresh blood in the sun.

Now she closed her eyes, wishing away the memories. Ronnie, her mind pleaded, where are you?

"Please come if you can," the note said. Well, she could. She was a lady now, and ladies sometimes visited the kitchens. Drawing a shawl over her robe, she left her apartment and waved an imperious hand at the guard who appeared in the wide hall at the sound of her door. She required no escort, the gesture said. She would walk alone.

The castle's east wing seemed deserted on this afternoon, which was not surprising. King Arthur was afield, and much of his retinue with him. His scientists should be working—he kept them always working—far across the enclosed lawns in the great, featureless tower that was their special place. It was said the tower was built over a hole that went to the center of the earth. Completed only two years ago, the great tower had been fourteen years in construction, supervised by Arthur himself. Standing tall and formidable in the prairie sun, it overshadowed the oldest part of the castle—the block buildings that had been the original complex of the Institute for Temporal Research, now totally enclosed within the fortress of Camelot.

Few ever went into that tower, and fewer came out. Even to speculate openly about it was to invite Arthur's wrath.

Only a few furtive servants, occasional cleaning crews, and

the stolid guards at their posts were abroad this afternoon in
East Wing.

For a hundred yards she traversed the quiet hallway, then
descended the great stairs that buttressed each end of the wing.
Three levels down she took a side corridor, then entered a service elevator and came out in the great, echoing chamber that
was the castle's kitchens. People labored there, but she ignored
them, wandering here and there, observing and inspecting,
until she was near the pantries. Then, unobserved, she turned
and ducked into the maze of storerooms, closing the portal
behind her.

"Here," a quiet voice said in the shadows. Lucy looked as
she had always looked—plain and freckled and endowed with
an impish humor. They embraced, and Lucy took her hand.
"Wait till you see," she said. "Come on." With Lady Sedgewick
in tow, she headed for a remote alcove deep in the pantries.

The boy was younger than the first one, no more than four
years old, but in his steady eyes was that same mysterious
intensity the other one had shown. And his face was the very
likeness of that other face, except younger.

"They must be brothers," Lindy ventured. "So alike. Lucy,
where do you suppose they come from? Did you find him
here?"

"He showed up in the spirit cellars," Lucy said. "It's just
luck that the one who found him is a—a friend. A young man I
see now and then. We brought him here in a basket."

"Then no one knows?"

"None who'll tell. But Lindy, what can we do with him?"

"I don't know. Can he talk?"

"Try him." Lucy grinned.

The child took it as his signal. "I been to sooks," he said.
"Got a tory."

"You have?" Lindy knelt beside him. "What does that
mean?"

"Wen' boo-oom," the child told her, nodding in secret
wisdom. "You like a fish?"

She glanced up at Lucy, who only shrugged. "If you say so,"
Lindy told the boy. "What is your name?"

"I got a fish-pish haven't any ears." This struck him funny, and he giggled. Dimples deepened in his cheeks.

Lindy grinned. "Well, great-oh, small corn, but what's your name?"

"Ed'in," he said. "Mane ruy staw?"

"What?"

"You're doing better than I did," Lucy said. "How old are you, Edin?"

"Ed-*win*!" the boy corrected her. "Edwin! Edwin Limmer!"

"Edwin? Wasn't that the . . ."

"Same name as that first one." Lucy nodded.

Lindy tipped her head, studying the boy before her. Same name, and so similar! But the other one had been an older child. "Edwin," she repeated. "How old are you, Edwin?"

He considered it carefully, then held up four fingers. "Hunnerd ninety-two," he said.

Lindy shook her head. "I guess you're three or four." She smiled. "And do you know where you live?"

He turned full circle, grinning. "There," he said. "Anywhen, anywhere. Whisplace!"

She tried again. "Where is your mother, Edwin? Your mama."

"Don' have any," he said, his bright eyes going serious. "Never-ever. Jus' Toocie. Whis!"

Lucy shook her head. "He seems well fed. And his wraps—those aren't peasant garb, but I don't know what they are."

Lindy took him by the shoulders. He was firm and strong, a healthy, vital child. "My name is Lindy," she said. "Can you say Lindy, Edwin?"

"Lindy. Lindy-lindy-lindy."

"That's right. And her name is Lucy."

"I know that," the boy said. "She told me."

"Okay. And what else do you know?"

"I know where I am."

"Oh? Where?"

He giggled. "Right here!"

Lindy laughed with him. "Oh, Lucy, he's adorable! How do you suppose he got into the cellar?"

"I haven't the slightest idea."

"Saw a bad man," the child said. "Kill people."

"You saw a man, Edwin? Who?"

"Niude nam a wass we." His expression said he was mimicking her, but the sounds meant nothing. "Nam a wass ya!"

"What's he saying, Lucy? Is that some foreign language?"

"Gibberish." Lucy shrugged. "Just baby talk, likely."

The child glared up at Lucy. "I did, too," he said. "I saw guns go zot. Man laughed. But Adam didn' let me look'a him."

"Who?"

"Adam! He came . . . pooh! Said le's slip outta here."

"Where you saw the man, was that where you came from?"

"No, here." He gazed around at the stacked crates and bales, distracted. "Here someplace. With Whispies."

Lindy glanced around at Lucy. "You don't suppose there were two of them?"

"No. Only this one."

"Edwin, do you know who the man was—the man you saw?"

"Sure." He nodded. "It was 'at sonabitch. Adam knows."

Ruffling the child's thick hair, Lindy stood. "Puzzle within a puzzle," she muttered.

"We can't keep him here," Lucy said, then hushed abruptly, turning.

Out beyond the stacked supplies doors banged and stern voices were raised. "All out!" a man shouted. "Clear the area! All to the midden yard and form ranks. His highness has returned!" A guard came around the stacks, peering. "Here, you! Out! All out! What's this, now? Whose child—oh, beg pardon, milady. The king has summoned all the household to the great court."

Frightened, Lindy stared at him, then mustered the dignity to wave him away. He backed off but remained, waiting. She paused in confusion. She had been a lady only five months, and her husband was away. She had no idea what to do. Almost in panic, she swept the child up and hurried to the pantry portal— and out into a seething, scurrying mass of humanity. Helpless, she was swept along, up the wide staircases and out the midden gates into sunlight. Around, armed men were barking orders.

The crowd at her back pressed her forward, across the flagstone ways and into the great courtyard.

Suddenly she was outside the crowd, stumbling, almost falling before a row of booted feet. She looked up at belted uniforms, zen-guns slung from vinyl-clad shoulders, menacing faces masked by the silvery faceplates of field troops. Behind and above them on the grassed slope were scarlet-and-gold-clad hussars, the king's own guard. And above them, atop the montret, was Arthur Rex.

Lindy tried to back away, but Arthur's quick eyes—eyes like agate chips in a wide, brutal face—saw her.

"Well, Lady Sedgewick," the tyrant growled, his voice carrying in the sudden silence. "From the kitchen gate? Why does the bride of Lord Sedgewick come from the kitchen gate?"

Off to one side, where nobles and various of the aristocracy gathered, there were murmurings and a few snickers. Lindy lowered her eyes, setting the little boy on the ground beside her. "Your Majesty." She bowed. "I . . . I was looking at the kitchens."

"Looking at the kitchens?" Arthur's gaze pinned her where she stood. "And whose child is that, Lady Sedgewick?"

She glanced down at the boy. Edwin stood unmoving, his eyes wide and fixed on the king as if to memorize each feature of the monarch's face. And on the face of the child was a look of utter loathing such as Lindy had never seen. "Zot," the boy whispered.

For a moment Arthur waited, then he scowled. In his youth, this man had been a precocious bully, and the bully had survived the turmoil of the dark times—survived, and emerged as absolute ruler of a realm. In whispers, it was said that Arthur Rex was more than a man. He was a demon. Brutal and determined, he had built a kingdom for himself, and his intuitions were as legendary as his ruthless dedication to his purposes. The will of Arthur Rex was law, and he tolerated no uncertainties. When he sensed an aberration in his realm, no matter what its nature, Arthur simply terminated it.

The king made a dismissive gesture and a hussar in the front rank stepped forward. "Guard," he said, "take the child."

Two armed guards paced forward, toward the terrified girl, then stopped, looking around in confusion. Lindy looked down. The boy was gone. It was as if he had never been there.

With an effort, Lindy squared her shoulders, every inch the proper lady. "I was about to respond, Your Majesty," she said. "I found the boy by the kitchen doors. I meant to question the registry staff about him. I don't know whose child he is."

For nearly a century it was believed that $E = mc^2$. Then Gilpin's Actualist Equations unveiled the prime proviso. $E = mc^2$, *only if* T1 (mc) = T2 (π). Without a temporal framework, the elements of relativity could not exist. Albert Einstein clarified the *what* of things but never quite grasped the *when*.

This illumination of the "relativity phenomenon" led to the review of many cherished "wavicles," absolute paradigms which proved to be incorrect.

Old knowledges must be reshaped in the light of new findings.

—*The Actualist Debates*

∞

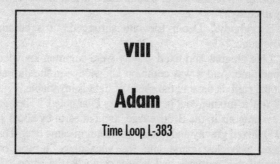

VIII

Adam

Time Loop L-383

"I am lying," Teal Fordeen muttered, as if testing and analyzing the syllables of it. He cocked a hairless head thoughtfully and said it again. "I am lying."

Several of the others paused in doing their various things and looked around at him, similar features in as many combinations reflecting curiosity. "What are you lying about?" Deem Eleveno inquired. "You haven't said anything."

"I said I'm lying," Teal Fordeen explained. "It's a paradox, you see. I state that I am lying. If I speak truly when I claim to lie, then it is a false statement. But if I am lying about lying, then I must be telling the truth. Theoretically, such a statement cannot be made. A person cannot say 'I am lying.' It's impossible."

"But you just said it, " Cuel Denyne pointed out. "You said it three times and referred to it as an accomplished statement twice. Therefore it is possible."

"Then you say it."

"I am lying," Cuel Denyne obliged.

"And are you lying when you say that?"

"Not if it's the truth." Cuel's large eyes narrowed in what might have been a frown. "Though I see what you mean. It can't be true if it's true. It's only true if it's false. A semantic paradox. But what's your point?"

"My point is that paradoxes may not be what they seem,"

Teal said. "Who knows for certain that true and false are mutually exclusive?"

"Everybody." Deem Eleveno shrugged. "It's common knowledge."

"Like dragons and fixed gravity were common knowledge at one time. And it was common knowledge in the dim ages that the earth is flat and the speed of light is invariable."

"You're mixing your periods," Elzy Pyar noted. "They gave up on dragons in the Bronze Age, and flat earth by about A.D. 1,000. Fixed gravity and photon momentum came later. That's where 'wavicles' came into the vocabulary. It was once believed that particles and waves could be the same. They didn't know any better."

"Ask Elzy what day it is and he'll teach you to build a star plotter," Deem muttered.

"But that's my point precisely." Teal smiled, running long, sensitive fingers across his bald head. "In each case human knowledge was stymied by a wavicle, and it took the presence of a paradox to make people look beyond their noses."

Signaling for continued attention, Teal crossed the smooth floor to where a huge, holographic chart stood waiting, a fifty-foot virtual cube of glowing traceries that seemed as substantial as it wasn't. It was one of several dozen virtual displays that almost surrounded the task chamber, all around and above. The displays hid the mind-numbing nothingness beyond them. "And here we have another paradox." He pointed at the chart, where dimensional displays swirled into context. "Magda Wilson is at this exact point—one and three-tenths miles west of Long Mesa on the Cimarron—at precisely 9:47:03.006 postmeridian on day 183 of the year A.D. 2040. There is no question of that. And yet she simply isn't there. She was, and she will be, but she isn't. And she isn't anywhen else, either. So where did she go?"

"That's what we're trying to find out," Cuel reminded him. "It's why we're dawdling here in this closed loop."

"Paradox," Teal pressed. "The riddle *is* the answer, if we can just understand it. We aren't locating the woman because we don't look past our preconceptions. We are laboring under a wavicle."

"By modern definition, possibly," Elzy clarified. "The ancestral definition—a phenomenon with characteristics of both a wave and a particle—would not lend itself to laboring under."

"A red herring, then!"

"Thank you." Elzy nodded. "But I knew what you meant."

"Then why didn't you let it go at that?" Toocie Toonine chirped, her wide eyes narrowing. "Sometimes I think you're as obsessive as Peedy Cue!"

"Peedy's preoccupation is with the mammary appendages of protomorphic women," Elzy noted, unruffled. "In particular, those of the bimbolithic cultures."

"He's a titmouse," Toocie scoffed. "And you're a buzzbee. Ancestral phraseology: gadfly . . . dingbat . . ."

"My specialty is clarity of definition and communication," Elzy said. "It is hardly the same."

"Clarity!" Deem scoffed. "You could obscure the Asian Abyss, Elzy. You'd explain it to death."

"Focus, please!" Teal snapped. "We are searching where Magda Wilson should be—by our present knowledge—and she isn't there. Obviously our knowledge is incomplete. So I suggest we try another approach."

"What approach?"

"We shall advertise," Teal said. Without waiting for concurrence, he returned to his console, activated the open link, and spoke to it. "To all World History Investigative Society parties in retrosync conduit," he said, "issue a T1 call for Magda Wilson in your sectors. Relay to observers. Respond searchloop 4.1."

"That is ridiculous," Cuel said. "Who's going to intercept a message like that?"

"Me," a deeper voice behind them said. The Whispers turned in unison, gawking at the newcomer, their faces registering various degrees of surprise and shock. It was not possible for the man—for anyone beyond their own crew, much less a man like this—to be in L-383. But here he was!

He was not one of them, not of their time or any time near it. He was taller, rangier, and heavier of frame than any of the group in the chamber, and he had a lot of dark hair. A primitive. The clothing he wore—boots and woven fabrics of several descriptions—gave no clue as to the era of his origin. Drab colors and a mottling of variety hinted at flexibility in his garb, as if with the turn of a garment he might alter his appearance to suit any occasion.

Slight bulges here and there might have been anything from concealed weapons to a change of underwear.

"You're looking for Magda Wilson?" The stranger glanced around at the hologram-bounded loop chamber. "She's quite safe. I got her away from the AATVs. Those laser-chasers were homed. You people would have been too late. You were too late, in fact. I've noticed before that your coordinates are a little iffy, especially on the fourth axis. I suspect it's the reaction time of having to plot a course before you take it."

"Who—who are you?" Teal Fordeen rasped.

"I'm Adam," the stranger said. "I'm a timer."

"Impossible!" Elzy blurted. "We don't know you."

"I'm not one of you." The primitive shrugged. "I'm independent." He glanced around the chamber, at the holograms, the virtual reality displays, the control consoles, the paraphernalia of retrosynchronization. "And I don't use crutches."

"You heard my call?" Teal squinted at him.

"Couple of days ago, by my duration. I was nearby, at Topeka, watching a legislature confuse itself—that would have been about 1985—and one of your shadows rushed past calling for Magda. So I traced him to now and here. Tell George Wilson that his wife is safe and in good hands. She'll rejoin him eventually."

"We've found no trace of her," Teal said. "Where is she?"

"Well, she isn't in your conduit." Adam smiled. "I wouldn't even have found this track except for your call. It's like a tunnel through reality. No wonder you're so hard to find."

"It's the only way to traverse time," Deem said, edging closer to the intruder for a better look. The man was obviously of primitive stock—a protohuman, like those who were the ancestors of the Whispers, like Edwin Limmer and George Wilson and all those other archaic humans who had populated Earth before the polar rift and the inaccessible age. The protos were fully human but lacked the diminutive proportions and sleek physical refinements of the race as it would be in the age of Teal Fordeen and his kind. The antepoluvian man's hands were large and strong-looking, his body well muscled, and his features pronounced. His dark eyes shone with the individualism and unpredictability that had characterized humanity before the Age of Common Reason. Deem estimated his genetic origins at not later than A.D. 2400.

"I was born in 1943," Adam said casually, as if reading the Whisper's mind. "But I'm from 2041. And I'm not in the chain of your science's developments. I learned time-jump on my own, without the burdens you bear."

"What burdens?"

"These." Adam swept a large, casual hand around, indicating the artifacts in the chamber—and the chamber itself. "Your crutches. They only slow you down, you know. Well, I've delivered my message. Good-bye, now. Have a nice time."

He started to turn, and Teal Fordeen shouted, "Wait! How do you know so much about us?"

"I grew up knowing about you." Adam grinned. He turned and strode across the chamber, long legs pacing easily while some of them scampered after him. At the "surface" of a virtual view of galaxies swirling in huge grace around the vortex of a gravitic singularity he paused. "Pretty," he said, then stepped into the hologram's pattern.

"You can't go there!" Deem chirped. "It's the conduit limit. There's nothing beyond."

"Nothing?" Virtual star-swarms spiraled around the stranger's head as he glanced back, a serene giant scattering galaxies around him. "Why, there's *everything* beyond. And all the time in the world."

He didn't seem to do anything except step deeper into the star system, and the sensitive instruments of the consoles registered no perceivable temporal distortion. But abruptly he was gone.

"Impossible." Deem gasped. "There is no dimension beyond the dimensions! Where did he go?"

"Paradox," Teal murmured. "A paradox of paradoxes. Unless, of course, he was lying."

"I thought only you were lying," Elzy snapped. "That business about paradoxes . . ."

Teal ignored him. "Maybe not a paradox at all," he muttered, stroking his beardless chin. "In pretemporal ages a person moving in the fourth dimension would have seemed to appear and disappear. He would have been untraceable—when only three dimensions were known. He would have gone in a direction that seemed not to exist. They didn't know that time is a dimension, so they couldn't visualize traverse within it. Maybe a paradox is not a paradox if one sees it from another angle. Maybe it's only a puzzle."

"What are you getting at?" Deem asked.

"I don't know," Teal admitted. "But if that indigenee is telling the truth, there's a flaw in the pattern of our science. A wavicle. Something here is certainly contrary to our view of things."

"Obviously." Deem nodded. "But what good is it if we don't know what it is?"

"We need a new paradigm," Teal decided. "Common knowledge has outlived its usefulness once again. It's time for a rethink."

"Send a CMWWK request upstream," Deem snapped. "We have our hands full here."

"They won't do anything with it." Teal shook his head. "They'll just send back the standard Concise Model of What We Know; I suspect the CMWWK itself is the problem. We need a fresh perspective. The Archaics were right in one of their attitudes. If you want a thing done right, do it yourself. We'll reanalyze here."

"Another closed loop?" Cuel protested. "No! First there was the Arthurian thing. We upset a self-sustaining anachronism by going around it, so now we have to fix it. And who volunteered? Teal Fordeen, of course! So we all came along. Then we inherited Edwin Limmer. Contratemporization and chronophasia! Complications stacked on complications!"

"And messy diapers," Toocie Toonine added.

Cuel chose not to respond to her interruption. "Now we're involved in a prototype Waystop," he pressed on. "We're supervising a travel agency and doing missing persons work on the side. Teal, if we keep following tangents we'll never get on with the expedition. If you will recall, our initial purpose was to investigate T-zero."

"To be precise," Elzy Pyar elaborated, "our mission purpose was to observe the near-creation ranges for evidence of branching conduits or similar phenomena."

"That's a contradiction in itself," Deem Eleveno asserted. "Nothing can be similar to a singularity."

Teal Fordeen gazed at Deem Eleveno and let his gaze encompass them all. He shrugged in elaborate resignation. "I'll do it myself," he decided. He turned toward his console, deep in thought. "I'll need the UEB archives on mainlink," he muttered, "and at least twenty wafers. Cuel, find Peedy and relay to Edwin Limmer what we've been told. He's a protomorph, too, like our visitor. Maybe he'll have some ideas."

"And tell Peedy to stop fondling the females at Waystop locus," Toocie added. "Or we'll send him home."

"Just what is it you intend to do?" Deem wondered.

"A compendium," Teal said impatiently. "I want to look again at our concepts of the chronoverse. Maybe we've missed something. It appears that this Adam person is out there somewhere, strolling around in open time, and we don't know how he does it."

"We don't even know who he is!" Cuel noted.

"But we know when he's from," Deem said. "Natal origin 1943. Yet he is 'from' 2041. He told us."

"What could someone from 1943—or even 2041—possibly know what we don't know?" Cuel scoffed.

"Maybe it's what he *doesn't* know that matters," Toocie Toonine mused, her big eyes bright with excitement. "Maybe he doesn't know what can't be done."

"The man is a primitive!" Elzy pointed out. "A—a barbarian! From far before the Age of Common Reason."

"He's from a time of *uncommon* reason." Teal shrugged. "The Age of Dreams, if you will. Keep in mind, Elzy, that it was his people who actually created virtually every science we now have. People like Ikebata and Tolafsson, like Magnus Opum and George Wilson. They were the inventors, those savage freethinkers each going his own way. All we have ever done, since the Refinement, is modify, apply, and perfect what they left us. The first person ever to see the fourth dimension wasn't one of us. It was one of them! I think it's time we considered whether the universal prime is four, or whether it's more."

"That's what we're doing!" Deem pounded a console with a dainty fist. "We started out to find the accesses to it, at the beginning of time."

"Common knowledge," Teal muttered. "Common reason. But maybe those accesses move forward on a time axis, right along with the solid dimensions. Maybe they're right here around us and we just can't see them."

"That is sheer sophistry," Elzy sneered. "Where's your evidence, Teal?"

"Evidence? Where did Adam come from, then? And where did he go?"

"And how did he get to Magda Wilson before we did?" Toocie Toonine wondered.

∞

Sudden entry into common duration from T2 transit can be a source of consternation to those indigenous to the time. Human instinct, reflex, and reaction should always be considered when scheduling a stopover.

—TEAL FORDEEN, *Etiquettes of Time Travel*

∞

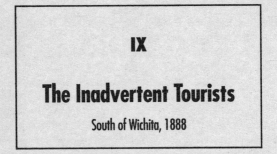

IX

The Inadvertent Tourists

South of Wichita, 1888

It was in the nature of Tsa'Vapiti to be cautious in his approach to the numberless problems and puzzles that were the fabric of everyday life. Long ago the man now called John Two Elk had observed that the incautious often came to disaster and usually didn't live very long.

So, faced with the unexplainable, Two Elk did what his experience told him to do. He assembled the elements of this latest puzzle and counted them.

The inventory included one cart with a broken wheel; one old horse called Horse; one wagonload of bleached buffalo bones—a lot of them now scattered all around; one fuzzy yellow thing from the sky; a squat, ugly metal thing with two tall posts, four wheels, and two outthrust iron teeth; and a strangely dressed man with a turtle-shell hat and no useful information.

Late spring storm clouds gathered above the flint hills as Two Elk built the small fire he had abandoned earlier and pondered the meaning of it all.

Li-tao "Larry" Hong squatted beside his forklift, watching as wisps of smoke lifted from tiny flames and angled skyward. Up it went, up into a sky still cobalt blue directly overhead though the sun was obscured by rising clouds. Meadowlarks darted there. The tendril of smoke rose above them, then abruptly ended, whisked away by errant winds aloft.

"Gonna rain soon," Two Elk said, more to himself than to Hong.

"Not according to the Weather Channel," Hong argued. "Less than a ten percent chance."

"Who told you that?" Two Elk sneered. "Gonna rain, sure as ever was. Smoke says so. Helluva rain."

"Not likely," Hong said stubbornly. Then his mood shifted again as he gazed out across endless miles of prairie. A deep, sudden grief glistened in his onyx eyes. "Musta been Apocalypse," he mused. "That's what it was. Ol' USSR's gone and we got lazy an' some nut got hold of the Ukranian arsenal an' cut loose. Or maybe it was Pritzyn or Gadhafi or one of them. Hell, maybe it was China. A billion Chinamen can't be wrong, they say. Bullcrap! A billion Chinamen are *always* wrong. My own grandfather told me that. Chinese people by ones and twos are the smartest you'll find, but the more of them you put together the wronger they get."

Old Li-tao knew, Hong thought. He had seen the Red Guard formed.

Everybody told these round-eyes, Never trust the Chinese. But Nixon thought otherwise. Even Carter—who never got it through his head that Menachem Begin and the Ayatollah Khomeini weren't both good Baptists—had thought otherwise.

"Shit," Hong mourned now, "there isn't a thing left anywhere except us. Not so much as a trace left. Not even ruins an' rubble. Just us an' a bunch of bones."

Two Elk frowned. The man was talking gibberish again. The old ones, back in the great days, would have said he was touched by spirits. But to Two Elk, he sounded just plain crazy.

"Which way's the river?" Hong demanded. He glanced at the sun, then at his wristwatch. "Over there," he decided, pointing westward.

"Which river?"

"The Arkansas! The only one around here, that and the Little Arky. They used to be right over there, seven or eight miles. Run right through Wichita. Even if everything's fried, the river ought to be there."

"River's there," Two Elk admitted. He gazed at the forklift, studying it this way and that, keeping a respectful distance. "This thing dead?" he asked finally.

"I shut it off." Hong spread his hands. "What good's a fork-lift when the world's wiped out?"

"Fork . . . lift," Two Elk repeated. He eased to the right, craning his neck, then walked entirely around the machine. "Steam engine," he decided. "Little locomotive. No rails, though. Go anyplace. Good idea. Take a wheel off of it, we can fix th' cart. You know how to take off a wheel?"

"What for?"

"Take it off that thing, put it on my cart. I need a wheel."

"The hell you say!" Hong snapped. "This equipment belongs to Sedgewick Sheet Metal Supply. I had to sign for it. Sam'd have my ass."

Two Elk stared at the stranger for a moment, then opened his belt pouch and hauled out Captain Jack's old six-shooter again. He pointed it at Hong. "Fix my cart," he ordered.

"Maybe we need to talk," Hong suggested.

Heavy clouds pregnant with spring storm filled half the sky when throngs waiting along the Arkansas River at its juncture with the Little Arkansas caught sight of the spectacle they had come out to see. Atop the low ridge above the south bank, people scampered ahead of and around something that crawled out of cloud-shadow into the receding sunlight. An apparition it was, a thing that became stranger by the moment as it trundled nearer—a thing of many parts all slightly askew. People gathered and gaped, mounted men splashed across the meandering streams in the riverbed, buggies and drays crowded the approaching thoroughfares toward Water Street.

The curiosity was followed by a growing crowd of men and boys, some on horseback and others afoot. It had been escorted for more than three miles—ever since it growled past Miller's Cross—and word of its coming had raced ahead to Wichita City. The escort maintained a respectful distance, except for a few yapping dogs that darted here and there around it.

Little by little, as the spectacle approached, parts of it became identifiable. There was a broken-wheeled old cart, piled high with buffalo bones, but the entire assemblage was off the ground. Instead, its hull braces rested on a pair of big iron teeth jutting from tall metal uprights on the front of another vehicle. This was a small, compact contrivance with four fat little wheels, which rolled under its own power. The horse attached to it was not in front pulling but behind, ambling along on a lead. A black-haired man with Oriental eyes sat behind the uprights, apparently guiding the contrivance.

And high atop the entire assemblage rode a familiar figure. He was enthroned on the pinnacle of the load of buffalo bones, where he sat in regal splendor, his arms crossed in disdain like a conqueror surveying his domain.

Despite the bright turtle-shell helmet above his graying braids, some recognized him. It was the old stockyard Indian, John Two Elk.

As the complex apparition approached the enthralled crowd lining the south bank, Two Elk gazed at the people around and below him, and his weathered face creased in a smile of satisfaction. Once again, as in times long past, Tsa'Vapiti of the Far Grass Kiowa was a famous man. There were people everywhere, pointing at him and saying his name.

His dark eyes lit on a covey of brightly clad females, entertainers and sporting women from the row of saloons along the waterfront. On impulse he retrieved the bright yellow, fuzzy ball from his pouch and tossed it in the air, showing off. Twice he tossed the ball up and caught it, then with a grin he flung it high, in the direction of the excited women.

The ball arced aloft, lazily, and started downward just as a flash of light and puff of white smoke erupted from the powder-frame of Howard Hughes, photographer for the *Wichita Eagle*. Hughes's photograph, after development, was marred by movement. The falling ball lacked detail, but it was unquestionably a ball. The picture clearly showed it falling, as Diamond Lil Hazlitt stretched upward to catch it with both hands. In the photograph were the crowds nearby, the sporting halls in the background, the elm and willow trees along the river, and a red-tailed hawk banking among storm clouds in the tumbled sky.

But John Two Elk was not in it. Nor were the wagonload of bones, the incredible thing that carried them, the man who drove it, or the horse following on lead. Where they had been was only a wide oval of cleared ground, as clean as if it had been swept with a broom. Not a loose pebble or grain of sand remained.

The fantastic assemblage had simply disappeared. Not a trace of it was to be found. All that remained to mark the odd event of May 27, 1888, at Wichita City—the unexplained phenomenon that preceded the deluge that flooded half the town that day—were Howard Hughes's peculiar photograph and a fuzzy, yellow ball named Wilson 2, which remained the property of Lillian Ruth "Diamond Lil" Hazlitt.

Waystop
The Present

If Amanda Brink had been skeptical about the fantastic story related to her by her sister Maude and Maude's husband, Lucas, most of her skepticism faded when Ray and the twins disappeared from Maude's metal-clad dining room. She chose to believe—and did believe—what they told her about the time-travel station, the booster apparatus, and all the rest of it. Being freed of the constant demands of Ray and the boys for a while was worth the price of credulity. Still, it was a lot to swallow.

Her best bet, she decided, was not to think about it right now. In Maude's guest room she disrobed, showered, and toweled off, then looked at herself in the mirror. Except for the traces of experience around her eyes and the hint of disillusionment in a chin too long held high despite Ray's constant, insistent criticism, the woman she saw there might have been a girl of twenty—a very pretty girl, with the wide-set eyes and stubborn, sexy lips of a young Vivien Leigh. She visualized maroon velvet, like Scarlett O'Hara's drapery gown in *Gone with the Wind*.

I'm wasting it, she thought. Ray Brink doesn't even appreciate what he has.

With a sigh, she opened her overnight valise and pulled on panties, then hesitated. A shadow had flitted across the room. Or maybe she had only imagined it. She looked around, then turned back to the valise. A touch that might have been only a current of air startled her, and again she thought a shadow had flickered past, just beyond sight.

Except for a brief and ill-considered excursion into and out of matrimony a decade earlier, Mandy Santee had lived—and flourished in—the single life until three years back, when a successful, respected attorney, freshly divorced and on the prowl, caught her in a moment of weakness. The voice inside her—that odd "knowingness" that she had always had—told her it was wrong, but for once she had ignored it and acted on mundane logic. She had accepted Ray Brink's opinion of himself. He was sheer, unsullied arrogance unmarred by any trace of conscience, but she had believed—chosen to believe—that his very blatancy was a pretense. Surely no one could actually be like that. It was protective coloration, she convinced herself. A mask to hide the real face of a sensitive, vulnerable soul.

She had married Ray Brink and had spent the ensuing three years wondering why. She knew now the truth of the axiom: What you see is what you get.

The thrills and the skills associated with being attractive, female, and single had gone mostly untried for three years now, along with those other odd sensations that felt like a skill but had never really surfaced. Ray Brink had wanted her for one purpose, it seemed, and she somehow went along with it. Systematically, unceasingly—when he thought of her at all—he pursued the destruction of her pride. All of her defenses now were focused against being demeaned, intimidated, dominated, and belittled.

But some of the old skills were still there, and Mandy had excellent reflexes. For the time being Ray was gone, and she could be Mandy again. Thus when next she felt that vague, not-quite touch at her right breast, she reacted. She whirled, grabbed, and squeezed, and a howl of anguish that was just short of true sound filled the room.

"Ohg tell!" a not-quite-soundless voice screamed. "Owaee!"

Instantly the room swam around her. She felt dizzy and disoriented, but she kept her hold and in her mind the strange sounds reversed themselves. "Yeow!!" the shriek said. "Let go!"

The room around her became indistinct, seeming to rush past in all directions. It seemed somehow an almost familiar sensation, and her mind registered what was too quick for her eyes to see—everything slowed to dark, and the dark flashed with a hurling brilliance. She felt it and nudged it with her mind. Abruptly she was somewhere else. She had a glimpse of the person whose crotch she clutched, and beyond him were dozens of people—mostly women and all dressed in 1930s attire. They were in a big, skylighted room filled with long tables that held antique, treadle-operated sewing machines and vast piles of brightly colored fabrics. The air reeked of heady dyes, and again there was the slowing, the darkness, and the light. The room swam and dissolved.

Her vision cleared. She crouched in a place beyond comprehension, but the contents of her locked fist were unmistakable. With grim determination she clung to the crotch of a soft blue coverall, and the genitals inside it. The individual attached to these was small, bald, bug-eyed, and frantic. He screeched, flailing about with small delicate-looking hands, and one of these hands held a tape measure—an ordinary cloth tailor's tape, its ends swinging wildly.

"Let go!" he pleaded. "That hurts!"

"And you deserve it!" another voice said. From somewhere aside another person stepped into view, this one even smaller and equally bald, though more delicately featured.

A female, some thinking part of Mandy's mind told her. And in that instant she knew who these people were. These were Whispers! The people from the far future, the ones Maude and Lucas had tried to tell her about. And the one with the tape was named Peedy.

"Let him go, dear," the little female said. "I don't think he'll bother you again."

Mandy hesitated a moment, looking around her. The place she was in was like nothing she had ever seen. There were several more of the little people and a lot of strange-looking furniture that might not be furniture at all. The room was less a room than an island in an endless sea of flowing, starry universes, interspersed with multidimensional charts, columns of figures that seemed to hang in space, roving lines and curves, spirals and diagrams that shifted constantly.

Almost unnerved by the strangeness and beauty of it all, Mandy released her grip on the little man's private parts. "Where am I?" she demanded. With a sob of relief, Peedy scampered back, protecting his violated area with both hands.

"I told him to stop harassing women," the little woman said. "I knew it would get him in trouble. Hello. I'm Toocie Toonine. This isn't exactly a 'where,' it's more like a 'when.' You might call it a time loop. We call it L-383. Who are you?"

"Mandy," she said. "Amanda Brink. You . . . you're *Whispers*, aren't you!"

"Yes, dear." Toocie smiled. "We call ourselves that. It means World History Investigative Society. I gather you're one of Edwin Limmer's volunteers."

"My sister is . . . I guess. I'm just visiting."

"She doesn't belong in the loop," another Whisper said. "This is very irregular."

"Oh, hush, Elzy," Toocie muttered. "Belong or not, she's here. It is an established fact. She obviously synced with Peedy."

"I didn't do anything with Peedy!" Mandy snapped. "I don't know what he had in mind, but I don't appreciate being fondled."

"I did no such thing," Peedy protested, still hunkered over his violated crotch. "Scientific measurement is—"

"He has a mammary obsession," Toocie interrupted officiously. "It's fairly common among males in our time. I believe contact with primitive—pardon, dear, but you are, you know—humans has triggered a latent reaction in them. A vestigial hormonal response to gender-specific morphology, I suspect. Probably a subconscious urge carried down from prehistoric times. Interesting, but anthropology isn't really our focus. We are more concerned with how it all began."

"How what began?"

"Everything. The universe. Time itself."

"With time out for measuring tits?" Mandy glared at Peedy, then let her gaze rove over all of them. They were obviously people—obviously human—but strangely alike in size, shape, and appearance. It was a little difficult, at a glance, to tell which ones were male and which were female.

"We have changed," Toocie admitted. "More dramatically than in any preceding millennium except the very early ones. Evolution is like that. It occurs in leaps. And ours may have been . . . well, assisted. We aren't quite sure. But we really are human."

"You actually are my—our—descendants, then?"

"Certainly. You and your kind are our ancestors, a thousand years back, at least. That's on the order of fifty generations, through some massively troubled times. There may have been some genetic manipulation involved, but evolution is part of it. Those best suited at each juncture survive and procreate."

"But, don't you? . . ."

"I'm basically just like you, dear. Only my topological components are less exaggerated."

"I . . . we made a double transit, Teal," Peedy reported to a thoughtful-looking Whisper nearby. "I'm sure of it. I blipped one, and only one registers, but we . . . went somewhere else first."

"Interesting," the thoughtful one murmured. "Get readouts, Peedy. We'll talk later." He stepped closer, cocking a hairless brow at Mandy. "We need Ed Limmer, I believe," he suggested. "Some situational adjustment is required here."

"I agree." Toocie nodded. "Mandy, this is Teal Fordeen. He coordinates our particular group—L-383. He proposes that we bring Edwin Limmer here—into the loop. Edwin can take you back to when you were, in open time."

"Good!" Mandy said. Then she blushed. "But I'm practically naked!"

"I'm sure Edwin will realize that." Toocie's huge eyes widened with curiosity. "Is that a problem?"

"Well, of course it's a problem! I barely—I mean, I hardly know him!"

Whisper-gazes flicked past her, surprised large eyes looking beyond her, and abruptly a garment—a simple cloak cut from a bolt of maroon velvet—was laid across her shoulders by large, gentle hands. Mandy turned, pulling the wrap around her, and stared up at dark eyes in a handsome, amused face. The man was thirtyish, tall and muscular, with the sort of face that had filled Amanda Santee's dreams before she outgrew them. Among the gaping little Whispers he was a large, amused presence, strong-seeming and assured, yet very gentle.

"This should cover the occasion," he said in a deep, soft voice. "Hello, Amanda. I'm Adam. Do you know the symbol for infinity?"

She stared at him, confused. "In—infinity? What do you mean?"

"The symbol," he repeated. "Like an ampersand for 'and.' How would you represent infinity?"

"Parentheses," she said slowly. "Like deep parentheses with an X connecting them."

"Wonderful," he murmured. His dark eyes seemed to fill her, to warm her, to be seeing everything about her all at once. She felt her heart pounding, slow and relentless as savage drums.

"Interesting way to time-jump," he said. "Clinging to a crotch."

"That was his fault!" she snapped, pointing at Peedy. "He tried to—to measure me! He'll be up a pickle if he tries it again."

"Up a pickle," he murmured, savoring the words. "Sounds like you're threading on thin grass, Peedy." His chuckle was deep and appreciative. "And your little side trip, Amanda? To the MGM costuming department, was that your idea?"

"That's right!" Peedy Cue burbled. "We *did* make a side shunt. But I don't know how . . ."

"This cloth!" Amanda exclaimed, fingering the velvet. "It's like Scarlett's dress!"

"Is that what you were thinking about?" The tall man gazed at her intently. "Interesting." To the Whispers, he added, "Why don't you show this lady around while she's here? You have time."

Again he searched her eyes, that same bemused, quizzical gaze. Then he grinned. With an amused wink and a gesture like a salute, he backed away, turned, and strode into the nearest starfield . . . and was gone.

"Who—" Mandy gasped, and started over. "Who was *that*?"

"He calls himself Adam," Teal Fordeen said. "We don't know who he is, exactly."

∞

There is no future in reality. Neither is there any past. Both past and future are fancies of the mind. One consists of memories and one of expectations, all products of the instant. For each of us there is only the reality of the present. We are a sequence of moments, each one the only moment we have. Life is but an instant, and the instant is now.

Live, then, for the moment, for we are slaves to our duration and for us there is nothing else.

—FREDERICK GATES, 1832

∞

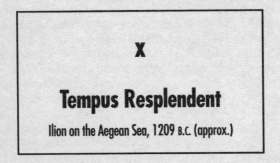

X

Tempus Resplendent

Ilion on the Aegean Sea, 1209 B.C. (approx.)

The two strangers entered the south gate at morning, making
no effort to blend with the crowds waiting there to enter Pallas
Market. Though the robes they wore were of common Mycenaean design, it was obvious that they were people of another
sort, from another place beyond even the lore of the merchant
princes whose maps and inscribed tablets descriptive of all the
known world were preserved in the Diantyne Crypt for study.

The two were a man and a pregnant woman, both extraordi-
narily tall—the man head and shoulders above most men of the
region, the woman not much less—and both as strong-looking
as palace warders. Their hair was dark—not the dull, dusty
black of the bubar and caspiate slaves who labored on the walls
and in the nearby fields, but a rich, lustrous dark umber like the
locks of young Pellonic warriors.

Keepers at the gate, and others in the marketway within,
moved to intercept them as they entered, then backed away.
There was something about the pair—especially the man—an
aura not hostile but simply entirely assured that said look but
do not accost. He carried no visible weapons, but no man
doubted for an instant that he had all the weapons he required,
ready at hand, should the need arise to use them.

His manner was harmless enough, as was the woman's,
and the guards were relieved that the two demonstrated no
hostility. They were not sure what they would have done in
such a case, but they were sure—each from his own observa-

114

tions—that the two would somehow be immune to javelins, blades, and arrows. It was as if they were surrounded by an invisible shield. Their very manner said so. They could not be hurt, and woe befall anyone who might try.

They did not seem as gods might, but it was certain that where they went, the aegis of gods went with them.

Here and there, among the crowd, some puzzled over vague recollections. A giant had visited here before, it seemed, many seasons ago. A giant who might have been like these. There were vague tales of such a one, who came and went in the days following the great upheaval. But these were not exactly the same. That giant, legend recalled, had yellow hair and eyes as pale as cold rain. They called him Quark, and some had worshipped him for a time. Then a mighty thing he promised had failed. Quark had been as a god and had foreseen the Troad as the center of the world. But the gods rejected him.

That had been in the time of Priam the First, sire of the warrior-prince Hector, now regent of Troy.

The two strangers said not a word in passing. They simply passed into the capital city of the Troad and went on, gazing at the splendors around them as innocently as serfs from the Idic foothills might.

Runners went by circuitous routes to advise the palace warders of the arrival of notables, and the guards went back to their business.

Where the market way opened out upon a wider, slab-tiled avenue, shoulders of broken stone surrounded a slightly higher level of ground. Beyond the avenue rose a double tier of crude, sturdy structures of wood and stone with the largest of the buildings—ranked by whole-trunk wood pillars above slabs of stone—standing against the western sky above them. Morning sunlight emboldened the raucous, gaudy hues of its many-colored murals and flashed off the bronze armor of the warders stationed along the porticoes. Here the two stopped and gazed.

"So this is fabled Troy," Magda Wilson breathed. "It really is kind of tiny and crude, isn't it?"

"These people don't think so." Adam shrugged, indicated the curious, motley crowds that flocked behind and around them, keeping a respectful distance. "This, to them, is magnificence. The seventh and greatest of the Troys. There are six other, earlier versions scattered and buried under this hill. And there will be more later. But this is the one Homer exaggerated. Fabled Troy! A wonder of the ancient world. For its time, though, it is a fair-size town. Believe me, it's far better than the earlier versions. Would you like some breakfast?"

The woman looked along the row of food stalls lining the end of the way and wrinkled her nose. "The odors are . . . interesting," she said. "Sort of overpowering. It's hard to separate the aromas of cuisine from the reek of the gutters. What kinds of food did they—do they eat here?"

"Whatever doesn't eat them first." He smiled. "This town has the pick of the whole region's agriculture as well as the harvest of hunters and some surprisingly capable fishing fleets. It's one of the places where cooking is becoming an art. They have discovered the use of herbs and spices, mostly from the Ethiopians. Among the local innovations that will last are sauerkraut and drained cheese. But it's best not to wonder too much about your meal." Adam grinned. "Just trust them. They know their world better than we do."

"What does that mean?"

"It means that any regional flora and fauna that are toxic have already been identified—the hard way."

"A platter of soyalon cakes and hot colata would sound good right now," Magda said.

"In my time it would have been pancakes, or bacon and eggs and a bowl of Wheaties." He nodded.

"Your time?"

"Well, it's the time I find most comfortable," he amended. "My favorite when. The early 1950s. I visit that time sometimes. It's when I was born, in 'real' time."

"I'd like to see that time," she said.

He glanced at her, as if searching for hidden meaning. His glance dropped for an instant to her swelling belly. "You will see it, Magda Wilson," he said slowly. "Soon enough. I promise that, just as I promise you will be with your husband again."

"So odd." Magda gazed up at him. "This thing you do, Adam. This jumping around in time. It's what Georgie used to talk about, though he saw it as a challenge for technology, not a personal skill. Do you suppose it's a natural talent, what you do?"

"Partly, I suppose. Certainly I'm not the first timer in history. There have been—are—others. So it's likely that the ability crops up now and then among humans. But unless they realize what it is and teach themselves to use it, they'd never know." He paused, frowning slightly, his eyes on the hillside ahead where bronze-clad warriors were coming into view. "Whoop, we're about to have company."

Across the slabbed avenue, citizens scattered as a tight phalanx of bronze-girt hoplites marched down the steps of the stone-walled rise, into the open area. Behind them came a double platoon of javelins and a company of ready archers, each with an arrow set in his short, Thracian bow.

On the avenue, the warriors spread out and halted, facing Adam and Magda at a distance of twenty yards. For a long moment the tableau was fixed, then atop the rise a trio of men appeared. The center one was a wide-shouldered, tousle-headed individual wearing a short kilt, corselet of silver-ornamented leather, and a lionskin robe. Though no taller in stature than those around him, the man was different. Morning sun highlighted the distinct auburn color of his hair and the lightness of his fair skin. Even at this distance, they could see his startling blue eyes.

"Is that the king?" Magda whispered.

"I don't think so," Adam muttered. "Hector would be older by now. No, I think this is his little brother. I suspect we're looking at Troy's greatest legend, Magda. I think that's Paris himself. The prince who stole the fair Helen from the Spartan king, Menelaus."

"Paris?" Magda gaped at the small, splendid man now pacing down the step-path with his counselors following him. "The 'chosen one' of Aphrodite?"

"So the classical legend says. I expect he wonders who the hell we are."

"Do you speak Trojan, or whatever their language is?"

"Only intuitively." Adam grinned. "Not the words. It's all Greek to me." Casually he took Magda's hand. His grip was firm and strong.

As Paris passed through the line of warriors, the line fell into step with him. Hoplites drew their stubby bronze blades, spearmen raised their javelins, and the archers' bows came up, aligned on the two strangers waiting just across the avenue. Giants or not, these were the elite of Ilium's fabled army, and it would take only a word from Prince Paris to unleash them.

Adam drew Magda close and edged in front of her, keeping his grip on her hand. "Be ready to jump," he whispered, keeping his eyes on the approaching Trojans.

Ten feet away, Paris stopped, arrogant blue eyes studying the strangers. The warriors nearest him halted, but those toward the ends of the line went on a few paces, forming a half ring around the visitors. When they stopped, every second man turned to face outward.

"Very good," Adam muttered. "Bodyguards and an honor guard, all in one. They're ready for anything."

Facing them, Paris listened intently to the whispers of his "counselors," two older men in bright robes, then took a step forward. Pointing an imperious finger at Adam, he spoke a few brief syllables in a lilting, musical language, then waited.

Adam's friendly smile didn't waver. "So you're the stud who started the Odyssean War," he said. "Well, I'm Adam and this is Magda. We're sightseeing."

Paris frowned and shook his head. Slapping a hand to his breast, he barked, *"Paris! Quel sura quille!"*

Adam imitated the gesture with his free hand. "Adam." With fluid gestures he indicated the village around them, nestled in its walls, then pointed at the palace on the hill. "We're visiting your fair city. We'd like to see the boss."

"Adam!" Magda murmured.

"They don't understand a word of it," Adam assured her. "But this one takes my meaning."

As if arriving at a decision, Paris nodded curtly. *"Mea pelona,"* he said. Turning his back, he strode away.

"I think he wants us to follow him," Adam said, glancing around at the armed men. They were two lines now, the outer perimeter facing the crowds on the streets, the inner moving in to urge their guests along.

Beyond the avenue, the step-path brought them atop a terrace where pole and split-log structures clustered and crowded in happy disarray. Here bakers, weavers, and metalworkers plied their trades in stalls and sheds nestled among three- and four-story sleeping quarters, and people gathered on rooftops to watch the procession pass. Little flocks of children, like diminutive wolf packs, ran here and there, herded loosely by women, some wearing robes, some only short skirts or kilts. It was hard to tell at a glance which of the denizens of Troy were citizens and which were slaves. They all looked and dressed alike.

Magda particularly noticed the children. They were everywhere, glitter-eyed little flocks of them, stealing from the merchant vendors, confronting the lame and unwary, running wild and untamed. Mostly they were ragged urchins, but in their gazes was a calculating, ambitious force that was startling. Like formidable little hunters, eyeing big game.

Wolf-children, she thought, and the thought made her shudder. What kind of people did such children become?

Another stone terrace led them up into the little walled courtyard of the palace itself. Here the distinctions were easier. There seemed to be people everywhere, in little groups, the patricians being attended by their plebeians. Then, almost in the entrance of the log-walled palace itself, Magda caught her breath. On a stone pedestal stood a young woman, naked and radiant in the full sunlight. She was being bathed. Servants came and went around her, carrying water in Mycenaean pots, little gold jars of oils and fragrance, and folds of flaxen cloth. The girl had long, raven-dark hair, drawn up in a ponytail wrapped in gold mesh. Nubile breasts, sun-bronzed, matched a pair of perfect hips below a small, trim waist. The curious eyes that looked their way were large, dark, lustrous, and wide-set.

Magda stared at the girl on the pedestal. "What a beautiful child!" she gasped.

Just ahead of them Paris paused, turned, and flicked a gesture toward the bathing girl. *"Helena,"* he said.

"No wonder." Adam nodded. "That is the 'face that launched a thousand ships.' That's no ordinary teeny-bopper, Magda. That's Helen. Helen of Troy."

Magda looked outraged. "That—that *baby* was some Greek king's wife?"

"Child bride." Adam nodded. "She probably wasn't ten years old when Menelaus claimed her."

"Va-deh!" Paris snapped, turning toward the palace entrance. Guards responded, urging them toward the heavy wooden doors that opened into a small, dim anteroom. Here most of the hoplites stepped aside as another set of doors creaked open ahead. Beyond was a large, roofless room like an inner courtyard, bright with sunlight.

Paris stepped through, signaling them to follow. In the center of the bright space a man sat stiffly on a tall, fur-covered chair. Sunlight shone on thick silver hair. His face was scarred, his eyes penetrating. Around him, away from center, were a dozen other seated notables, including three women. Flanking each chair were two or three liveried hoplites, holding javelins and blades. At the far end of the room, between wide, twin hearths, stood a large wooden sculpture of the goddess Pallas Athene.

"Hector." Paris waved a casual hand, indicating the silver-haired man. *"Regis e fraternis."* Then, turning to the seated man, he bowed slightly. *"Adama, Regis. Vadate. E sororis Magda."*

"He's introducing us to his brother Hector, the regent," Adam whispered. "He says you're my sister."

"The language sounds a little Latin," Magda noted under her breath.

"Probably is." Adam nodded. "Those wild children outside, in the markets—some of them could become the founders of Rome."

"Remus and Romulus?"

"Could be. And a lot more like them. By the time they're grown, a lot of those wolf-children will be running loose, all over this part of the world."

"Qui vadaetes." Hector signaled them to approach. *"Adama e Magda? Doneas tue anatoleia?"*

"I wouldn't tell you where we're from, Hector, even if you could understand me," Adam said politely, his grin amiable but unreadable. "But I'm here to save your bacon if I can. I'm looking for Viktor Schlemann. *Vur bist du, Viktor?"*

Around the room, heads were cocked and brows lifted. To most of them, it was simply more gibberish—a language alien to their ears. But by the far wall, behind Hector, a stooped, robed figure gasped audibly and jerked upright at the final words. The robe parted and a hand appeared, holding a nasty-looking bronze dagger. "Ah, Viktor!" Adam pointed at the man. "There you are!"

Heads turned and people gasped as the cowl fell away. The man revealed was certainly no Trojan. His bald head and rimless eyeglasses shone in the sunlight. *"Adamische schweinhundt!"* he hissed. *"Ich bin so weit gekommen! Ich bin entschlossen mein diel zu erreichen! Hektor muss sterben!"* Like a panther he sprang, raising the dagger, aiming for the defenseless regent of Troy.

"Hector!" a woman cried. *"Victor paedatenes! Iliul ti Hector!"*

At Adam's side, Paris barked a command and a dozen javelins flashed in the sun, from several directions.

The assassin jerked and danced as spear after spear pierced him. He was dead before his face hit the slab-stone floor.

"Time to go bye-bye," Adam muttered. He squeezed her hand, and Magda felt again that sudden, vertiginous dizziness as the room swam around her, slowing and darkening. A bright bronze blade slashed through the air and thudded against an upraised arm. Then light too quick to be light flashed and everything was gone, and she was standing in a vast field of ripening wheat, where startled meadowlarks darted away on the hot wind of midday.

Her hand was still in Adam's, but as she turned he staggered, cursing between clenched teeth. Blood dripped from a gash along his left forearm.

"That pissant Paris," he hissed. "I save his brother's life, and he tries to kill me."

"Let me see that," Magda commanded. She stripped off the linen robe covering her tattered ITR jumper. With torn strips, she began wrapping Adam's wound. "You could use some stitching," she said. "Where and when are we?"

"American central plains, summer of 1942. Southwestern part of Kansas."

"Then let's find a road. What was that all about back there?"

"It was about time," he said. "And history. I told you, there are others with the temporal skill. And some of them know they have it. That Nazi, Schlemann, was one of them. He's been in the vectors since a few years from now, messing things up. I've tracked him through four eras so far, and this is the first time I ever saw him. But I've cleaned up after him. This time I was lucky. He'd sneaked into Troy as a visiting cousin of Priam's, and Cassandra—Priam's daughter—made note of it. The archaeologists found a clay tablet . . ."

"Why was he trying to kill Hector?"

"To change history, I guess. To make things go his way. Some people are like that. And Troy was a natural focus, the boiling pot from which other cultures arose. Schlemann wasn't the first to meddle there. Quark was there, too. Earlier."

"Is that what you do? Trace people like that? You . . . *police time*?"

"I guess you could call it that. I stumbled into it and just kept on."

"Who is Quark?"

"I'm not sure. By his behavior, I'd say he's a dangerous lunatic, at least. Maybe the worst of them. I think he'd wipe out humanity if he could. But I'm not sure he's alone. I think there's someone else—or *something* else—directing him. There's a kind of pattern there, if I can puzzle it out. It has something to do with the symbol delta. At any rate, I'll find him, sooner or later."

"But why, Adam? Why you?"

"Because I can." He shrugged. "If not me, then who? History is a rat's nest of accumulated occurrences, by its own volition, but it could be worse. There are people without scruples, Magda."

"Like Arthur."

"Arthur's a fair example. A simple psychopath. But Arthur isn't an adept, only a tyrant. My concern is the real timers, those who won't let history alone." With his bandage secure, he squared his shoulders and looked around. On the western horizon, a rectangular shape stood above the waving fields. "There's a grain elevator yonder," he said. "Let's go that way."

"So you hunt down the bad guys?" Magda gazed up at him thoughtfully. "You balance things?"

"Somebody has to. The vectors are getting busy. Timers, temporal technology, and now a bunch of tinkerers from the future. Whispers. They mean no harm, but they'll muddy things up. And now they've spun off a travel agency! Of course, that's years from the present *now*."

"Why don't you do something about them, then?"

"The Whispers? They aren't malignant. Weird, maybe, but they're part of the fabric—part of the natural course of events. They're not really timers, just a bunch of curious travelers from somewhere in the future. They're a natural occurrence. With them, dimensionality enters a new phase. Everything intertwines, Magda. Real history happens, and it's a mess, but at least it's real and everybody had their choices. It's altered history that worries me. Especially when it's altered by eradicators like Quark and lunatics like Schlemann. I know what Schlemann was trying to do. He bought into Hitler's Aryan dream. Or maybe Hitler and Himmler got it from him. But Schlemann found a way to make it real. He was at Telemark, probably got the idea there. Anyhow, he learned to time-jump.

"If Hector had died before Agamemnon launched his attack on Troy, three thousand years of history and culture would have changed. Graeco-Roman culture would never have evolved. There'd have been no Rome to keep the barbarians in check, no Constantinople to thwart the Muslims, no Frankish armies to hold western Europe. Maybe we'd have had a Eurasian culture eventually.

"Certainly the Hebrews would have been wiped out in the later Bronze Age and the Semitic and Arabic tribes scattered, so half of our present religions would have been lost. There'd have been chaos, and Teutons might have dominated the western world before modern history even began. Maybe Persia would have been overrun by Celts. So much for Darius and Xerxes.

"Schlemann wanted to completely reshuffle the deck of history."

"Nobody could predict all that," she objected.

"No. Nobody could. Quark seems to have a purpose behind him, but Schlemann just thrived on chaos. He didn't care. There are people like that, Magda. 'If it doesn't work for me, then I'll just break it.' Like Ghengis and Attila, like Borgia, and a couple of the Henrys, and Stanton and Perón. Like Hitler and Stalin and Johnson. Like Arthur. Heaven help us when the lunatics among us have time on their hands."

They found a road, and they found a ride, and they found a remote little town in western Kansas with a doctor. And somewhere along the way, Adam said, "You'll have your wish, Magda. You'll see the Great Plains in the early 1950s. I'm going to leave you here. Just blend in, become one of these people. Your name is Magda Wills, and your husband is in the army. Get a post office box. All the documents you need will be in it. And don't worry. Your George will be with you soon, I promise."

She looked stricken, but after a time she asked, "Why, Adam? You saved me from Arthur's AATVs. I'm important to you, but you've never told me why. Am I like Hector? Am I a pivot in history? Tell me."

"I can't." He shrugged. "Just accept it, please."

"Where will you go?"

"I'll help you get settled in, but then I have other things to do . . . other places, other times."

"Will I ever see you again?"

"Yes, of course. I promise." Again the ironic grin tugged at his cheeks. "You'll see a lot of me."

With Adam's usually unseen help, Mrs. George Wills took up residence in an unassuming house on a quiet street and began getting acquainted. It wasn't difficult. In the months since Pearl Harbor, a lot of people were moving and resettling. Older women in little towns all over the country were appointing themselves to look after "displaced brides," and in Faye Jones, Magda found a friend.

Then on a quiet, breeze-blessed evening, Adam told her he was ready to leave.

She took his hands. "Bring Georgie home soon," she said.

"He'll be here when his son is born," he promised.

She nodded. "We'll name the baby Adam, after you."

"Yes." He smiled. "I know you will."

∞

Science cannot at this point deduce the possible effects of overlapping focal fields in the T2 continuum. Theoretically, an occurrence of this nature would simply contradict itself, resulting in no occurrence at all. In any case, the likelihood of an accidental overloop is extremely remote. Theoretically, a perpetual redundancy might result, but little study has been given to such eventualities. As an accident, it could not occur. Literally, such an incident would have to be intentional.

—J.L. THORNE, Ph.D., T.T.D.,
Chief of Instrumentation, ITF, 8/12/46

∞

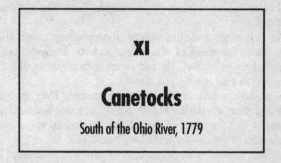

XI

Canetocks

South of the Ohio River, 1779

Barely a breeze stirred in the frail undergrowth beneath the interlinked pine boughs above. The morning was fresh, cool, and still. Beyond the deadfall clearing, blue shadows held hints of autumn fog and the only movements were small ripplings where life stirred—twitch of a squirrel's tail on a chestnut limb, flutter of wings where an oriole flashed the morning, ripple of wide leaves on a berry vine, and the slight, slow rise of lustrous gray fur from behind a stump. Beneath the fur, the shadowed eyes of Jack Higgins widened as he studied the clearing just beyond.

The clearing was full of people—busy little tan people, all dressed alike in garments he could not describe and all as bald as pigeon eggs. Big-eyed, small-featured, and energetic, they looked like a gang of hairless, agitated children, searching here and there for something on the ground.

Higgins studied them from cover, speculating. The fine fur of his coonskin cap touched his ears, soft as goose down in the tiny breeze that stirred it. By its motion the hunter knew the course of the wind and knew that he was concealed. From his flowing whiskers to his fine rifle, long knife, and tomahawk, from buckskin shirt to high moccasins, he blended with the thicket behind him and the ground where he lay.

It was part of his skill, and a measure of survival in this wild land, that Jack Higgins could blend with his surroundings as easily and naturally as the creatures he hunted. Once a Shawnee buck had actually stepped on him as he lay concealed beside a stream. It was the last thing that Shawnee ever did.

As well as any man this side of Boonesborough, Jack Higgins knew the ways of the forest and its denizens. Now, though, he was baffled. He had never seen anything like the gathering in the clearing just ahead.

Nine, he counted. Nine diminutive persons. They scurried here and there, chattering in fast, soft speech that he could not make out, and the fabric of their clothing—various grays, reds, and shades of green—looked like Chinese silk.

Injuns, he reasoned. Some kind of Injuns, but no kind he had seen before. Their bald heads might have been Mohawk or Huron, their large eyes might have indicated Cherokee—but not exactly. He could see clearly the thing one of them had dropped. It was small and gray, with a shiny surface and a strap like a doll's belt. It lay twinkling beneath a clump of sedge, a foot from his free hand, and they were looking for it.

One of them now wandered close, and the eyes of Jack Higgins narrowed. She—he wasn't sure why he thought "she," but it seemed right—was less than four feet tall, as bald as the rest, and her eyes were as big and dark as rain-wet walnuts. She carried various odd things about her—attached to a gold-fiber belt at her waist and slung from slight shoulders—but nothing that looked like a weapon.

The little female was very close now. She half turned, looking around, her eyes roving past the hidden woodsman. Then she looked down, nudged the sedge with a fabric-booted toe, and said, "Comlink."

As she bent to pick up the shiny gray thing, Jack Higgins moved. Like a great cat springing from cover, he erupted from the sheltering vines and grabbed the little person's wrist. In the same motion he lifted her, snugged her under his arm, and brought up his long rifle, cocked and ready to fire.

For an instant the other little people stared dumbly at the apparition before them. Then some of them shrieked, and they darted away in all directions, seeking cover. They were not good at it. The underbrush writhed and waved around them. Birds flew up ahead of them, twigs snapped, and rocks clattered. Jack Higgins raised his rifle, picking out one of them. But before he could level it a sharp pain in his left armpit made him flinch. The flinch gave the scampering little people time to disappear into the underbrush, though he could still hear their retreat.

"Dang!" Higgins muttered. "Skittier'n bugs, they be." Muffled cries came from the captured one, struggling and straining under his arm. Glancing around at the still-noisy wake left by the fleeing creatures, Higgins snorted his disgust. "Wonder they ain't et up yet, the clumsy thangs," he mused. Then, setting Betsy against the stump, he swung his prize around and held it up for a better look. His armpit throbbed where it had bit him.

"Let me go, you savage!" the stranger snapped. "You smell terrible!"

"Dang," Higgins rumbled. "It talks American. What be ye, small-fry? You a heathen Injun, maybe? Or some kind of critter?"

"Critter? I'm more human than you are, you hulking primitive!" The little creature's angry voice was high and musical. To Higgins it sounded like the sweet wail of a fast fiddle. "Put me down!"

"So's ye can light a shuck, I reckon. How's come ye got no hair, if ye're a human bein'?"

"Put me down, oaf!"

Higgins considered it, then set the little creature on its feet, atop the stump. It would be no trick to catch it, should it try to bolt.

"That's better," it said. "Hello. I'm KT-Pi. Who are you?"

"Katie, huh?" Higgins pulled off his coonskin cap. A gentleman acknowledged the presence of a Christian-speaking female, even if she was the strangest-looking child he recollected ever seeing. "Jack Higgins, Miss Katie. At your service. Lose yer hair, did ye?"

"Of course not! Papillary filamentation is an aboriginal vestige. My people have evolved past such crudity!"

"Yes'm." Higgins nodded. "My, don't ye talk fine!" A slight smile parted his dark whiskers. For all of her strangeness, the little creature was oddly attractive. Her fine, small features were expressive and pleasant, and those oversize dark eyes were almost hypnotic. Her diminutive size and lack of contour were like a child, but something about her said that she was no child at all. In his adventurous life, Jack Higgins had encountered many kinds of people—Negroes and Greeks, Dutchmen and Frenchies, and even a shipload of Chinese, not to mention more Indians than he cared to remember. But never had he seen a person like this.

"I reckon I'd best take ye home," he decided. "Maybe th' squire'll know what to make of ye."

"I think not," KT-Pi said.

Never since childhood had Jack Higgins been caught unawares in the wilds. He knew these woods like he knew his own cabin, and nobody—certainly not a clumsy bald midget—could ever catch him off guard. But he knew when he heard Betsy's hammer click back that this had happened. He whirled around, to face another of the little people. This one was a bit taller and less fine-featured, apparently a male. And it was holding his own rifle, aimed at his gizzard.

"Are you damaged, KT?" the newcomer asked.

"Not excessively," KT chirped, climbing down from the stump. "Have care with that artifact, Sev. It could discharge." She knelt, retrieved the lost gray thing and held it up. "Here is Deejay's comlink. Where are the others?"

"They're ..." Sev turned to point and Betsy's muzzle waved wildly.

"Careful!" Jack Higgins flinched. "Yon's a hair trigger—" but it was too late. Betsy's roar, sharp as the crack of a whip, echoed through the thickets and Higgins doubled over, his knees sagging. Bright blood welled between the fingers clenching his belly, and his face went ashen above his beard. "Aww," he moaned, "I surely wisht you hadn't did that." For a moment he crouched there, pain and accusation in his eyes as he looked from one to the other of them. Then he folded and sagged to the ground.

Sev stared at the fallen man, horrified, and dropped the long rifle.

Matthew Bullock heard the shot and knew it wasn't right. Ears attuned to wilderness knew the sound of a rifle loosely held, and long-honed reflexes did the rest. "Injuns!" he barked. "Come on, boys!"

Elem Threeby was just gathering his frightened scouts when the shot rang through the forest. "Sev and KT," he deduced. "They're in trouble. We must go back."

Big eyes peering this way and that, they followed him as he retraced his steps through the forest. The clearing wasn't far away. Bald heads bobbing above the undergrowth, seven Whispers headed back.

They paused at the edge of the clearing, looking across. Sev was there, fidgeting beside a tree stump, and KT knelt in the screening fronds a few feet away. "There they are." Elem Threeby pointed.

They were halfway across the clearing when Deejay's recorder pouch exploded, and a sharp crack like the strike of lightning reverberated around them. Fifty yards away the foliage erupted with tall, bearded primitives.

"Bald devil Shawnee!" a man yelled. "Li'l Injuns, by God! They done got Jack!"

Rifles waving in big fists, tomahawks and long knives flashing, the savages bore down on the startled time explorers. Elem Threeby tapped frantically at his wrist com, and the Whispers turned and ran. The savages were right behind them, towering over them, bright deadly blades flashing in the mottled sunlight. One of them stooped as he ran, reaching for something to clout. His big fingers closed on a bald head and slipped away. He reached again, raising his rifle to swing it like a club.

At the first shouts, KT-Pi looked up from her inspection of the fallen barbarian, then ducked as a flung tomahawk embedded itself in the tree stump beside her. "Oh, mercy," she breathed, flinging herself down across the large body of the woodsman. The comlink in her hand slipped from her fingers and fell into a fold of his buckskin shirt. Frantically she searched for it.

There was pandemonium all around, the sounds diminishing slightly as pursuit began. Then, abruptly, the world around her darkened and shimmered, and was replaced by the nothingness of undefined T2.

Little fingers closed on the lost comlink and she grasped it. It was covered with blood.

Time Loop L-383

"Around and around and around he goes, and where he stops, God only knows."

Deem Eleveno paused in his studious consumption of a glazed doughnut direct from 1942 and looked around. "What?"

"It's a segment of a children's rhyme," Teal Fordeen explained. "Circa 2080, I believe. It refers to the legend of King Arthur." He set down a half-filled cup of dark liquid and repeated, " 'Around and around and around he goes . . .' I suspect the implication here is that Arthur trapped himself in his own closed loop—or possibly overloop—thus causing the anachronism that so disrupted the flow of time during the postregime period. Tempus Rampant, some of our ancestors called it."

"Periods of persistent improbabilities," Toocie Toonine noted. "Like ring waves in a pool. My favorite is the story of the hoodlums who fled into a department store, filled the cash tills with money, and disappeared into the crowd after all the police went away."

"Folk legend," Deem Eleveno scoffed. "An example of the peril of attributed understandings. And that rhyme . . . the people indigenous to 2080 could hardly have deduced that Arthur became a closed loop. They didn't know about time manipulation then."

"Obviously some did." Teal shrugged. "They certainly

knew that *something* very strange had happened, and the technology for gravitic acceleration was at least thirty years old."

"Well, they certainly didn't know about loops yet, much less closed loops and overloops." Deem frowned at a partially consumed sugared pastry. "But let's attend to the business at hand. This pastry is nothing but aerated gluten and sucrose. It has almost no nutritional value."

"The coffee is even less nourishing," Teal Fordeen commented. "Boiled extract of a pungent seed, moderately high in caffeine. Yet these two things, coffee and doughnuts, were a cultural icon for generations. In combination, they somehow represented serenity—a respite from the trials and frustrations of daily life."

"It makes one wonder how we ever evolved." Deem nodded. "Our ancestors seem intent on placing value on things that have no value."

"And have we changed so much? Aren't we preoccupied with seeking the answers to questions that have no redeeming significance?"

"There is no such thing!" Elzy snapped. "If we don't seek answers, we have no purpose."

"Everybody has purpose," Peedy Cue said. He fingered his tape and glanced curiously at Toocie.

"Forget it, Peedy," Toocie warned, though a faint flush crept past her ears.

"A mystery," Cuel Denyne agreed. "Please pass the doughnuts."

Abruptly the cozy loop was filled with alarms. All around, virtual universes receded before displays of urgent data.

"Stations," Teal ordered. "Party coming upstream, emergency mode. They're signaling for a shunt."

"We have no shunts," Toocie reminded him. "This colony is the only offstream loop in this sector."

"Then bring them here," Teal said. "They need our assistance."

Whispers tapped out codes and a virtual display dissolved into a featureless tunnel. Almost before it cleared, panicked explorers darted in—eight of them. As the last sprinted into stable duration, looking back over his shoulder, he shouted, "She's still back there!"

"Close the shunt," another ordered.

The tunnel dissolved. The final Whisper pushed forward, through his milling companions. All of them wore the garb and equipage of field scouts, an exploration team from somewhere in the real-time past.

Spotting the insignia on Teal Fordeen's breast, the leader of the newcomers nodded. "Elem Threeby," he said. "Gateway log eight eight point five. We've encountered hostiles. They're in the conduit."

"Hostiles?" Teal blinked at him. "How? Who?"

"We don't know," Elem Threeby admitted. "Indigenees from circa 1790, we believe. They are armed, aggressive, and definitely hostile. They—they *shot at us*!"

"*Shot* at you?"

"They have propellant weapons. They chased us along the conduit. They wrecked Deejay's recorder!" He pointed and another of the new arrivals held up a sling-tied pouch with a visible half-inch hole in its fabric. Inside, something rattled. The Whisper folded back a flap and lifted out a battered, tangled thing that rattled brokenly. Hair-fine wires and little electronic components dangled from it. It looked as if it had exploded. "This hit it." Deejay displayed a flattened, oval blob of gray metal.

"Smelted lead," Elem pronounced. "Impregnated with residues of carbon, sulfur, and potassium nitrate. Those savages used a primitive explosive—Sev has analyzed it as a substance called black powder—to propel lead balls at us."

"They shouted at us, too." Deejay raised an offended, hairless brow at the indignities heaped upon him. "Called us 'Shahnee devils' and 'li'l Injuns!' "

"And you don't know who they are? How many of them were there?"

"Seven or eight, at least," Elem Threeby hissed. "Bunch of howling savages!"

"Primitive indigenees," a fugitive noted. "Native to the period. They call themselves Canetocks."

"But how in the Divine Multiples of Four did aborigines get into our conduit?" Elzy Pyar demanded.

"It's happened before." Toocie Toonine glared at Peedy Cue. "Maybe they grabbed somebody."

"They did," Deejay admitted.

Elem Threeby turned slowly, his large eyes moist as he looked around at his scouting party. "We are minus one. KT-Pi is missing."

"That can't be helped now," Teal Fordeen decided. "Those hostiles can't be more than seconds away. Clear the shunt."

"They could emerge anywhen!" Toocie protested. "We need coordinates."

A virtual display wavered and the sounds of angry men came through. "No time." Deem Eleveno dived for a console. "We'll use what's linked."

"Clear the shunt!" Teal ordered.

Springfield USO Club
1942

Patsy Morrison stared open-mouthed at the big face gaping down at her. The man was very tall, his face half hidden by bushy, unkempt whiskers and his eyes fierce. He held a heavy-looking antique weapon in one massive fist, as casually as another man might grip a serving fork. He wore stained, slick-worn buckskin garments and a wide, floppy hat, and various pouches, axes, and blades hung about him in ominous array. He reeked of stale sweat and woodsmoke. Behind him were several others just like him. She hadn't even heard them come in. Except for Sergeant Raines and Corporal Dobbs, she thought she was alone in the USO club. All the usuals were gone, most of them on their way to the depot.

Patsy tried to speak, swallowed, and tried again. She was already distracted, trying to account for a large platter of doughnuts and three jugs of coffee that had disappeared into thin air   and now this. Hands trembling, she offered a laden platter. "Doughnuts?" she squeaked, trying for her best USO smile.

Behind her a chair clattered and Master Sergeant Cato Raines strode forward. "You men are out of uniform!" he growled. "Your name and rank, mister?"

The bearded man gawked at him, then lowered his ancient rifle and drew himself to attention. Moccasins shuffled as those behind him followed suit. "Matthew Bullock, sir," he said. "Squad leader, First Butler Crick Rangers. Ah, beggin' pardon, sir, but where in God's creation be we?"

"Shut up!" Sergeant Raines snapped. "And don't call me 'sir'! It's 'sergeant' to you! Rangers, huh? Well, I guess that explains it. Where you are, Corporal, is the Springfield USO. Where you're supposed to be is out in that street, formin' up for duty! This regiment's shippin' out at twelve hundred hours! Now git your butts out there and report! 'Bout face! March!"

Patsy Morrison scuttled around them, to present her tray as they filed out into the busy street. At her insistence, they helped themselves to doughnuts as they passed.

Poor souls, she thought. They all look absolutely lost. Just like those kilted Canadians who had shipped out from Springfield last week.

Behind them, Sergeant Raines frowned and tapped a spit-shined boot on the linoleum floor. "Rangers," he muttered. "Army's goin' straight to hell, looks to me."

At the roll table, Corporal Danny Dobbs tore a page from his desk calendar—April 11, 1942—grinned, and shook his head. "Special force, I bet," he said. "Boy, wait'll ol' Mussolini gets a load of that bunch comin' down his road! He'll crap his britches for sure!"

Right out of the picture books, Patsy Morrison thought, watching through a window as the Butler Crick Rangers were herded into formation, motley and garish among the ranks of uniformed GIs with their packs and slung helmets. In five months with the USO, she had seen all kinds of soldiers—hundreds of GIs, of course, but also Canadians, a French unit, several turbaned Ghurkas from Special Forces . . . and now these. She wondered where they were from but decided not to speculate. "Loose lips sink ships," the big sign over the dance floor said.

Right out of the picture books, they had been. Fur caps and rawhide, laced moccasins and muzzle-loaders . . . they even smelled of woodsmoke and forest paths.

Usually it was best not to wonder too much.

∞

In terms of duration, from the first practical application of Magnus Opum's theories by the World History Investigative Society (WHIS) in 2744 to the perceived present (Closed Loop L-36, Day 36-343), is a T1 span of 169 years plus 86 days. In that entire period, WHIS has encountered a total of two—or just possibly three—anomalous, practicing time-jumpers. One of these is Edwin Limmer, whose presence in T2 retrosync is accounted for. The other certainty is a true anomaly, a protomorph identified only as "Adam."

This presents two puzzles: Assuming our discoveries in retrosynchronic bioduplication are—as we believe—the ultimate breakthrough in practical time travel, opening the way for unimpeded use of T2, then who and what is Adam, and how many others like him might there be? And second, why have we encountered no one except ourselves traversing our conduits to the past? *Why, for that matter, have we not met others—from our own future—making use of our discoveries?*

—Teal Fordeen, memos to WHIS

∞

XII

Visiting Dignitaries

Decatur City, County of Illinois, 1802

The Reverend Jacob Ross considered himself, with pious humility, as a wise and educated man. For forty-three of his sixty years he had devoted himself to the studies of Holy Scripture, doctrine, and theology, while pursuing also the secular arts of mathematics, composition, humanities, and the classical philosophies.

As much as a mortal man might be, the Reverend Jacob was intellectually prepared for even the most bizarre of occurrences. He had never witnessed a resurrection or the raining of manna from the skies, any more than he had ever actually seen an elephant. But should such phenomena present themselves to him, he was prepared to accept and welcome them.

What he was not prepared for on that bright, crisp Sunday morning was the sudden appearance in his very dooryard of a wild Indian, an oddly attired Oriental person, a dilapidated old horse, a broken cart suspended at eye level and heaped with bleached bones, and a mechanical monstrosity he could identify only as a—a *thing*.

For long seconds he stood transfixed—one freshly waxed shoe on his porch and one still planted on the tile of his vestibule, his left hand still holding the brass knob of his open front door—staring at the apparitions in his dooryard, two of which were staring just as dumbly back at him.

Nothing moved except the Widow Ferguson, who had been passing by when the outlandish conclave appeared abruptly in the reverend's yard and who was now pounding wildly away down Elm Street, her skirts flying.

The widow's receding wail barely registered on Jacob Ross. He stood astonished, simply staring.

The frozen moment was shattered when the old horse tethered to the mechanical thing decided to vent its own astonishment in a fit of equine panic. Wild-eyed and twitching, it looked around, bunched its haunches, and lashed out with its rear hooves. The Reverend Jacob's carefully whitewashed picket fence collapsed behind it and his gate splintered from its hinges to sail out into the shaded peace of Elm Street. Across the way, windows were raised and doors opened.

"Here, now!" the pastor yelled. Long, skinny legs flying, he cleared his porch in two strides, vaulted down his steps, and headed for the offending animal. It kicked again and bits of shattered picket fence flew, along with gouts of the trimmed spirea hedge.

John Two Elk, just climbing down from his buffalo bones, was almost bowled over by the racing preacher. He thudded against the solid upright of the forklift, spun around, and sprawled across the lap of Larry Hong at the controls. With a crash, the forklift dropped its load. Buffalo bones rattled and bounced merrily across the Reverend Jacob's carefully tended little lawn.

Jacob reached the horse and grabbed its tether. "Stop that this instant!" he demanded. Horse rolled its eyes again, ears back, then changed its mind and nuzzled the reverend's hand, entranced by the scents of bay rum lotion and floral soap.

With the animal under control, the Reverend Jacob turned to gawk again at the unexplainable entourage around him. His impeccable little lawn was a disaster. "In the name of God," he breathed, "what is going on here?"

The old Indian had recovered his balance and was looking around, turning full circle as his stricken eyes took it all in. He pointed an accusing finger at the Reverend Jacob's neat house. "House," he stated. Still pointing, he turned half around again. "More houses. Houses everyplace. Damn!"

Hunkering in the saddle of the mechanical monster, the Oriental gentleman moaned, "It's the Gathering. Holy Mother! We're all dead. Everybody's dead, and we're gathered here for Judgment." As he glanced around at the Reverend Jacob, a spark of futile hope lit his dark eyes. "I don't suppose this is still Kansas, is it?"

"It is not, nor ever has been," Jacob assured him. "This borough is Decatur City, Illinois Territory of the State of Indiana, and you people have wrecked my garden."

Beyond the assemblage, Mistress Augusta Ross peeked from the doorway, while Ambrosia peered over her shoulder. The mistress of Cottage Ross had not yet donned her Sunday bonnet, and tightly pulled silvery hair framed a frightened face above the lace of her collar. "What is it, Jacob? Do we . . . do we have guests?"

A crowd was gathering beyond the smashed gate, people from surrounding homes joining those who had been walking past, east or west according to their religious persuasion. A pair of buggies passed in the street, slowed, and stopped as their occupants gawked at the commotion in front of Jacob Ross's house. The murmur of curious voices grew to a babble with questions of "What's happening?" and "Has there been an accident?" and "What in heaven's name is that thing with the poles and chains?"

Now a big man in frock coat and old-fashioned knee breeches pushed through. In his wake came the disheveled Widow Ferguson. "What seems to be the trouble here, Jacob?" the big man asked, staring past the minister in wide-eyed astonishment. "Who are these persons? And *what is that thing*?"

"I assure you I don't know, Amos." The Reverend Jacob shook his head. "This entire spectacle was here when I opened my door."

"Devil's work!" the Widow Ferguson proclaimed. "That's what it is. Wasn't a soul yonder, then *pop!*"

"Pop?" Amos inquired.

"That's right. Pop!"

"Hush yourself, Mistress Ferguson," Jacob said. "There's

no devil's work here and no pop. This rectory is the legal property of the church."

"No church of mine," the Widow Ferguson assured him. "Heathen Indians and creature remains! And on the Lord's day, too. You ought to be ashamed of yourself, Pastor Jacob!"

"The late Mr. Ferguson was a Democrat," Amos explained to John Two Elk and Larry Hong, who looked mystified. "I reckon that's why Hazel gets this way. Hope you gentlemen speak English. My name is Amos Miles. Where'bouts are you folks from?"

"San Diego, originally." Hong shrugged. "Now I live at Pratt. That's between Wichita and Dodge."

"Can't say I ever heard of it. That in Illinois?"

"Kansas."

"Where's Kansas?"

"That's what the Expansionists are calling the western Missouri Plains," the Reverend Jacob explained. "It's out in the Purchase."

"That's all wild Indian territory!" a farmer declared. "The Great American Desert! Not good for anything a'tall. I believe Jefferson's lost his mind."

Amos frowned, trying to recall his geography. "And the heathen—ah, the Indian gentlemen yonder? Is he yours?"

"Him?" Larry Hong shook his head. "I don't even know him. He made me carry his bones. Threatened to shoot me if I didn't."

"Does he . . . ah . . . speak any English, like you do?"

John Two Elk answered for himself. "Talk damn good 'merican," he asserted. "Which way to th' stockyards?"

"What about my fence?" the Reverend Jacob put in. "What about my garden?"

"Gypsies," the Widow Ferguson decided. "The Decatur City Unity Church is harboring Gypsies."

"Spaniards!" someone beyond the broken fence asserted. "You heard that Chinee, Amos. They're from the Spanish Territories."

"The Chinee ain't speakin' Spanish, is he?"

"If they're Spanish out there," someone else shouted, "then how's come we're buyin' them from France?"

"We ain't buying 'em from France, Zebulon!" a man in the rear rasped. "We're buying 'em from Napoleon. Napoleon ain't Spanish *or* French, he's Italian! Said so in the newspaper. Can't ye read?"

"Course I can!"

"Don't believe he's Corsican, Zeb. More Sicilian."

Amos Miles swung around, big fists on his hips, stern eyes roving the crowd. "Why aren't you people in church?" he demanded.

"We're waiting for the preacher, Amos," a gaunt man with a drooping cravat explained. "How 'bout it, Reverend? We gonna have services today or not?"

Augusta Ross had come out onto the porch now, followed by the dutiful Ambrosia, who brandished a heavy broom and glared at the motley crowd. Augusta's hands were clasped at her chin. "My goodness!" she said, over and over again.

The Reverend Jacob Ross stood perplexed, his mind straining for a clue as to what was happening here. In the crowd beyond his wrecked fence he saw two or three elders of the opposition True Faith Church, staring gleefully. Worse, he spotted at least three of his own deacons. At a loss for solutions, the Reverend Jacob knelt and bowed his steel-gray head in prayer. All around, hats were doffed and heads lowered. For a long moment, the pastor knelt in silence, seeking wisdom. What came to him was inspiration. With a quiet "Thank you, Lord, amen," he rose to his feet and spread his arms, turning slowly.

"My beloved," he intoned in that fine voice that could soothe babies or rattle the rearmost pews, "behold a mystery, a sign sent among us to test us on this, the Lord's day! Just as the Scriptures promise in the Book of Revelations! Before us stand weary travelers, unfed and unwashed. We know not who they are, nor from whence they come among us! No one of us may say how they came to be here, yet behold, here they are, a scorned and unredeemed heathen, a stranger from the other side of the world . . ."

"I'm from Kansas, for Christ's sake," Larry Hong muttered, but Amos silenced him with a glare.

". . . divine travelers here to test our hearts and our hospitality. Just as all of these bones test our patience and that—that *thing* there tests our faith. Thus might the Lord's own angels have appeared in the day of Lot!" The Reverend Jacob held out open hands toward Two Elk and Hong. "Welcome, strangers," he said. "Come ye into the bosom of our family. You will be bathed and anointed among us. Your needs will be attended. You will be given food and wine . . ."

"Hallelujah!" Two Elk cheered.

"For this we do in God's name, and in the knowledge of God's mercy. The Lord be praised!"

"Amen." A Unity deacon grinned, casting a victorious glance at one of the elders of the True Faith Church.

"Fill a washtub, Ambrosia," Augusta Ross whispered to her servant. "And see that there's plenty of yellow soap. I'll ask some of the ladies to set a nice table out by the shed."

"Gee, John Two Elk," Larry Hong muttered, "I don't think we're in Kansas anymore."

The Stowaway Journal

May 12, 1996

Oddity among oddities—as I try to recall those years of rejuvenation following the night in 1952 when I finally broke free from retrosync, it is the little inconsistencies that emerge in memory. One would think that, with a purpose like mine—to someday reach the end of life so that I might somehow have a hand in how it all began—one would focus on the main weave of those myriad patterns leading toward that end. Yet more and more I find myself dwelling on discrepancy.

For example, I think often about a puzzling episode one morning in 1961 in the park at the end of 11th Street. I had gone there to listen to Walter

Wall's farm reports, a routine that in my case required privacy since the Walter Wall report I was hearing was not the same as the Walter Wall report numbing the ears of everyone else around me. Theirs was today's report. Mine was tomorrow's.

I had done well in futures—so well that the Limmer Trust was now a substantial holding discreetly bedded in several banks, and its earnings had become the bedrock of the Limmer Foundation. This was primarily to mollify the IRS, which had a nasty habit of bumbling around in things it didn't understand just because it didn't understand them. But the Foundation had developed a life of its own and was doing good work.

At any rate, I went to the park for privacy, and usually found it. On this morning I saw only one other person, a tall, distant figure wandering across the north picnic area toward the flower displays. He was some distance away from the bench of my choice, to my left.

I was hearing Walter Wall tell me about sunflowers as a cash crop when I glanced right and noticed a young man walking toward me some distance away. He was just crossing Lexington, just entering the park, maybe a hundred yards away. I didn't think much about him. It was a public park. He looked vaguely familiar, but then living in a small town is like that. After a while everybody looks familiar.

He might have been a student just home from college or even a local young buck still in high school—a tall, strapping, dark-haired young man past adolescence but still plagued by the appearance of youth. I wouldn't have noticed him further except that at that instant he paused, clenched his fists, and closed his eyes, the picture of intense concentration.

Something subtle happened to the morning. For just an instant there was a stillness, a sense of "slowing," an impression of abrupt darkness and light—like a loop shunt, done before it was really perceived. Yet in that instant I looked around and saw the other park visitor, closer now, over by the Methodist Ladies' tulip garden. I thought I was seeing double. It was the same young man! Fifty yards, at least, from where I had seen him an instant before. But when I glanced back to the right, he—that young man just entering the park—was gone. As if he had never been there at all. He was off to my left, right where he had been before. He *was* the figure I had seen moments before, already in the park when I got there.

I put the playback away and watched him. He strolled nearer, and I knew him. One of the local boys, one I had seen around town off and on for nearly ten years.

He approached, glanced my way, and said, "Morning, Mr. Limmer."

"Morning." I nodded at him. "Nice time of day."

"Yes, it is." He walked on, then paused and looked back. "All time is nice time, isn't it?"

I watched him leave the park, and knew where I had first met him. He had been about ten years old then, and I had been only a couple of days old in real time. He was the boy who brought me a note, when I was in the bank that first time—the one who cared that I had a place to stay.

Price, the banker, had called him by name that day, I thought. But I couldn't remember the name. Who remembers kids, in a busy world like this?

The mind is an astonishing thing, and we're never ready to give it the credit it deserves. Within moments I had pretty well decided that it wasn't a time-jump I saw that morning—a time-jump accomplished by a mind unassisted by T2 temporal reverse technology—but only a trick of perception played by my own mind. A century-plus of duration was bound to have some side effects, after all.

It was thirty-some years later, in durational time—and I was thirty-some years younger—when I mentioned that odd morning to one of the Whispers. Zeem Sixten heard me out and put the memory to rest with a word.

"Dream," he said. "Possibly you dozed off and dreamed it."

Clear logic. A person could easily doze off, listening to Walter Wall's farm reports. But still, I think about it sometimes.

∞

Infinity is all in how you look at it.

—AMANDA SANTEE BRINK

∞

XIII

Anywhen, Inc.

Waystop, The Present

"The kids probably think we're crazy," Maude admitted, "but then that's what they usually think. Janet called, said Joe had called her. I guess they just want to be sure we're all right."

Mandy scanned the PC screen, tapped in an adjustment, and pulled out the printer's paper tray. In the next room, a tiny bell sounded, twice. There were Whispers in the conduit. They heard George Wilson coming in from the back patio, to read the settings. Rhythmic guitar music drifted through the open door. Edwin Limmer was out there, chording Lucas's old guitar to a Clint Black song on the radio.

"So what do they think about you and Lucas going into the time-travel business?"

"Janet didn't seem concerned. I tried to explain it, but I know she's imagining museum tours and group junkets to historical sites. She said Joe just asked about 'Mom's latest bizarre adventure.' "

"Like when you tried to patent edible forks and your petition to macrame the Houses of Congress? You do get some stirball ideas, Maude."

"The word is screwball. Or at least it used to be. Maybe *stirball* is better. I suppose. Where do you get these kooky expressions, Mandy? Have you been sneaking peeks at the future or something?"

Amanda glanced up at her. "I don't know. Sometimes it almost seems like it. When I think a phrase used now I

149

sometimes hear it as it originated . . . or as it might become. Maybe it's just progressive semantics."

The kitchen was long and tidy, a cool oasis lighted by the glow of sunlight on lace curtains. At the oak table, Maude had Rolodex cards spread out, entering addresses and phone numbers in a ruled ledger book. Mandy was monopolizing the computer. Since her excursion into "Whisper Central," as she called it—clinging to a handful of far-future testicles—Maude's little sister had become an enthusiastic part of Waystop operation. She had learned to calibrate the TEF system, displayed an almost uncanny accuracy in four-dimensional plotting, and had several times "chronigated" and boosted groups of Whispers on their upstream journey toward the distant past. She had learned everything George Wilson could—or would—teach her about the technology and theory behind temporal relocation and had quizzed Edwin Limmer for hours about his experiences in retrosync.

For all intents and purposes, Mandy Brink had become the chief technician for the first booster station on the Whisper line. She had even modified Wilson's calibration tables, to adjust for geographic placement as a function of time differential. "No reason not to kill several steps with one stone," she explained to the bemused Wilson.

Now she activated the PC's printer, let a few cards slide into the collecting tray, and handed one of them across to Maude. "How's this?" she asked. "Grab your attention?"

It was a simple business card, on 20 percent linen stock. Imprinted on it was an odd-looking, sideways figure-eight and the inscription: ANYWHEN, INC., followed in smaller typeface by Lucas's unlisted business telephone number and a fax number.

"What's this, a brand?" Maude squinted at the card. "Lazy 8?"

"Of course not! That's infinity. Or as close as I could come, with your Graf-Ex and EZ-Comp programs. Why don't you update, sis? This is antique software. It's really old hash."

"I don't chase trends in graphics," Maude muttered. "The only reason we have a computer is to keep Lucas's material inventories and payroll records. What did you do, put an X between parentheses?"

"There's a lot more to it than that! Infinity is hard to get, when you're working with five-year-old bookkeeping software."

"Well, it looks fine, I guess. What do we do with these?"

"We hand them to people," Mandy explained. "Good business practice."

"Oh. I suppose so. Anyway, Janet said they'd let us know if anybody they know would like to take a time trip. She said she'd like to send Jamie forward about three years. He's being a pill."

"It doesn't work that way," Mandy said seriously. "To slide him past the rebellion phase, she'd have to send him back in time, then recover him when he's a little older." Tilting her head, she scowled at the Anywhen business card, then went back to the keyboard. The card needed a slogan to go with its logo.

"Like with Ray and the hoodlums?" Maude looked up, studying her sister. "Are you ready to bring them back yet?"

"No. Not quite yet, anyway."

"It's hard to imagine what would make those monsters grow up," Maude said. "Sorry, but you know how I feel about Ray and his twins. Lucas is right. You took on two outlaws and a lawyer, and it's hard to tell the difference. Ray's a twit."

"I know," Mandy agreed sadly. "Honestly, I don't think it's their recovery I'm concerned with right now. It's mine. I've been maxed up for quite a while."

"Fed up, you mean. Or maxed out. You're having fun now, though, aren't you?"

"Yes, I am."

"I've seen that dreamy look on your face, little sister." Maude nodded. "Somehow I don't think it's thoughts of dear old Ray that put it there."

Mandy shot a glare at her sister. "Are you saying you think I've? . . ."

"No such thing," Maude assured her. "But you certainly glowed when you told us about Whisper Central . . . and Adam. Even Lucas noticed it."

"I did not glow! I was just excited!"

"I can imagine," Maude drawled. "The way you described that Adam . . ."

"I was excited about the time-travel thing! And those people from the future. They look so strange, like little bald-headed dolls with big eyes. The biggest eyes . . ." She gazed out the kitchen window, where elm trees shaded a manicured Bermuda lawn. "Those eyes. So gentle and—and amused, kind of. As if he were looking right through me."

"Just like I thought," Maude chuckled.

"What?"

"He! Adam! My God, sis, you sound like a schoolgirl. And that piece of velvet on your pillow! You sleep with it, huh?"

In what had once been the dining room, a tiny bell trilled happily. The conduit was clear. They heard George Wilson heading back to the patio. The sad-eyed "technician" spent a lot of time out there now, just strolling around or sitting in the shade, lost in his own thoughts. They all knew what bothered him. He was lonely for his wife. As Wilson left the house, Ed Limmer entered from the garage, pushing a two-wheel dolly loaded with boxes and crates. He rolled through the kitchen, into the transport chamber. "All clear for private use," he told the women in passing. "No more Whispers today."

The first several times Whispers had passed through the new booster, Lucas and the two women had stood in the open door with Limmer and watched—or tried to. They had seen the passage each time, but what the eyes registered was more than the mind could register. To Mandy, it had seemed a sudden blur appeared in the empty booster chamber, a blur that swirled just beyond perception, then slowed abruptly and there were figures within it—small, agitated people, standing crowded like people in an elevator except they faced in all directions.

But it was only the barest fraction of an instant. Then the chamber was empty, except for the nagging suggestion of having gone from light to darkness to light.

Some of the Whispers at Whisper Central had tried to explain to her how the process worked. The TEF, they said—the temporal effect focalizer—was actually a sort of infinite mirror reflecting back and back within itself. It gathered light from a radiant source and "slowed" it within an intense magnetic field that simulated, then gathered and focused gravity. Like steam and ice, the two elements—light and gravity—streamed together, becoming one substance midway between the two. But unlike water, the elements remained in flux, each reversing its polarity. Light became gravity, gravity became light, and the result was a "slingshot" effect that propelled anything within the TEF's projected magnetic field ahead of the wave of newly formed light.

In essence, whatever was in the way of the wave was instantly moving faster than the wave, to stay ahead.

To travel in time, they explained, an object must move faster than light. So the light was slowed to nothing, then rereleased, and the transported object rode the ripples ahead of it.

This was the principle developed by George Wilson. It was the paradigmatic basis of practical time travel—the basic principle behind the TEF. The inspiration for Wilson's discovery, some thought, came from the simple workings of the ubiquitous inertial energy light source, the common lamp of his time.

In theory, they all understood it. Seeing it was something else. To Lucas and Maude, it was simply indescribable. But its effect on Mandy was different. Each time she watched a transit, she had a feeling of limitation, as if there should be more going on than there was. The whole thing seemed, somehow, constricted and mechanical. Something important was unaccounted for.

Like a Cadillac chassis on bicycle wheels, the TEF technology had an awkwardness about it, to her. It was almost right, but not quite. Something seemed askew, but she couldn't grasp what it was. Thinking about it gave her a headache.

They had all given up watching, though they remained awed at the magnitude of what each little bell sound signaled. People were passing through here, propelled beyond light speed by a pulse of raw, universal energy.

The immense power to accomplish such feats lay in the heavens. The generator drew light from the sun and gravity from a black hole somewhere in space—which were both the same source in some inconceivable weave of dimensions. Both occupied the same time but at different places, or the same place at different times. The full range of energy in a universe composed of nothing else. Matter is mass. Mass is energy bounded by dimension. The dimension of movement is time, and its only limit is infinity.

Infinity is as each of us sees it. To Amanda Santee Brink it looked like two parentheses and an X.

Now the gate alarm flashed, and Maude went to the front window. "They're here," she called. "Our first outside customers."

Mandy ran a few more cards on the printer, then carried three brand-new folding lawn chairs into the focalizer chamber. Edwin Limmer was right behind her, trundling the two-wheeler with another load. There were cases of canned goods and some camping equipment. He stacked the load on the steel floor, wheeled his cart out, and returned with a load of bottled water, flashlights, and an expensive nylon all-climate tent, still in its box.

While he unloaded, Mandy checked the inventory. "All accounted for," she said.

"All the comforts of home." He nodded.

When Lucas Hawthorn went on a recruiting trip, he chose his hunting grounds carefully. The type of client he was looking for would, in his opinion, most likely be found either in a prison cell or in a high public office. But since Lucas had only limited connections in such strata, having never indulged in either crime or politics, his next best bet was a large city. For his purposes—a full-scale dress rehearsal of the services of Anywhen, Inc.—he had decided he needed the most useless subjects he could find. Therefore he ventured among the urban rich, with a hunter's eye for those individuals whose primary passion was the pursuit of conspicuous consumption.

Ed Limmer had suggested the time and place to be visited. "It's an island," he said. "Very remote. Believe me, it's nearly anachronism-proof. Even if something were to go wrong, there'd be no serious harm done to the historical pattern of events. Of course, the chances of anything going wrong are remote, but why take chances at all with history?"

It was Limmer's "why take chances" that made Lucas decide to seek out specific clients, at least for this first full-scale test since the Swains' visit to their deceased aunt. What he wanted were influential people, of course, but particularly those whose continued existence was of no particular value to anyone but themselves.

"I'm looking for a few worthless big shots," he told Maude. "Somebody who can do us some good when they come back, but it wouldn't really matter if they didn't. *Prestigious*-type people, you know, but useless as tits on a rake handle, that's what I'm looking for."

"Go to Topeka," Maude suggested. "It's full of those. D.C.'s even better."

"Politicians." He shook his head. "We need somebody with credibility."

"Sounds to me like you already know who you want," she said.

Lucas grinned. "I do. But I want to be systematic about this."

Systematically, he ruled out Denver, Oklahoma City, and Kansas City as hunting grounds because none of them was in Kansas, where Anywhen, Inc., was registered as an incorporated venture. Thoughts of the legal furor that could ensue if anything went remotely wrong—"Useless But Prestigious Citizen Sues Building Contractor for Interstate Contratemporization; Claims He Was Subjected to the Seventies"—kept running through his mind.

He was sure there were no specific laws against interstate contratemporization, but Lucas was a product of his time—a small-business entrepreneur in a litigious society. Anybody could and did sue anybody for anything, law or not, and there were glitter-eyed plaintiff's attorneys crawling out of the woodwork just to keep the pot boiling.

Crossing state lines simply multiplied the jeopardy. So Lucas decided to recruit strictly within Kansas.

He ruled out Lenexa and Overland Park because they were

too far from home and because they were so much a part of Kansas City that they might as well have been in Missouri.

That, then, left Wichita. And that satisfied him. A discreet call to an old KU buddy there got him three unlisted telephone numbers and some vital statistics. A little research in the local newspaper's morgue gave him the slant for his pitch. Three days later he met a gold-striped LearJet at the local airport and drove its occupants to his house.

He had no doubt that the three were fully apprised of his credentials, his personal authenticity, and probably his bankable assets by then. He also knew what had lured them more than anything else. His offer had been simple: an exclusive, ten-day package junket to a pristine, idyllic Indonesian island exactly as it was in the late 1800s, even including some "extinct" flora and fauna. In return, his clients would allow restricted use of their names in conjunction with limited, exclusive presentations to future potential travelers.

Lucas knew without doubt that Francis "Fry" Murdock, L.K. Hemingway, and Chad Ryan—the heir apparent to one of the nation's largest fast-food companies, the owner of two professional sports teams, and a local television superstar on his way to network fame—didn't believe a word of it. What had lured them to agree was nothing more than terminal curiosity.

But for whatever reason, they agreed. And all three fit Lucas's criteria: They were rich, they were widely known, and—in Lucas's opinion—they were all three absolutely useless. All were single, all childless, all self-centered, narcissistic, and self-indulgent, and not a one of them had any redeeming social value that Lucas Hawthorn could see.

As he drove through his gate, Lucas could almost hear the sneering skepticism in the minds of his guests. *What is this? This isn't anyplace. It's just somebody's house.*

Unperturbed, he stopped in the curving drive, got out, and held the back door open for Murdock and Ryan while Hemingway let himself out on the passenger side.

"Where are we?" Ryan demanded. "Why are we stopping here?"

"Please bring your own luggage, gentlemen," Lucas said.

"You'll be departing in just a few minutes on an adventure you will never forget."

They followed him in, glaring around at the living room and its furnishings. "Cheap," Hemingway muttered. "Tawdry."

Maude closed the door behind them, pretending not to hear. "Welcome to Anywhen, gentlemen," she said. "Right through there, please."

In a stage whisper, Chad Ryan asked Murdock, "Who's that? His wife?" Then as they entered the kitchen he caught sight of Mandy, and his flawless features took on the famous smile that most of America had seen on the numbing screen. "Now we're getting somewhere," he muttered.

"I wonder if she's part of the package," Murdock leered.

"Right through here," Lucas growled, and led them into the former dining room.

"What's this?" Hemingway demanded, his eyes roving the stacks of goods and equipment, the lawn chairs on the steel floor, then flicking to the glistening cone of the TEF on its I-beam tower. "I've seen better waiting rooms in junk shops."

"You have a chopper pad out back?" Ryan asked. "What airport are we going to?"

"Please be seated." Lucas indicated the lawn chairs. "Be with you in just a moment."

Ed Limmer met Lucas in the doorway. Mandy and Wilson were already in the alcove, confirming the settings.

"You found a real prime bunch of assholes." Limmer grinned. "Sure you want to bring them back at all?"

"A deal's a deal," Lucas said.

Mandy came from the kitchen and handed each of the "tourists" a manila envelope. "This will tell you about your island adventure," she said.

"You going with us, hon?" Murdock leered. "I'll spring for a grass skirt."

Mandy ignored him. As she disappeared into the kitchen, Hemingway growled, "This is crazy. What kind of a scam is this, anyway?"

"Give it a chance." Ryan shrugged. "Maybe there's a pad out back. Maybe we're waiting for a chopper."

"Let's see what this stuff is," Hemingway said. He seated himself in one of the lawn chairs, fumbling with the flap of his envelope. The others joined him. As Ryan's package opened, a business card slid out. He picked it up. ANYWHEN, INC., it said. There were some numbers and an odd-looking little logo like a patched-together 8 lying on its side. In the center were the words: HAVE A NICE TIME.

Abruptly the room seemed to swirl dizzily, spiraling into an infinite dimness. Then it disappeared entirely. The three stared around them, open-mouthed. They were still sitting in their lawn chairs, still holding their packets, and the stacks of supplies still stood behind them, but nothing else was the same.

Dappled sunlight danced around them, and the fresh, salty breeze carried the sweet scents of distant seas and tropical vegetation. Birds of a dozen varieties were visible just from where they sat.

"What the hell happened?" Murdock roared. "What is all this?"

"Jesus Christ, they have special effects and everything!" Ryan marveled. "How did they do that?"

Hemingway gawked this way and that, rising to his feet as he studied the unexpected surroundings. Then he remembered the packet in his hand and tore it open. In addition to the Anywhen, Inc., business card and some photocopied lists of flora and fauna, there was a neatly typed letter. He glanced at it, then read it aloud.

Good afternoon, gentlemen:

It is the first day of May 1883, and you have just arrived on the beautiful peninsula called Polish Hat, which extends from the northeast quadrant of an island in Sunda Strait. The waters here are said to offer some of the finest wade-fishing in the world, and the slopes above you abound in small wild game of many varieties. You will find hunting and fishing gear among the supplies provided for your comfort by Anywhen, Inc.

Indigenous life in the vicinity includes several species listed as extinct in our time.

There is no permanent human settlement on the island in 1883, though primitive fishermen do visit occasionally. Merchant seamen who have voyaged here have reported that these people are courteous and not aggressive. Be cautioned, however, that indigenous persons encountered here, as in any primitive environment, should be approached as one would approach any unfamiliar plant or animal—cautiously and with respect.

The three peaks you see are Rakata, on the south, Danan in the middle, and Perbuwatan on the north. Rakata is highest, estimated at more than 2,600 feet above sea level. It is rumored that a fabulous treasure of gold artifacts and precious stones was concealed in a cave on Perbuwatan during the late 1700s, and may still be there.

We hope your stay on Polish Hat will be a pleasant one. Feel free to explore, to take photographs, and to sample the many delights of life in this tropical paradise.

Your return is scheduled for noon, May 10, your time.

Have a nice time.

He crumpled the letter and thrust it into a pocket. "What the hell is this, Fantasy Island?"

Chad Ryan was scampering here and there, looking for concealed props or backstage gear. "This is marvelous," he kept saying to himself. "How did they do this? It's almost *real*! I want these people! God, what CBS would give . . ."

Murdock hadn't moved from his lawn chair. "Crap," he muttered sourly. "I don't believe any of this."

Hemingway stared at him. "Do you believe that snake under your butt?"

Murdock went one way, the lawn chair the other. "What? Where? Jesus Christ!"

"Just wanted to see if you were still alive, Fry," Hemingway sneered.

A deep, almost subsonic rumble filled the air and flitting birds erupted from treetops. The three tourists gasped, then flailed and danced for balance. Far beyond them, clouds of steam shrouded the peak of Perbuwatan.

The earth's motion lasted only a moment, then stilled. "What in God's name was that?" Hemingway gasped.

"Earthquake," Ryan said. "My God! That was an earthquake!"

"Hell it was," Murdock growled. "We don't have earthquakes in Kansas."

Back in the present, Ed Limmer looked at the empty room that, just moments ago, had been full of travel gear and prestigious assholes. The brazed steel floor gleamed between cheery residential walls and the TEF was dark.

In the hallway beyond, Mandy Brink was complaining to her sister, "Did you hear what that Murdock suggested? What does he think I am, some kind of dimbo?"

Limmer grinned and shook his head. He hoped the settings for the TEF were as precise as George Wilson assured him they were. If so, his host's trio of urban dignitaries from Wichita had just been deposited safely and neatly on the peninsula called Polish Hat. More important, they should have arrived there precisely on the first day of May 1883.

They would have ten days to themselves there, exactly as advertised, to do anything their monomaniacal little hearts desired. Then they would be whisked back to Kansas.

Nothing they could possibly do in the interim would make any historical difference. Exactly nine days after their departure from Polish Hat, the entire island of Krakatoa would blow itself to smithereens, along with any evidence that the three had ever been there.

∞

Consider the simple Möbius strip: to one who perceives dimensionally, a visible and tangible impossibility. A mark extended along either surface of the long axis will traverse both surfaces and meet itself where it started, without ever crossing an edge. The Möbius strip, therefore, is a two-dimensional solid object of finite size, with one dimension being infinite.

Ability to see a two-dimensional solid in this fashion indicates the perceptive skill to view dimensions as neither invariably finite nor limited to three.

A high percentage of children between the ages of eight and sixteen have this skill naturally, though the percentage apparently diminishes following puberty. While most adults can readily understand the mechanics of the Möbius strip, fewer than one in five can actually "see" the dimensional paradox it presents.

Without this perception, a Möbius strip is simply a loop of tape with a half-twist.

—ALICE M. HAMMOD, *Perceived Parameters: Notes on Dimensional Topology,* May 1964

∞

XIV

A Touch of Perpetuity

Southwest Kentucky, 1779

As KT-Pi's hand closed around the bloody comlink, Jack Higgins's hand closed around hers. Big, strong fingers like leather-hard saplings engulfed her tiny fist, and his other hand cupped the back of her head, crushing her to him. He rolled, and she was smothered beneath him. Holding her motionless, he got a hand on Betsy and dragged the long rifle close to his side. "Hold still, missy," he rasped deep in his throat. "Those ol' boys are Rangers. They'll kill you quicker'n a snake, do they spot you."

He shifted his position slightly, a groan of pain escaping his lips, then lay still. Facedown, unmoving, he lay in the wild underbrush, letting his shape and texture blend with the natural colors of the wilderness. Beneath him, KT-Pi lay inert, stunned by the weight—by the massive, easy strength—of the huge man on top of her.

Around them the forest echoed with the sharp cries of fleeing Whispers and the howls of Kentuckians in hot pursuit.

Camouflage and concealment came as easily to Jack Higgins as bears to a honey tree, and he used all his skills now as Matthew Bullock's buckskinned Rangers swarmed through the clearing, bounding and howling their fury. Mulehide boots and tarred moccasins raced past the hidden pair. Rifle butts swung here and there, knocking aside clumps of underbrush as sharp eyes searched in passing.

For a moment a pair of high-top moccasins with beaded

crosses on them were planted directly in front of Jack Higgins's eyes. "Was I a buzz-tail, I'd bite you, Linus," the woodsman whispered to himself.

Then the chase was gone, and the forest around was silent. With a growl of pain, Higgins raised his head, peered around, then rolled over onto his back. Released of his weight, KT-Pi lay gasping for air, her huge eyes staring into the pristine blue of the forest sky.

Higgins tried to sit up, winced, and gave up. Fresh blood flowed, its deep-red, wet stain soaking the buckskin shirt at his midriff. "I fear yer friend's done fer me, missy," he gasped.

KT-Pi sat up, then came to her knees. She hovered over the prone man, studying the wound in his belly with great, dark eyes. She raised her free hand, and tiny fingers pulled back the buckskin flap gently, revealing a neat little hole in his skin, just under his ribs.

"Be still," she commanded. She tried to free her other hand, but he clung and she gave up. With her free hand she shifted her little belt around, opened a concealed pocket there, and brought out a small device like a gray lily petal. Even in the mottled sunlight, it pulsed with radiance as she cupped it in her palm and pressed it against his wound. When she lifted it, her fingers were wet with blood but not a trace showed on the heart-shape device. Instead, little symbols danced there, bits of green light in various shapes.

"No foreign material," she murmured. "The projectile must have gone entirely through."

Still on her knees, she turned, lowered her shoulders, and pressed her head to the ground at his side. The upthrust little silk-clad bottom of her, to Jack Higgins, seemed no bigger than a child's bottom. But its roundness was not that of a child. "Mercy," he breathed.

"Here it is," KT-Pi said. "It came out right back here."

Upright on her knees again, bending over the big barbarian, she brought out other items from pockets in her belt and spread them on his chest. "I wish you'd let go," she said. "I'll need both—"

Abruptly, everything around them swirled and dimmed,

then disappeared. Higgins's startled eyes stared past the little bald head into a sky no longer blue but filled with cold rain. In the rain were the smell of woodsmoke and dim outlines of big, square-topped buildings and people passing by. He could hear hurried footsteps on wet pavement, muted voices, and the clatter of shod hooves and carriage wheels on cobblestones.

"—hands for this," KT-Pi finished, then glanced up. Intensifying rain ran down her smooth cheeks. "Uh-oh," she said. "We've been shunted."

J-Bar Ranch, The Cherokee Strip
1882

"Like as peas in a pod, ain't they?" Ansel Flagg's sardonic eyes glinted beneath his hat brim. He hooked a knee over a corral post and began to roll a smoke. "Been thinkin' I might sell 'em out to a medicine show for curiosities." In the corral, a matched pair of hulking, sullen young men cursed and struggled with a neck-roped mustang. Both of them were covered with ice-flecked mud, and neither seemed to be really in charge of the horse. But they kept at it with grim determination, slipping and sliding in the mud as they tried to get a loop around the animal's hind foot.

Elliot Pender stepped down from his worn saddle and shrugged his wool coat higher around his ears. "Why not just run 'em off, Ans? How's come you keep 'em around a'tall?"

"Dunno," Ans admitted. He turned slowly, surveying the far, bleak horizon in the way a man does when all his world, for all his life, has never had closer boundaries. A north wind that hadn't hit anything taller than a range fence since it left Canada tugged at his upturned collar and toyed with the silver fringes of his mustache. "Greenest greenhorns I ever seen, but I can't say they don't try. They done some tall thinkin' since Cook an' T.J. got through with 'em. I swear, though, sometimes I almost believe what they keep sayin', about comin' from the future an' all."

"You ain't serious," Elliot drawled. "How could anybody be from the future? It ain't happened yet."

"I know that. But they surely can lay out a line. You wanta hear it?"

"No, I don't," Elliot said firmly.

"Then how's come you to ride all the way over here from Bootheel? It ain't but March, Elliot."

"I know it ain't but March! An' colder'n a well-digger's ass, too. But I come anyhow, because of my merciful nature. I thought them pair ought to know their daddy's in jail over at Blackwell."

"In jail? What for? He shoot somebody?"

"Bounced a feller wearin' a ladies' dress, they say."

"Prob'ly do that myself, did I see one," Flagg growled. "Transvestitutes is an abomination."

"Nobody'd argee that point." Elliot nodded. "But the sissy feller come with a road show out of St. Louis, an' they hauled him up on charges. Then the damn fool practiced law without a license. In Orville Boone's court."

"Hot damn," Ansel swore. "He must be crazy." The ranchman turned to yell at his top hand, "Holly! Bill Holly! Run them Brinkses up to the house! Need words with 'em!"

"Yessir!" By the corral gate, Bill Holly took a final snip at the bobbed tail of a finished mustang and hung up his shears. "Ain't one thing it's another," he muttered.

There had been changes in Leslie and Leland Brink in the months since Bill Holly flushed them out of a prairie dog town southwest of Wichita. Nine days of refusing to eat anything Cook Ferguson had to offer had melted some of the lard off their frames, and five months of hard work on the J-Bar had replaced it with muscle.

Long gone were the shoplifter pants, rap-rags, and cross-trainers of a previous life. Ansel Flagg had seen to that. "I won't have anybody on my place lookin' like the world's biggest midgets," he rasped when Holly's crew brought them home.

Flagg had staked the pair to some decent britches, boots, shirts, long johns, and wool coats, to come out of their pay if they ever earned any. Then he had turned them over to T.J. Hastings for instruction.

Hastings drew his wages and quit J-Bar on the spot. He would saddle-break broncs or wrestle moss-horns out of mud bogs, he announced. He'd even mend fence. But he'd be hanged if he was going to be schoolmarm to a brace of hundred-and-sixty-pound bawlin' infants.

In the months that followed, Hastings quit six more times and pitched a fit twice. And Flagg was out the price of a Mexican guitar that Leland ruined trying to do heavy metal. But little by little, as the winter months passed, the Brink twins had begun to shape up. They still weren't much use that anybody could see, but they did simple chores now without too much complaint and even provided some entertainment from time to time.

The livid scar on Leland's forehead came from trying to ride a cow pony with a loose cinch. Leslie still walked funny from his first encounter with a range steer. His hatred for cow critters now matched that of any man in the Strip.

Mostly, though, it was the outlandish tales they told that provided amusement on cold, firelit evenings—tales about times and places that never had been. They both insisted they were born in July of 1981, which by anybody's reckoning wouldn't come for another hundred years. They went on about teevee and peetza, and they called sarsaparilla "root beer." Every sentence was salted with odd colloquialisms such as "like, hey, man" and "y'know," and puzzling references to "high-dollar hype" and "chillin' out," and "beat the rap," "cyberspace," and "internet."

Mostly, nobody could make heads or tails of what the pair was talking about when they talked, but there was an odd consistency to it, like they had been someplace where folks actually talked that way. But every time anybody asked about where they were from, they said, "Kansas." Sometimes, then, one or the other would add, "Bummer, man. L.A.'s where it's at."

Still, the winter months had slimmed and toughened them in appearance at least. Now with their floppy hats in hand and some of the icy mud sluiced off of them, the twins looked almost like ordinary cowboys as they stood before the big oaken desk in J-Bar headquarters.

Ansel Flagg leaned back in his chair, glaring up at them. "Y'all recollect Mr. Pender?"

The boys glanced furtively at Elliot Pender. "We didn't do it," Leland said.

"Didn't do what?"

"Didn't do nothin'." Leslie shrugged. "What's he say we did?"

"Was it me," Elliot advised Ansel, "I'd run 'em off. Teach 'em some manners."

"Mr. Pender rode all the way over here from Tucker just to do you boys a kindness." Ansel glared. "So mind your tongues or I'll give y'all to Mr. Holly yonder."

Bill Holly stood by the door, a wicked grin on his face. He'd made it known all along that he was in favor of shooting the scutters, and as top hand he wore the iron to do the job.

"Yes, sir," Leslie muttered. "Sorry."

Flagg glared at the pair a moment longer, then lowered his eyes. "Tell 'em, Elliot."

"They got y'all's daddy in a jail cell up at Blackwell," Pender said. "Judge Boone's got him. Boone's a hangin' judge an' he holds with the dignity of the law. He don't favor folks that scorns it."

The brace of Brinks stared at him dumbly.

"What I'm sayin' is, that daddy of your'n claimed under oath that he was a lawyer."

"He *is* a lawyer!" Leland turned to his brother. "Isn't Daddy a lawyer?"

"I think so." Leslie shrugged. "He makes a lot of money."

"Well, he's gonna need testifyin' witnesses," Elliot said. "Or God help him."

"Right thing for me to do," Ansel Flagg decreed, "be to cut you boys loose to go help your daddy, I reckon. Y'all know where Blackwell is?"

The boys looked at each other. "No," Leland decided.

"Or have any way to get there?"

"No."

Flagg scowled. "You do want to go, don't you?"

"No."

"We do, too, Leland!"

"I mean, yes. Yes, sir."

Elliot Pender grinned. "God help their daddy."

Flagg crossed his big hands over his mustache and muttered into them as if in prayer. "Sometimes the right thing ain't enough," he decided. "Man's got to do th' Christian thing now and again. Bill Holly!"

By the door, Holly lost his grin and straightened. "Sir?"

"I want you to take these boys up to Blackwell and get their daddy out of Judge Boone's jail."

"Yes, sir." Holly scuffed his feet. "Uh, that ain't gonna be exactly easy, Mr. Flagg. That Orville Boone, he's had folks thrown in prison just for trackin' mud on the courthouse floor. They say Buck Sims got six months' hard labor for snorin' in court. An' Judge Boone hanged a Mexican two years ago just for sharpenin' his knife!"

"Sharpened it on a deputy marshal's ribs, the way I heard it," Pender noted.

"But I never heard of him lettin' anybody much loose," Holly concluded. "So how'm I supposed to get that stampeder out of jail?"

Flagg stared at his top hand, a sardonic glint in his eyes. "Bill, you recollect takin' forty head of cull stock up yonder three summers back, on court requisition?"

"Yes, sir." Holly reddened, remembering. "Them marshals done us out of that herd, sir. Skinned us nose to tailbone."

"They did for a fact!" Flagg snapped. He looked around at Pender. "Filed a counterclaim on the brands, an' th' judge confiscated all forty head. Why J-Bar doesn't do business at Blackwell anymore."

"I swear," Elliot said.

"Been thinkin' about that ever since," Flagg muttered. "Bill Holly, you go ahead on, like I said. Go get these young gentlemen's daddy out of that jail."

"Yes, sir." Holly nodded. "I'll take some of the boys. Uh,

after we free that poor innocent soul from the injustice of his bondage, can I shoot the scutter for a damned stampeder?"

"We'll think on that later," Flagg assured him.

Time Loop L-383

"We have an unreconciled comlink trace." Teal Fordeen indicated a minute section of virtual reality above Toocie Toonine's tracking console. "Is it one of yours?"

Elem Threeby peered at the pattern and tapped harmonic codes into a cuff-mem. "It is the missing comlink," he said. "The one Deejay dropped. When is it?"

"Not 1779," Toocie assured him, scrolling data on four screens. "It was picked up in the take."

"But it isn't in this loop," Elem snapped, "so obviously it was shunted. Then those barbarians have it."

"I don't think so." Toocie frowned, concentrating on her data. "We shunted them to a prelinked . . . ah, here it is. 1942. But the trace isn't then. It's—that's odd. It is sometime in 1703. And of course farther east geographically."

"Of course. Where?"

"The city of Philadelphia, Pennsylvania, by these readings."

"Is it activated?" Elem asked Teal Fordeen.

"Activated and in contact." Teal nodded. "Give me your missing person's resonance scan."

The object looked like a tiny playback disc, except for its size. It was smaller than a drop of morning dew on a petal, yet it contained the entire harmonic resonance code of a person. "This is KT-Pi," Elem said.

Teal dropped the tiny record into a receptor and read it against the virtual resonance of the comlink trace. "That's her," he said, "She has it."

"Marvelous." Elem sighed. "You can bring her in then."

"There is a problem," Toocie warned, peering past Teal at the virtual scan. "Your KT-Pi's resonance is occluded. She is in contact with someone else . . . let's see. Male, protomorphic to a scale of four, injured somehow but . . . yes, there's a mender blip . . . and another." She turned to the leader of Sector 1779 Whisper scouts. "I'm afraid if we lock your associate now we'll also bring in one of the barbarians who chased you. She's with him. They shunted together. He's been hurt, but—"

"Then he's the one I . . . ah . . . shot!" Sev looked horrified. "I really *did* hit him when his weapon discharged. I swear, I—"

"He isn't dead," Toocie interrupted. "See the blips? Your friend is mending him. But still, do we want to bring them both here? What would we do with him?"

"Leave her for now," Teal decided. "We'll wait and observe. Will the comlink respond to her?"

"It does, enough to read her resonance."

"Then we should know if she needs immediate withdrawal. We'll wait. Meanwhile, I want to see those readings from WWKN. We have a paradox to deriddle."

"And a new assigned task," Cuel Denyne advised him. "Control wants us to begin survey immediately for a second Waystop. Traffic is piling up in the conduit. They want a new booster at 1887."

"I knew it!" Elzy Pyar griped. "We've become a modification platform. We'll never get out of this closed loop!"

"I'll go," Peedy Cue volunteered.

Toocie glared at him. "You and your measuring tape, I suppose. For your information, Peedy, those depictions you saw on that recovered poster were of dancing women of the time, wearing whalebone corsets beneath their attire. The corsets tended to compress them at the center and push everything malleable upward.

"The women of 1887 were not proportioned any differently from those of the centuries before and after."

∞

TO: WHIS Control
FROM: Teal Fordeen, L-383
RE: Coms CS-1114, CS-1115, CS-1116; initial recommendation TLI-13; ImAttReq

CS-1114, folio 19: Urgently request further historical data: incidents suggesting temporal displacement by persons extraneous to WHIS. Specifically, references to "Adam" in any unusual, nonbiblical context.

CS-1115, folio 1: Be advised: Your request for a second Waystop booster premature. First Waystop not yet fully debugged. One WHIS teamer (KT-Pi 3622) presently situational in reshunt. One Waystop I indigenee plus one mechanized self-propelled lift unaccounted for. Group of eighteenth-century indigenees inadvertently displaced to 1942.

Please hold *CS-1115* tempo.

CS-1116, folio 6: Discontent quotient among L-383 volunteers rising. General feeling is that we get all the dirty jobs. Please address.

Recommendation TLI-13: Tangent Colony

The origin of the Asian Abyss, in the period 2000 plus, is accepted historically as a massive act of collective madness resulting in detonation of a thermonuclear holocaust on the eastern Asian mainland. The result was an event of global proportion. Following the seven-day darkness, Earth's surface had massive alterations. Most of eastern Asia no longer existed. Coastlines were inundated, then left as barren islands as waters receded. Massive tectonic shifts realigned landmasses.

But was the event caused by human activity or merely triggered by it? Startling similarities present themselves—the mysterious disappearance of the subcontinent Atlantis in antiquity, the more recent Siberian Implosion, which, apparently, nobody caused, and the Deep Hole disaster a century later in North America, among the examples.

Is Earth in fact a globule of compressed dust covering a gravitational singularity? And has the substance of that singularity—the theoretical neutronium—been separating into smaller particles and surfacing? Such could explain each of the improbabilities. More important, the resulting surface implosions might provide clues to the "gates and bridges" of temporal configuration found in the hypothetical origin of the universe—the "time before time."

In view of these questions, it is proposed that WHIS authorize creation of a tangent colony of volunteers, in closed loop, to map the global patterns of tectonic shift back to origin, for a T1 grid overlay.

It is considered likely that the resulting wide view might lead to recovery of the "lost loop," L-270, and its occupants, whose untraced reports in T2-3004 first revealed the "gates" phenomenon.

This action is most strongly urged. How can we claim mastery of the dimension of time when we lose people in it?

Also urged: In view of situation re L-383 personnel (ref: CS-1116 and 6 [six] folios) make every attempt to assign this task to someone else. *Not us!*

∞

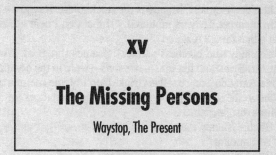

XV

The Missing Persons

Waystop, The Present

"Who on earth would have filed a missing persons report on Ray Brink?" Lucas demanded, cocking one eyebrow at the large, phlegmatic man standing in his living room. "He's just a lawyer."

Detective Sergeant John Soames shrugged. "His wife," he rumbled.

"I did no such thing," Amanda said.

Soames leafed through a stained notepad. "Not you, ma'am, this was another wife. A Mrs. Flotilla Johnson. She alleges that—"

"That's Flossie," Amanda corrected. "It's Flotilda ... Flatin ... *Flosilda*! Not Flotilla. She's his first wife."

"Yes, ma'am. Flosilda." The detective scratched at his pad. Across the room his partner, an inquisitive, cynical-looking man named Myers, was peering around the door frame into the steel-clad dining room. "Weird," he remarked.

"She alleges," Soames continued, "that is, Mrs. Flosilda Johnson does, that Mr. Brink and sons—her sons Leslie and Legion—"

"Leland."

"Leland ... were last heard from about nine A.M. on the twelfth of July, at which time Mr. Brink stated they were headed for this address, to visit Mr. Brink's business partner—"

"Brother-in-law," Amanda corrected.

173

"Ray isn't my partner!" Lucas emphasized. "He's just a stockholder. Actually, Mandy is the stockholder. Ray just—"

"Iron carpet," Myers muttered. "If that don't beat all. And what's that thing? A stereo?"

"The lady said business partner." Soames shrugged. "Anyhow, Mr. Brink and his sons—her sons—were in the company of one Amanda Santee, alias Brink. Don't blame me, ma'am. It's how the complainant stated the circumstances of the victim's disappearance."

"Bitch," Mandy muttered.

"Yes, ma'am."

"What victim?" Lucas demanded. "You think there's a victim here?"

Myers turned from his scrutiny of the unique room beyond the kitchen. "The word is 'subject,' John. Not 'victim,' for Christ's sake. Did you see that room in there with the iron floor? I'll bet that rusts like crazy when the humidity's high."

"It doesn't have a speck of rust on it," Maude asserted defensively. "It's self-cleaning."

"What'll they think of next?" Myers shook his head.

"Anyhow," Soames pressed on, "that was more than three weeks ago, and the vic—the *subject* hasn't been heard from since. Neither have the other subjects, Leland and Lester—"

"Leslie."

"Yes, ma'am. How do you account for that, Mrs. Brink?"

"They're away for a time," Amanda said. "But they'll be back."

"When?"

Maude brightened. "About 1887, isn't it, Lucas?"

"Eighteen eighty-two. Eighty-seven's when Ed and George went, to scope out that next booster."

"He means when will they be back?" Myers explained.

"Probably tomorrow," Lucas said. "We'll be doing several retrievals."

"Several . . . retrievals."

Amanda nodded. "Mr. Limmer wants Mr. Wilson to train us in that technique."

Soames and Myers looked at each other. "Retrievals,"

Myers muttered. "Sure." He pivoted abruptly, to stand face-to-face with Lucas Hawthorn, and the lazy, cynical expression was gone from his eyes. His look was as cold as winter rain. "Do these *retrievals* by any chance have anything to do with a few other disappearances lately, Mr. Hawthorn? Disappearances such as one Louis K. Hemingway, one Francis Murdock, one Charles Damon Ryan, and a felony suspect named Larry Hong?"

"Lot of missing persons lately." Soames grinned. "All of them last seen here at your house."

Lucas didn't bat an eye. "Of course they were. L.K. and Fry are clients of ours. So's the Mouth of the Arkansas. Hong was a crewman on a remodeling job I did."

"Then you know where they all are?"

"Sure. The terrible trio are wreaking havoc on an island off Java, and Hong's killing time someplace between 1838 and 1822. He bounces around. You said felony suspect? What's he done?"

"He's wanted in connection with theft of equipment," Soames volunteered. "A missing forklift."

"Oh, that. Yeah, he probably has it with him. Well, Fry Murdock and his pals should be back tomorrow, though I don't know why anybody would want them back. Same goes for Ray and his hoodlums. We'll pick up Pete Swain and his tribe, too. Hong may be a little harder to find. He's caught in a wobble."

"A . . . a wobble." Myers seemed to be glazing over.

"Time can do that." Maude nodded. "Mr. Limmer explained it."

Myers and Soames looked at each other for a long moment. "Maybe we'd better look around," Myers growled.

"Help yourselves," Lucas offered. "Anything in particular you'd like to see?"

"Yeah. I'd like to see the shining faces of some of these clients of yours."

"Right now?" Mandy asked.

"If it wouldn't be too much trouble," Myers drawled.

A little bell tone sounded in the dining room. Soames moved aside, glanced through the doorway, then stared, his eyes going wide. At his gasp, Myers peered around the frame. "What—" he squeaked, then coughed and tried again. "What the hell is—"

"Whispers," Mandy said casually.

A moment later the little bell sounded the all-clear. The two detectives were still gaping at the empty room a few feet away.

"I guess it wouldn't be too much trouble," Mandy decided. She glanced at Lucas.

"Right." Lucas shrugged.

Mandy turned and went through the hall, into the little control chamber. It had been a utility closet, but now it housed the displays and controls for the booster system. With the door closed it was dark enough inside to read the little virtual displays easily. A narrow slot provided a view into the TEF chamber.

"A quick bounce," she murmured, reading virtual patterns and adjusting dimensional calibrations. "Ray's blip is stationary. Him first, then Lucas's customers. Just a quick hop."

The detectives were in the kitchen now, peering into the chamber. "I don't know what I saw in here," Myers growled. "What was it?"

Lucas was right behind them. "Whispers," he said. "Just passing through."

"Whispers," Myers muttered. "We saw whispers?"

"They're hard to see," Lucas assured him.

"They were right here," Soames breathed. "What do you do, project on smoke or something?"

The two stepped through the open doorway onto the steel floor, hands near their holstered guns.

The TEF glowed slightly, and the room dimmed and flickered. Then the two were gone.

"Bingo." Mandy's voice came from the control chamber behind the bell tower.

"You sent them?" Lucas asked.

"To see Ray first, then the islanders. Double set, three minutes apart."

"That's cutting it fine." Lucas frowned. "Did Wilson okay short intervals?"

"Nothing to it," Mandy's voice assured him.

"But Ed Limmer said the calibrations are erratic in short durations."

"He did? I must have missed that."

Territorial Jail, Blackwell, Oklahoma
1882

There were no rooms in the lockup of Judge Boone's tidy little prison. The cells were iron-bar cages, three by six feet, five feet high, and stacked four deep along one side of a roofed shed behind the courthouse. They weren't built for comfort, and they weren't built for sanitation. They served only one purpose—the secure holding of prisoners awaiting trial and sentencing in Judge Boone's court.

Ray Brink had bumps on his head from trying to stand up in his cage and bruises on his back from trying to lie down on the bottom bars. He was sore in places he didn't even know he had, and he reeked of urine from failing to dodge when the man above him, a half-Choctaw bunch cutter named Amos Sand, relieved himself.

Brink had long since given up his loud protests against such indignities and inhumane treatment of an officer of the court. Now he simply sat, cross-legged in his cell, counting his miseries in a mumbling monotone.

Nobody—not the men above, below, and around him, not the laconic guards idling across the shed upwind—showed the slightest interest in anything he had to say. The only human discourse Ray Brink had experienced in four days, aside from the twice-daily slopping and watering of the prisoners, were the intermittent attempts of the prisoner directly below to catch him off guard and poke him in the crotch with thumb or boot heel. Ray had learned to keep an eye on that one. Sooner or later, he swore to himself, he would catch the bastard's arm coming up through the grate and methodically break all his fingers.

Twice a day parties of burly guards accompanied by armed

marshals visited the shed, called off a dozen or so names, and released that many wretches to haul them off to the scouring troughs for cleaning and grooming in preparation to be dealt with in his Honor's courtroom. And early each morning there were raucous crowd noises beyond the wall, where the top of a three-rope gallows was just visible from the cells.

Sometimes the gallows trap thudded twice, sometimes just once, but it hadn't missed a day since Ray had been there.

The second thump of the morning had just sounded on Ray's fourth day of incarceration when a ruckus erupted in the shed not ten feet from his cell.

Ray banged his head on the grating above, then hunkered and pressed his face to the bars, trying to see what was going on.

In the reeking walkway between the cells and the guard-path, two men crouched back to back, both holding large automatic handguns in waving fists. Around them, startled guards shouted, dodged this way and that, and edged back in a tight ring.

The two strangers looked bizarre and totally out of place, attired in clothing that wouldn't be around for a century or so.

"Freeze where you are, all of you!" one of them was shouting. "We're police! Drop those weapons! You heard me! Now!"

All around, stubbed-off shotguns and lever-action carbines clattered to the stone floor.

The larger of the two men looked around, wide eyes taking in the stacked cells. "Holy shit!" he rumbled. "What is this place?"

Ray Brink's breath caught in his throat as he recognized one of them. "Myers!" he rasped. "Hey, Myers! Detective Myers! Here, it's me! Raymond J. Brink, attorney-at-law! Right here!"

The man squinted at him, then muttered, "Shit, it *is* him!" and wheeled around, his cocked automatic showing its tonsils to various guards. "Who's got the key here?" he demanded.

Hesitantly a man raised his hand. "I got it," he said. "Just take it easy with that—whatever that thing is."

"Get that cage open!" Myers spat. "Now!"

"Yes, sir," the guard said. With a skeleton key the size of a cudgel, he unlocked a strap-iron cinch and hauled a plank away. Instantly the exposed sides of six cages fell open and filthy, ragged men erupted from them. One of these was Ray Brink—a leaner and definitely meaner Ray Brink, but still Ray Brink.

"Cut that out!" the second detective barked, swinging toward a knot of guards lining up for a rush. At sight of his strange but lethal-looking weapon, the men faded back. But now others behind him crowded forward.

"I said everybody freeze!" Myers roared. He raised his gun and its bark was a roll of thunder in the shed. Dust and splinters flew from the roof above. "Watch them, Soames," he hissed.

"Gawd damn," a man in the crowd gasped, staring at the hole overhead.

"You men are under arrest!" Myers shouted, his free hand indicating virtually everybody in sight. "Kidnapping, false imprisonment . . . hell, you name it! You all have the right to remain silent. If you give up that right, anything you say may be used against you in a court of law. You have the right to an attorney. If you cannot afford an attorney—"

"Whut'n hell's that scutter yappin' about?" someone in the crowd asked.

"Watch it, Myers!" Soames tried to whirl toward a flash of movement, and something heavy hit him across the shoulders. He staggered, saw a hand reaching for a revolver lying on the floor, and kicked the gun aside. "Freeze, you bas—you citizens!" he roared. "What the crap's going on here?"

"You ain't got any right to let these men loose," a bearded guard protested. "They're 'pendin'!"

"Waitin' to be tried," another corrected him. "This here's the Honorable Orville Boone's lockup."

"Sure it is," Myers gritted. "And I'm O.J. Simpson. Freeze!"

"I think he means stand still," a guard whispered.

"I wish you'd stop pointin' that thing at me, Mr. Simpson," another pleaded.

"What in thunder's going on here?" a deep voice echoed

through the shed. Men scuttled aside, opening a path for a big man with a handlebar mustache and long, dusty black robe.

"I won't tolerate this!" Judge Orville Boone thundered. "You men! Disarm those two!"

As if kicked by mules, the entire circle of guards and two or three released prisoners pitched forward, engulfing Soames and Myers. The entire center of the shed became a swirling, gouging melee, collapsing upon itself.

Ray Brink caught a boot in his midriff, fell against a still-occupied cell, dodged the clawing hands that shot through the bars, and rolled aside. Then with a screech he scuttled away, around the lockups and out of the shed.

The kicking, battering pile of men flailed on the floor for a moment longer, then began sorting itself out. As space was cleared in the center, men gawked. "Where be they?" somebody gasped. "By doagies, they're done gone!"

Krakatoa Island
May 9, 1883

Soames went down under the weight of his attackers, weaving and dodging even as his knees buckled. He heard the whuff of Myers's breath as a blow landed, and another, and then he was smothered beneath a squirming, kicking mountain of men. The gun in his hand was under him, and he thumbed the safety, his head swimming. He felt stifled and dizzy. He tried to clear his head.

A gunshot roared, clear and unmuffled, and Soames thought at first it was his own. Then the floor pitched beneath him, and he realized he was in the clear. Beside him, a spent shell case from Myers's .38 Super *pinged* and rolled on a floor of wooden planking. A startled voice shouted, "Here, now!"

Soames got his hands and knees under him, shaking his head. It was nearly dark, the moving shadows aglow with lantern light. Cold spray hit him in the face, and it had the taste of salt. He looked up.

There was no shed roof overhead, only skudding clouds in a

glow-lighted, angry sky. Big, billowed sails drummed in a fresh wind, framed by heavy timbers ringed and ranked with taut ropes as thick as his forearm.

There were men here and there around them, and the floor beneath was a wooden deck. Beside him, he heard Myers's "Holy shit!"

The men around them were not the ones who had piled onto them. These were other men, and with a glance Soames thought, Sailors. These were seamen, and this was the deck of a sailing ship. Among the sun-baked and bewhiskered white faces were other faces, as well—dark faces, black in the gloom. And these, too, seemed to be sailors.

He surged to his feet, wild-eyed, and almost fell as the deck rolled beneath him. " 'Ere, mate!" a grizzled man with a lantern warned. " 'Ave a mind wi' that cannon now!"

"Fair dinkum bark to them, eh?" someone else remarked. "Easy, cobber. No 'arm done yet."

"Stowaways," another voice decided. This was one of the black men—wide-nosed, thin-lipped, and haloed by raven ropes hanging from his tar hat. "Tuckered in th' bilge, most like."

"Police!" Soames said in his best authoritative voice. He fished his badge wallet from his pocket and held it out, open, beside his weapon. "Detectives Soames and Myers, Sedgewick County Metro Section, assigned. Who are you people?"

The grizzled man squinted in the rolling gloom. "Police? Stone th' bleedin' crows, we've swagged a brace of constables." To Soames he said, "Rankin's th' name, mate. Cap'n of this 'ere tub, th' *Skibberoo*."

"Nobbut sails an' salt rot," a black-faced sailor muttered.

Rankin glanced at the man. "Stow yer yob, Beejum! Bloody aborigine!"

Behind him a corpulent, pouty man pushed forward, two others following him. These three visibly were not sailors. They were not even of the same century, by their attire. "Sedgewick County?" the first one demanded. "As in Kansas?"

"That's right," Myers said. "Sheriffs' Metro Section, assigned to Butler jurisdiction."

"It's about time," the man spat. "My name's Hemingway. This here is Francis Murdock, and that's Chad Ryan back there. Get us out of here!"

"It's them," Myers confirmed. "That's Ryan, all right."

Yellowish light flared above, limning the high sails with a sudden, unearthly glow. On the receding horizon beyond the stern of the vessel a gout of brilliance shot skyward.

"Perubuwatan's puttin' on a show," the grizzled man remarked. "Fetchin', w'at?"

"That's a damn volcano!" Hemingway growled. "Tropical paradise, shit! Nothin' but stinkin' smoke and lava flows the past three days. I got better things to do."

"I wish I knew how they do that." Chad Ryan shook his head. "It's—it's almost *real*!"

"I'm going to make Lucas Hawthorn wish he was never born," Fry Murdock rumbled. "When my lawyers get through with him . . ."

"Are you stating that Lucas Hawthorn kidnapped you men?" Myers asked.

"I'm saying the son of a bitch misrepresented this—this *excursion*!" Murdock hissed. "He said we'd see a tropical island like it was in the 1800s! He didn't mention earthquakes and lava flows and stinking steam!"

" 'At's like it is, righ' enough," Beejum said cheerfully. "Nobbut a blinkin' volcano."

"We'll get to the bottom of this," Myers muttered. He faced the grizzled Rankin. "Where's the nearest telephone or airport?"

"Th' w'at?"

"Just tell me where we are!"

"Maybe three leagues off Polish Hat Point, mate." Rankin shrugged. "We watered yon an' picked up these blighters. We're bound from Java to Port Jackson, wi' tools an' tucker for all them lovely convicts at Sydney."

"Where's that?" Fry Murdock demanded.

"New South Wales, mate. 'Ome of th' kangaroo an' th' dijeridoo, not to mention Beejum 'ere an' 'is mates on walkabout."

"Sydney's no 'ome to us." Beejum bristled. "Foul, stinkin' 'ole. Us lot's from Dirambandi, mostly."

"Yer bleedin' aborigines can 'ave all that." Rankin returned the sneer. "Won't find me in th' bloody outback."

"I think he said we're on our way to Australia," Soames explained to Myers.

"When did we leave Kansas?" Myers muttered.

∞

Anachronism A person, object, thing, or event that is chronologically out of place.

Anomaly An incongruity or inconsistency; someone or something deviant from the common rule.

Paradox A statement or proposition seemingly self-contradictory or absurd but in reality expressing a possible truth.

Infinite Unbounded, unlimited, endless, inexhaustible.

Infinity The state of being infinite, as the length of a loop.

∞

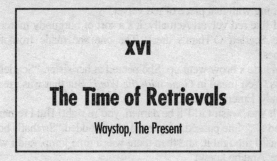

XVI

The Time of Retrievals

Waystop, The Present

"You could just leave him there, you know," Maude Hawthorn told her sister. "Just let Ray Brink remain a thing of the past."

"I've thought about it," Mandy admitted, looking up from her calculations. "It would be easy to just—just not find him for retrieval. It wouldn't be like I'd murdered him or anything. He could still live out a full life, only in another century. But that wouldn't solve anything, would it? Horse's ass or not, Ray Brink is my husband. I married him of my own free will, and I meant the vows I made."

"So you just chalk it up to a nice vacation and go back to being his doormat?"

"No way!" Mandy scribbled a notation on a page of mathematical diagrams and set the page aside for data entry. Maude's little PC had grown in recent weeks, starting with a new motherboard and two added CD drives. Now it occupied most of the breakfast nook and part of the kitchen counter—a maze of components linked by great webworks of electronic conduit. The wires formed a sort of buffer between Maude's cooking zone, where cherry cobbler was being created in wholesale volumes, and Mandy's calculations for the TEF booster.

"No way you'll go back to being Ray Brink's subdued little bauble?" Maude asked hopefully.

"We're going to make some changes. I've had time to think about my life lately—"

"And met Adam." Maude grinned. "I notice you're still sleeping with that piece of red velvet."

"I like red velvet! Actually, it's a sort of burgundy maroon. Like Scarlett O'Hara's dress. The one she made from the drapes."

Maude's brow went up. She peered at her sister. "Scarlett's dress? You mean in *Gone with the Wind*? But that was green, Mandy. Emerald green."

"It was, wasn't it! I'll be darned, you're right! But I remembered . . ." She paused, perplexed, then nodded. "So that's how it was! I thought it, and then there was a time jump, and I was there. And he knew!"

"Knew what? Who did?"

"Adam. He knew my focus. He—he *tracked* me! That's why he came to the Whispers' loop. He *knew*! And he gave me an anachronism to show me how it worked."

Maude was staring at her openly now. "You lost me way back there, sis. What the devil are you talking about?"

"Scarlett O'Hara's dress was green! But it wasn't originally. It was maroon red! That was the material he brought me. The . . . the visual image that I focused on. He took that and somehow it changed history. They were cutting drapery for stage setting, but because we were there for a moment, they used the green instead of the red. Then they costumed Vivien Leigh in that same forest green!"

Maude shook her head. "You get stranger by the minute, little sister." She topped off a cobbler and slid it into the oven. On the rack next to it a previous cobbler simmered, sweet juices seeping over a browning crust. "Forest green," she said. "Maroon red. My lord, you're like the old Mandy again! Whatever that Adam did, it certainly returned you to your sweet little abnormal self. I think you should dump that jerk you married and go find Adam. Certainly he's somewhere in time."

"Oh, Maude, come on! I'm a married woman. But I *have* set some new standards for myself. Ray Brink is just going to have to realize that he isn't the only fish in the sink."

Maude shook her head. "Fish in the . . . the *sink*? You're weird, Mandy. You always were weird—except after you started trying to live up to Ray Brink's ideas of how a wife should be."

"I was never weird!"

"You were, too, Like the time you stole my frozen M&Ms."

"I never stole M&Ms from you."

"You most certainly did. It was when I was in high school. I guess you were about twelve at the time. I had a package of M&Ms that Jerry McCarthy gave me. I put them in a Ziploc bag, with my name on it, and hid them in the freezer. That night I went to get them and they were gone. I found the Ziploc bag in your room."

Mandy shrugged. "I don't remember that."

"The thing was, you weren't home that whole week. You were at Grandma's, three hundred miles away. I never figured out how you did that. What do you mean, you don't remember?"

"Oh, I remember the M&Ms, all right. They were good frozen. And I remember they had your name on them. But it seems like I ate them at Grandma's, not at home."

"You were always doing spooky stuff like that," Maude said. "Things you couldn't have done but did anyway." She chuckled. "Remember Junior Denton? He always thought there were two of you. He swore you had a twin."

"Junior was a twit," Mandy pointed out.

"Well, he wasn't the only one. But it was just the way you were . . . like sometimes you could be in two places at once."

"You always said that. I grew up wishing it were true. Be neat to have an eager alto."

"Alter ego," Maude corrected.

"Yeah, whatever. Two heads are worth a bird in the bush."

"And that business!" Maude said, as if scoring a winning point. "Talking to you sometimes is like talking to a jigsaw puzzle. I used to think you saw the world from different angles from anybody else because of that. You don't just mix metaphors, Mandy. You pulverize them. Then you put them back together so they almost sound the same but mean something better.

"You were always a weird kid, sis. And you still are. I keep wondering what you're going to do next." Maude reached past the computer cables to pick up one of Mandy's Anywhen, Inc., business cards. She gazed at it, squinting at the odd little patched-together emblem that somehow looked more like infinity than the normal symbol for infinity. "Weird but a lot of fun," she added. "What did you do, bury all that when Ray came along?"

"I guess." Mandy brought up her data file and started entering figures for today's retrievals. The equations would be right. They were always right. George Wilson swore that Mandy's calibrations were field-tested before they were entered. They were unerringly accurate.

The little bell rang, and men's voices filled the TEF chamber. ". . . experience?" Lucas Hawthorn was arguing. "How are you going to find somebody experienced in time travel in the 1880s?"

"How did we find you in the 1990s?" Ed Limmer pressed.

"I was already here, cocked and primed. You and the Whispers saw to that."

"Same principle," Limmer said, leading them into the kitchen. "Mornin', ladies."

"What principle?" Lucas demanded. "Hi, Mandy." He crossed to the counter and planted a kiss on Maude's cheek, ignoring the flour smudges there. "Hello, sweetheart."

"Manure." She wrinkled her nose.

"What?"

"You smell like cow crap. Go take a shower."

"That's how the 1880s smell, babe. Like cow crap."

George Wilson came in, carrying a pocket computer no larger than a flip-top cellular phone. He stood behind Mandy, frowning at the equations on her monitor. "Exact coordinates, quadrangulated," he said. "How do you do that, without range grids and projectors?"

"It's easy," she said. "If it isn't right, it doesn't look right."

"Fantastic," he breathed. "Let's start bringing people home."

"Do we have to include her husband and his twin disasters?" Lucas spat.

Maude shrugged. "She says we do."

Lucas turned to his sister-in-law. "Better for everybody if we didn't, Mandy. Ray is a pompous, self-centered ass. But he's no joke. He'll find a way to make trouble if he can."

Mandy turned. "He probably will." She sighed. "He usually does. But we have to bring him back. And the boys, too. I only hope they've had a good time back there in the past."

"We'll get your policemen first, ladies," Ed Limmer decided. "I'm sure they've seen enough."

Lucas grinned. "I'd like to hear them explain where they've been to Clay Connors. The Butler County sheriff doesn't care much for unusual circumstances."

"Neither did his grandfather," Limmer mused. "Good man, though. He was a policeman, too, back in the fifties. Friend of your father's, Lucas—and of mine, back when I was old. You might want to offer Clay a family visit. Be good for him to spend a little time with old B.J."

"I guess we're ready," Wilson said. "Mandy, you run the retrievals. Lucas will observe."

"Me?" Amanda punched her data into the main drive. In the TEF chamber, equipment hummed softly as lenses and coils adjusted themselves. "I haven't done retrievals."

"No time like the present." Ed Limmer nodded. "You folks will be on your own in a few days."

Maude opened the oven to peer at her cobblers and said unladylike words. "I wish you'd look at this!" She pulled the door wide. "There were two pans in there. Now there's only one."

"That was Peedy," Mandy said. "He's developed a new obsession. He's into antique pastries now."

"I hope he burned his fingers," Maude growled. "That was for our returning guests."

The Neutral Strip
Spring 1882

Its name was Splinter. It sprawled where Badger Creek crossed the Haymeadow trail, barely a mile west of the jurisdictional limits of the Nations, an unsightly jumble of sheds, rickety barns, and lean-tos assembled mostly from stolen lumber. It was considered a town simply because it had a sign that said it was. The only real building in the place was a garish little two-story fortress that served as trading post, general mercantile, saloon, watering hole, and momentary haven for citizens in a hurry. Generally, anybody riding west from the Territory was either running from somebody or chasing somebody.

Now Leslie and Leland Brink hunkered in the shelter of a claybank, peering out at the dismal scene indicated by a smelly citizen named Clyde.

"He's still in there," the man rasped, pointing an accusing finger at the two-story building. "Just went loco, I reckon. Shot the place up, run out everybody but Herman's whores, an' been there ever since."

"He's been in there since Wednesday?" Leland marveled. "What's he doin' in there for three days?"

"Drinkin' an' fornicatin', I reckon." Clyde shrugged. "Got hisself six whores and a month's supply of whiskey. What else would he be doin'?"

"We got to get him out," Leslie decided.

"Wish you would," Clyde said. "Man's a menace where he is. Ain't shot anybody yet, but he's bound to hit somebody eventually."

As if to punctuate the sentiment, dust erupted from the pole roof of the building and a bullet whined away into the sky. Muffled by enclosure and distance, a slurred, strident voice demanded, "Order in the court! I won't tolerate these outbursts, by God!"

"That's Daddy," Leland muttered.

Leslie cupped his hands to shout, "Daddy? Is that you in there?"

Another bullet erupted from the front wall of the place. "Who's out there?" the drunken voice roared.

"He's in that front room upstairs," Leland observed. "Keep talking, Les." Sliding back into cover, he crouched and ran.

"It's us, Daddy!" Leslie yelled. "Leslie and Leland! Are you all right in there?"

"Having the time of my damn life!" Ray Brink responded. "Go 'way!"

"We come to get you out of jail, Daddy! Mr. Flagg gave us horses to ride!"

"I already got out, an' I got somethin' better than horses to ride!" Ray chortled, slurring the words. "Six of 'em, by God!"

"Daddy, can we come in?" Leslie raised himself to his knees. "It's cold out here!"

Distantly, a door chain rattled, then there was the rending sound of hinges being kicked loose. "What's that?" Ray Brink yelled. "What's going on?"

For lack of a better notion, Leslie swatted Clyde on the shoulder. "Give me your gun," he demanded.

Obediently, Clyde drew a well-worn Colt revolver from his belt and handed it over. "You gonna shoot your daddy?" he wondered.

Leslie fumbled with the firearm, got it cocked, and pointed it straight up. Eyes shut tight, he touched it off and flinched violently at the discharge.

Instantly another bullet whanged through the wall of the emporium. "I know where you felons are!" Ray Brink shouted. "Order in the court!"

Leslie slid backward down the claybank and ran, trying to keep to cover, heading for the building. Another wild shot, this time from an upstairs window, and his crouching run became an all-out sprint.

"Take your damn hands off me!" Ray's voice shrilled inside the building. "I don't know you!"

Leslie hit the barred front door of the emporium at full speed. Long months of hard work had toughened him, and his shoulder crashed through the portal as if it weren't there.

Upstairs, women were chattering and Ray Brink was raving. "Leslie!" Leland yelled. "Help me!"

Leslie flew up the stairs and burst into a smelly little room to see his brother and his father rolling on the floor, struggling for a revolver. All around them were women, wearing very little clothing. Leslie blushed, trying not to look at them. "Excuse me," he mumbled. Then he stepped forward, got a firm grip on the contested gun, and wrestled it free.

"Get up, Daddy," he said. "Leland, let him up! This is no way to act!"

Waystop TEF Chamber
The Present

The TEF glowed for an instant—that distinctive instant of enormous energy-matter transition too big and too quick to comprehend and registering on human senses only as a flicker. Where there had been an empty room, now there were two large, rumpled men, a wooden keg, and a swooping seagull. The gull squawked, shifted its wings frantically, and executed a straight-up roll, missing the east wall by inches. Then it circled once in flapping confusion and landed on the head of the man seated on the water cask.

"Get off of me!" Myers yelped, leaping to his feet and reaching for his gun. The errant bird flapped upward, circled once, and settled on the cask.

Soames turned full around, gawking at the transport chamber. "Iron floor," he marveled. "We're back."

Maude Hawthorn peeked around the door frame. "Hello," she said. "Would you gentlemen like some coffee and . . . get that bird out of my house!"

"Yes, ma'am," Soames said. With a quickness belying his size, he scooped up the bird and followed Maude through the kitchen. At the back door he released the outraged creature, which nipped his hand, drawing blood.

Myers recovered his composure as Lucas stepped into the chamber. "Welcome back," Lucas said. "Did you boys find everybody you were looking for?"

"I got to write a report on this." Myers glared. "How in hell am I going to write a report on this?"

"Give it time," Lucas said. "How about some coffee?"

From beyond the slitted wall behind the bell tower came other voices. "Ready to activate again," George Wilson said. "Quads?"

"Same base plus 11:0331 running," Mandy advised. "ES base plus 1,480 feet 8 inches south, 77 feet even west running. What about that barrel in there?"

"It will trade out," Wilson said. "Everybody clear the chamber!"

"Come into the kitchen," Lucas told Myers. "We've got more retrievals coming through."

Mandy sounded the warning bell. "Clear!" she called.

Chad Ryan was, in media parlance, a "personality," not a reporter. In front of the camera, he could don sincerity and righteous concern as easily as most men pull on their socks. But the world behind the camera had never been of much interest to him. Thus it took Krakatoa's monolithic smokes on the horizon to remind him of the little Minolta 35 that had been resting in the deep pocket of his custom-designed safari jacket for the past ten days.

"I could have been taking pictures," he muttered, suddenly realizing that the camera was there. "God, NBC would give a bundle for this, even stills."

The little *Skibberoo* rolled slightly as he fished out the Minolta, fumbling at its unfamiliar lens cap with unskilled fingers.

The aborigine Beejum wandered close, curious black eyes peering at the object in the passenger's hand. "W'at's it, then, mate?" he asked.

"Camera." Ryan muttered. "Gotta get some stills."

"Eh?"

"Photographs. Pictures."

"Oh, aye." Beejum shrugged. "Pic-chers, eh?"

"Pictures." Ryan squinted at the lens ring, then peered through the viewfinder. The great column of smoke appeared tiny against a vast sea. "Wrong lens," he decided. "Here. Hold this."

Beejum took the camera gingerly. He had never seen anything remotely like it.

Ryan searched in his pocket. "Here somewhere," he
muttered.

"What's 'at, mate?"

"A long lens. Telephoto. I know I brought one."

"Tel-fodo." Beejum nodded. "Aye." He held the camera to
his face as he had seen Ryan do. Through the viewfinder he
saw an image—as if in miniature—of *Skibberoo*'s stern sheets.
" 'Ullo!" he gasped. "It's a bleedin' glass!" His finger touched
the shutter button and the camera's tiny strobe flashed. The
thing made quick, smug little sounds as it advanced its film,
auto-focused, and readied itself for the next shot.

"Don't waste that film!" Ryan warned.

"Blimey!" Beejum swore. He turned the camera and peered
into its face, searching for the source of the abrupt light. Again
his finger triggered it, and it flashed. He almost dropped the
camera, scampering backward.

" 'Ere, now!" Captain Rankin's harsh voice called from the
afterdeck. "No bloody sparks on deck, mates! Yer want ta fire
our sails?"

"Here it is," Ryan said. He pulled a five-inch lens assembly
from the depths of his pocket and removed its caps. "Hold
still," he told Beejum. With the aborigine holding the camera,
Ryan removed the stubby 2.8 lens and snapped the long lens
into place. "Know how to use this, do you?" he said. "Well,
how about a shot of me with that volcano in the background?"

He situated himself beside the mainmast, assumed his
anchorman face, and said, "Go ahead."

Beejum looked through the viewfinder again. The image
was much better now. Everything was larger and closer. "Stone
th' crows," he muttered. "A bleedin' marvel 'ere." With Ryan
in the frame he tripped the shutter again, getting the hang of it.

"Now me with my fellow adventurers," Ryan decided. He
headed forward, past Beejum, to where Hemingway and Murdock sat on a fife rail, watching. "This is about right," he said.
We'll . . . ah, where are those policemen?"

Everyone looked around. Just moments before Myers and Soames had been right there, at the foredeck cask. Now there was no sign of them. The cask was gone, too.

"No matter." Ryan shrugged. "Just get the three of us."

"To hell with that," Murdock rasped. "My ad agency says no unapproved photographs."

"I'm not endorsing your station," Hemingway told Ryan. "Not until we renegotiate game coverage."

The two left Ryan standing among curious seamen and headed aft. They passed Beejum, then turned. "*Now* you can take his picture," Hemingway told the man.

"Right-o, mates," Beejum said.

Waystop
The Present

"Double retrieve locked," Mandy said. "Retrieving . . . now." She closed the circuit and that odd, instantaneous slowness filled the TEF chamber—an instant only, then it was gone. Beyond the kitchen doorway Maude Hawthorn, Edwin Limmer, and two sheriff's detectives blinked as a motley, disarrayed crowd appeared in the steel-floored room. Murdock and Hemingway stared back at them with startled eyes. Between them, shoulder to shoulder, an ebony-skinned man with cutoff breeches, striped shirt, inky braids, and a tar hat leveled a small camera and its flash lit the room.

Just beyond them two tall young men in rough, Old West clothing held a filthy, bearded, squirming Ray Brink upright and blinked in astonishment.

"Lor' luv a duck!" Beejum swore, lowering the camera.

"Oops," George Wilson said, behind the slitted wall.

Mandy squinted through the control room slit. "Ray? What in the world? . . ." She rushed out of the control cabinet and a moment later appeared in the double door of the transport chamber. "Ray, are you all right?"

"Daddy's drunk, Mandy," Leland said.

Ray's bleary eyes focused on his wife. "Bitch!" he roared.

"You did this!" With a violent twist he broke free of his sons' hands, lurched past Beejum, and confronted Mandy. With his closed fist, he swung at her. "Told you to stay out of my private life!" he spat.

∞

Hindsight is only useful to someone going backward. Even then, hindsight can be misleading. For example, I thought I had made a mistake once. But I was wrong.

—EDWIN LIMMER

∞

XVII

The Intruder

Waystop, The Present

"I think we'll find that there is a direct correlation between Krakatoa's final eruption and the Siberian event," Teal Fordeen said, helping himself to a piece of Maude's cherry cobbler. "It may approximate the relationship between Vesuvius's recorded eruption two millennia past and the subsequent 'Day of Dancing Death' that devastated the Toltec empire centered at Tenochtitlan. Events half a world apart, but linked by tectonic phenomena, accompanying a global 'wave.' Such occurrences in prehistoric ranges have caused polar shift. We know that the resonance associated with Vesuvius and Tenochtitlan caused a wobble in the axis, and we know that wobbles can upset both temporal and geographic coordination."

Maude stared at the little person sitting on the kitchen cabinet. It was the first time she had actually seen a real Whisper, unblurred by temporal transit. "You're saying that because Krakatoa exploded and there's a hole in Siberia, we lost a TV personality in some kind of time warp?"

"There actually is no hole in Siberia," Teal corrected. "That's one of the odd things about Tunguska. But the 'time warp' idea has some merit. It's only a theory, though. Elzy Pyar is still tracing vectors."

"Right now?" Maude asked. "Where?"

"Loop L-383." Teal tilted his bald head. "Actually, that isn't anywhere in the three-dimensional sense. It's a closed loop, part of the temporal conduit but not actually attached to it. As to *when* he is, *now* is a relative concept. In terms of actual, expired T2 time, L-383 is nowhen. But in terms of duration, you might consider him as 'now.' "

"Huh?" Maude blinked.

"It's a dimensionality thing," Mandy explained. "I can visualize it but I can't explain it." As she spoke, she concentrated on the equations spread out on the breakfast table. Her voice sounded thin, and her position hid the livid bruise on her cheek.

The strange, picturesque aborigine sitting cross-legged on the floor at the end of the counter tried to say something, swallowed, and started again. Beejum held a huge plate of cherry cobbler in both hands, demolishing it with glee. Globs of thick juice streaked his indigo features. Bits of crust clung to his whiskers, and there were traces of whipped topping on his wide nose and his braids. He wore a Minolta pocket-35 on a string around his neck.

" 'E says ther cobber's trackin' wi' us but on th' next bloody trace," the bushman explained.

"Exactly." Teal Fordeen nodded.

"Oh," Maude said.

"The question is, where is Chad Ryan?" Mandy pursued. "Everything and everybody has to be somewhere, some time. I understand how we lost him to a wobble, but we have to get him back."

"Bloody right," Beejum agreed.

"Absolutely," Teal said. "He isn't in the conduit, so he has to be somewhen. Elzy's premise is that a triangularity occurred. There was a ship's water cask in the transit chamber at point of displacement. Its mass might have served as a pivot. Somehow the retrieval track caught this indigenee Beejum—"

"Mind yer tongue, mate," Beejum growled. "It's *aborigine*, not that other thing."

"—caught Mr. Beejum in a transposition with Mr. Ryan—"

"An' none o' that talk, neither!" Beejum demanded. "I'm no blinkin' follywog."

Teal shook his bald head and sighed. "The resulting triangularity could have created a slingstone effect, with that water container as the fulcrum."

"So?" Mandy pressed.

"Well, obviously Beejum is here, and Ryan is not. We know that a tempronic retrieval occurred and that a trade-out was made involving the water barrel and Mr. Ryan's camera. Beejum now has the camera, though the policemen took the film from it. And it's fairly certain that the water barrel is back aboard *Skibberoo*. We can assume that the combined topographic surfaces—and probably the combined mass—of Mr. Ryan and Beejum roughly equaled the water barrel, since the other two retrievals executed by that particular gravitic-photonic reversal—Mr. Hemingway and Mr. Murdock—were not affected. Nor did the simultaneous retrievals of Mr. Brink and his progeny in any way impact upon the wobbled retrieval.

"Elzy should be able to determine the placement of Mr. Ryan from these parameters."

"*Should* be able?"

"*Will* be able. It's just a matter of time."

Maude edged close to Mandy, sensing her sister's tension—the determined set of her profile as she hid the bruise on her face. That bastard Ray, she thought. "What's all that about, Mandy?" she asked. "What's a triangularity?"

Mandy didn't look up, but the tight set of her shoulders eased with concentration. "Imagine a three-dimensional 'snap the whip,' " she explained. "The TEF 'reels in' a traveler at something more than light speed—slowing and turning around, but still light speed. Then say the 'line' gets fouled around something heavy. The retrieval occurs, but that first turn is a doozy. The line breaks. In a three-dimensional world, the resulting spinoff occurs in two dimensions. The freed 'fish' snaps right or left, and that's the way it goes. But this is four-dimensional stuff, so Mr. Ryan had three dimensions to sail off into—right-left, forward-back, or past-future."

Maude struggled with it. "What about up or down?"

Mandy shuddered. "Galactic launch or splat? Yuck. Let's don't even consider that possibility," she suggested.

Maude wrinkled her nose, understanding. "Okay, let's don't. But how about you, sis? Where do *you* go from here? Up or down?"

"Up," Mandy said softly. "Ray's done a lot of things, but he's never hit me before. I know he was drunk, but that just makes it worse. It took his mask away. I wonder if you'd mind putting me up a little longer, Maude . . . until I find a place of my own?"

Maude nodded. "It's about time. I'll get out the Lincoln as soon as Lucas gets back. We'll go to Wichita and pack up whatever you need."

"I won't need a ride," Mandy said. "We have dimensional travel right here. I'll use the TEF. I can be there yesterday, pack my things, and be back here an hour or so after I leave. I'll clear the conduit and set an automatic retrieve."

A tiny sound came from the direction of Teal Fordeen, and the Whisper pressed a dainty palm to his ear. His huge eyes widened. "Emergency," he said, retrieving his comlink from somewhere in his garment. "Excuse me."

Mandy turned. "What's happened? What is it?"

"L-383 is penetrated. Elzy is . . . excuse me, please."

With a quick tap at his comlink, Teal flickered and was gone.

Time Loop L-383

Virtual starfields swam lazily, columns of characters racing through them as Elzy Pyar fed data into a plotting console. "Slingstone," he griped. "I question the logic of allowing indigenees access to our technology. This is just the sort of thing I would have expected."

"We could as easily have done it ourselves," Toocie Toonine objected. "They made no error. It was crustal shift, Elzy. We wouldn't have foreseen that, either."

"Why do you defend these primitives?" Elzy closed a file and began a new one, adding dimension to dimension.

"I like them," Toocie said simply. "They haven't discovered their limits yet."

"Maybe it's time they did! We're skirting major anachronisms here, Toocie. We might not be, if your antique friends

would stop improvising and limit themselves to what they
know."

"Like we do? Maybe that's our shortcoming, Elzy. Maybe
we've lost what they have—an absence of perceived limits."

"They're primitives!" Elzy snapped. "They—" Above and
before him, a virtual field spun crazily, columns of data scattering among the stars. "Here, now! What? . . ."

The field darkened and a man stepped through it. He was a
protomorph, thickset and heavily muscled. Hair the color of
moonlight hung around his ears, and his eyes were like gray
ice. Just above the bridge of his nose was a little tattoo—a triangle. The linen robe he wore hung open, revealing a belt and
shoulder straps arrayed with weapons.

"Adam has been here," the man growled, narrow eyes
darting around the virtual peripheries of L-383 as if seeing
right through them. "What is this, a dimensional conduit?"

"A—a loop," Toocie said. "Who are you?"

"I want Adam," the man said. "Where is he?"

"We don't know." Elzy gaped at the apparition. "We don't
even know *who* he is . . . or who you are."

"No." The man shrugged. "I suppose you wouldn't. You're
just Whispers. But he was here. I have his trace."

"Who are you?" Elzy demanded. "You can't just come into
a temporal loop like this! I insist . . ." He started around the
console, wagging an outraged finger at the stranger.

Hardly seeming to move, the big man drew a weapon and
discharged it. Its roar echoed away among the virtual stars. As
if slapped by a giant hand, Elzy Pyar tumbled backward, across
the data console. He sprawled facedown on the luminous floor
and lay still.

Toocie knelt beside him, scanning his body frantically with
a palm-size gray pad. Then she raised her head. Huge, stricken
eyes gazed at the man towering above them. "You killed him!
How could you just—just kill a person? What are you?"

The big man looked down at them disinterestedly. "Adam
may come back here," he said. "Tell him Quark is looking
for him."

He turned away and was gone, into the starfields.

* * *

Sheriff Clay Connors's office was spacious by most court-house standards—sixteen by eighteen feet. But right now it seemed crowded to the point of insanity, and the sheriff would have considered that a fair description of the assembled crowd.

Two of his detectives were present, both prodigiously unkempt, unshaven, and smelly. The crowd also included two very prominent Wichita businessmen, both wearing stained and ragged safari suits; a well-respected Eastwood building contractor whom the sheriff knew slightly as Tombo Haw-thorn's younger brother; a matched pair of young men who looked like working cowboys; a lean, touseled man who had been introduced as a temporal technician; a robust middle-aged man who claimed to be a hundred and forty years old; and a raving lunatic who just might have been—in another life—Raymond Brink, attorney-at-law.

The four others present were District Attorney Sam Adams, a sleepy-eyed court stenographer, and two uniformed deputies standing by to keep order—if any order ever was achieved. Both of the deputies hovered near Ray Brink—partly because he was drunk, belligerent, and offensive, and partly to defend him from some of the other men, who had witnessed his unprovoked assault on a woman. The detectives had brought him in cuffed, after he struck his wife.

The strangest baker's dozen of misfit people ever assembled in Clay Connors's memory—and the overlapping stories they were telling him were the wildest things he had ever heard. But patience and pragmatism were beginning to pay off. Nine times in the past fifty minutes Clay had repeated the words "Everybody shut up! Now, you. You talk." The various parts of the assembled puzzle were fitting themselves into place.

Myers and Soames had left this office three days earlier, pursuing a routine missing persons report. They themselves had been missing since then. But now they were here, with the missing person and all these other persons in tow. Yet nobody had been truly missing, it seemed—just gone. The subject of the primary missing persons report, Ray Brink, was wall-eyed drunk and smelled like a sewer, and if he began that judicial ranting again Connors intended to arrest him as a public nuisance and let him cool off in the tank.

The two cowboys were Brink's twin sons, who apparently had rescued him from a whorehouse somewhere in Oklahoma. The building contractor, Lucas Hawthorn, was present because it was his house Brink had disappeared from. The businessmen, Hemingway and Murdock, had been brought in because they, also, seemed to have disappeared for a time and because they threatened to charge Hawthorn with everything from kidnapping to early-morning volcanoes.

Ed Limmer claimed to have been a longtime friend of the sheriff's grandfather, and George Wilson was there for reasons as yet unknown. Both, apparently, were house guests of Lucas Hawthorn.

Connors pursued his inquiries until his patience ran out. Though a dozen felonies had been charged, none had been substantiated. There were probably any number of misdemeanors here, but he couldn't seem to sort them out. Finally he stood, hooked an authoritative finger at Sam Adams, and said, "Let's step outside. The rest of you, don't move!"

In the hall beyond his office, Connors frowned at the district attorney. "Well?"

"Well, what?"

"Did you get all that?"

Adams shrugged. "Sure I did." He flipped through his notes. "Mr. Hawthorn has built a time machine in his dining room. Mr. Limmer helped him finance it, and Mr. Wilson runs it for him. They're both from the future. And there have been a lot of whispers."

"Don't be comical, Sam," Connors snapped.

"Me?" Adams turned innocent eyes on the sheriff. "They're yours, Clay. Not mine. You called me, remember? Anyway, Ray Brink is married to Mr. Hawthorn's wife's younger sister. The two junior wranglers in there are his kids from a previous marriage. Brink claims that Hawthorn and his friends sent him and the boys back in time, willfully and with malice aforethought. Claims they were dumped into a nineteenth-century cattle drive." The district attorney's stern expression quivered like Jell-O. He turned away, shaking his head. His shoulders sagged with suppressed merriment.

"Come on, Sam!" Connors snapped. "I got a situation here."

Adams got himself under control. "Don't you, though," he muttered. "Okay, there's conflicting testimony, to the effect that the . . . the time trip was Brink's own idea. Matter of fact, three witnesses say he insisted on it. Same witnesses corroborate Hawthorn's claim that Brink physically attacked his wife—Brink's wife—in their presence.

"Which brings us to the Messrs. Murdock and Hemingway. They allege that Mr. Hawthorn defrauded them and subjected them to an unnatural experience. He pretended to send them to a volcanic island, they say."

"And Lucas Hawthorn says they went voluntarily," Connors pointed out.

"Right. If they went at all. If not, then there *might* be a fraud involved here, except that no money changed hands. But those photographs your boys brought in are definitely pictures of Hemingway and Murdock, among others, and they sure weren't made anywhere around here.

"Then there's the matter of Chad Ryan, who allegedly went along on the Murdock-Hemingway excursion and didn't come back. But it's his camera the photos came from, and he's in the photos, and there is no evidence of foul play of any kind. I don't suppose anybody has filed an M-P on him?"

"Who'd care if Chad Ryan is missing?" Connors growled. "Son of a bitch cost my office a bundle with that tornado story three years ago."

Adams nodded. "Very dramatic piece of showmanship. It made him famous."

"Yeah. He's famous, all right. Except there never was a damn tornado. Just a dustdevil in a field. Bastard made the whole thing up. Scared hell out of half the county and cost county services a fortune." Connors gritted his teeth, controlling his temper. "Anyhow, what do we do here? Who should I arrest?"

"You can arrest anybody you want to, Clay." Adams put on

his innocent look again. "You're the high sheriff. But I don't see a thing here I'd want to prosecute in court. Do you?"

"I guess not," Connors allowed. "Like to have something on Ray Brink, though. Sleazy bastard. You could give lawyers a good name if you'd prosecute that twit. Soames says he knocked his wife halfway across the room."

"Up to her, if she wants to press charges. Otherwise it's just a domestic matter."

"Soames and Myers said she declined charges."

"Maybe drunk and disorderly, then," Adams suggested. "You could probably make that stick."

"And have all the rest of this crap come out in court? For three days of county jail time? Hell, no. Not worth it."

"It might come out anyway, if Hemingway and Murdock file civil suits."

"That'll be the day." Connors snorted. "Where they gonna say they went? They got stockholders to answer to."

"Then you're going to drop the whole thing?"

"Maybe so," Connors decided. "But I *would* like to see for myself what turned two of my detectives into tongue-tied morons."

"Why don't you, Clay?" Adams suggested. "Eastwood's in your jurisdiction. Why not drop in on them? Lucas *did* offer to arrange a visit with your grandfather."

Connors snorted, then pulled out the little business card Lucas had handed him and looked at it again. "Anywhen, Inc.," he breathed. "You know, maybe I will. Maybe I'll take Lucas Hawthorn up on his *travel agency* offer."

As he led the way back to his reeking office, Clay Connors muttered to himself, "Wouldn't that be something! A travel agency. *Time* travel yet! Ye gods!"

∞

The "Adam phenomenon," we know now, is not unique. We have confirmation of two such "timers," Adam and the subject called Quark. There is also convincing evidence of a third, though that individual may not realize—so far—the presence of autotemporal ability.

All three of these subjects appear to be pre-upheaval protomorphs with physical, cultural, semantic, and behavioral characteristics of the twentieth century. Subject number one has claimed 1943 as his birth year, though he stated he is "from" 2041. Subject number two—Quark—is of unknown nativity but appears to be of twentieth-century origin as well. The third possible subject, of unconfirmed ability, was born in 1972.

All three of these subjects have been encountered by personnel of L-383. All three have, in fact, penetrated the dimensionality of the closed loop. We must conclude, therefore, that the existence of "timers" is not an isolated phenomenon. These people have the ability—latent or realized—to move freely and at will in four or more dimensions.

That timers are rarities is obvious, but they are not unique. How many more of them are there? And, most crucially, how do they do what they do?

—TEAL FORDEEN, memos to WHIS

∞

XVIII

The Hands of Time

State Highway 254, The Present

High, lazy cirrus horsetails defined a vast sky full of evening twilight as the Explorer rolled to a stop on the shoulder of the road. Lucas squinted ahead, then turned to look back the way they had come. The road was empty, just a ribbon of asphalt between horizons studded with stubby grain elevators and the low outlines of little towns.

Lucas muttered something, peered at his rearview mirror, then swiveled to look back again. There was no one back there. Yet, in the mirror, a man on foot plodded toward the car, walking in slanting sunlight along the edge of the pavement. But the sun had been down for several minutes. It was brighter in the mirror than in the scene the mirror was supposed to reflect—as if the mirror were seeing an earlier time.

"Why did you stop?" Edwin Limmer asked from the backseat. "What are you looking at?"

In the front passenger seat, George Wilson gazed around at the serene twilight, then leaned to glance at the outside mirror. In the dusk, its glow projected an oval pattern on the window's dust and lighted his face within. "Slow light," he said. "Who's that behind us?"

"The engine quit," Lucas said. He turned the ignition key. The starter's whine was a low growl. "Damn."

"Energy drain," Wilson said. "A light-gravity conversion. The mirrors catch it first."

Lucas looked again at the reflection of the man walking up

the road. He was a tall, youngish man, strangely dressed. He wore tight, soft-leather pants, flared at the bottoms over dusty boots. A stained linen shirt with wide sleeves covered his arms, and a piped silken vest revealed open collars above a lithe, muscular torso. Uncropped dark hair curled beneath a wide-brimmed, concho-banded hat, and a big, drooping mustache framed a wide, strong mouth and chin. He cradled a lever-action rifle in one arm, and a large revolver dangled at his hip.

From his door pocket, Lucas drew a stubby Smith & Wesson. "Weird," he muttered. "What's he supposed to be, Pancho Villa?"

As the stranger approached, the evening light seemed to brighten. Lucas felt warmth on his face and realized that the sun's edge was again visible, above the horizon ahead. With an oath he glanced at the Explorer's console. In their little black frame, green numbers were moving, spinning backward: 7:31–7:30–7:29–7:28– . . . "What the hell?" Lucas growled.

Sudden movement on the pavement was a blue pickup racing past, going backward at impossible speed. For an instant it was there, in the eastbound lane, then it was a speck on the sun-blazed horizon ahead, then nothing.

The walking man approached on the passenger side and rapped on the front window. "Watch it," Lucas said.

George Wilson lowered the glass. "Yes?"

The man outside leaned down, peering in. He glanced at Lucas, then at Ed Limmer, then fixed his attention on Wilson. "Are you ready to go home?" he asked, his voice respectful. "Magda is waiting."

At the wheel, Lucas bristled. "Did you do something to my car?" he demanded. "What is this, anyway?" The gun in his hand came up defensively. In the back, Ed Limmer leaned over the seat and forced it down.

"Wait!" he said. Then, to the man at the window: "You're Adam, aren't you?"

"Yes," the stranger said. "I'm Adam. I apologize about the machinery. Its electronics are sensitive to grav-resonance. But it isn't harmed. I simply backed things up about five minutes, right around here." He looked at Wilson again, gazing at the technician as if memorizing his features. "Have you completed your work here for the Whispers?"

"All I can do now is more of the same." Wilson shrugged. "The people here are as qualified as I am to maintain the TEF. Have I paid my debt?"

Adam looked past him, at Limmer. "Has he?"

Limmer nodded. "I think he has. The Whispers want another booster activated east of here in 1887. We've scouted the time and place. But someone else can do the work. There are others who can be qualified."

"Where—where and when is Magda?" Wilson's voice shook just a little. "Is she all right? And the child? . . ."

"You'll see in a moment," Adam said. "Mr. Limmer, what do the Whispers report about me?"

"Their loop was penetrated again. L-383, the one you visited. This time it was a hostile visitor. Someone named Quark. He said he is looking for you, that he has your trace."

In the shadow of his wide hatbrim, Adam's eyes glinted like ice. "Quark," he muttered. "I know about him—a timer. But there's somebody else behind him."

"Do you remember Elzy Pyar? Quark killed him."

"Yes." The hatbrim lowered, a sad salute. "Yes, I remember Elzy."

"How did this Quark know where you might be?"

"The same way this vehicle's electronics knew. Somewhere I left a trace—a residual pattern in the harmonics. He found it and followed it."

"Then he can do it again," Wilson said. "I can barely conceive how you do what you do, but I understand dimensional harmonics. To someone attuned, a displacement in resonance could be like a beacon on a dark night. And its polarity might last for years."

"Then I can't take you home now." Adam sighed. "I might lead Quark to you—and to your family."

"Maybe the TEF . . ."

"No. I'm sorry, but your technology is crude and messy, compared to . . . to what timers do. Too much energy is involved. The TEF leaves huge tracks. If Quark is monitoring Whisper transports . . ."

"But there are so many!" Limmer objected. "How could he know the focus of any single transfer, or even which ones to track?"

"He isn't alone," Adam said sadly. "Obviously, he is connected, and I assume they have the senses—or the sensors and equipment—to do multitrack."

"Gravitic polarity," Wilson murmured. "That's what they would sense. It must be the same thing we use to track for retrievals. We—the Whispers, I mean—never investigated it. We just know it's there. And we know the 'trace' of a person of our time is different from a Whisper's. The Whispers themselves recognize the difference. They call us 'protomorphs.' We have different energies. If Quark can read traces, he'd know when a TEF activation involved a 'proto,' someone like us."

"I can't avoid him," Adam agreed. "He has all the time in the world, just like I do. Unless I can find him first . . ."

"Why is he after you?" Lucas stared.

"To kill me, I imagine. There are renegade timers who'd like me gone. And I've been looking for Quark. Now he's killed a harmless Whisper. I guess that was part of the message."

"But *why?*"

"I don't know for sure. Something I've done, obviously . . . or will do."

"You used your ability to come here now," Wilson said thoughtfully. "So there is a fresh trace at this locus."

"Yes."

Wilson had his pocket computer out, tapping in data. "Your means of transit, what is the energy source?"

"Light and gravity. Just like the TEF, but without electromagnetic stimulation."

"What is your stimulant, then?"

Adam raised curious eyes to study the technician. Then he pointed at himself, his finger touching his forehead just above his nose. "This," he said. "The energy of synapses."

"Barely a spark, by comparison," Limmer muttered. "The TEF uses conversion of analogs."

"I told you it was crude." Adam nodded. "The TEF technology, to me it seems incredibly overpowered. Like using a bulldozer to move pawns on a chessboard—an enormous, clumsy, limited crutch for people who can't walk on their own feet. But I guess that's the whole point. Most people can't 'walk' in time. They can't move in multiple dimensions without a technological crutch."

"Like ladders and lifts," Limmer muttered.

"Yes. So the TEF gives people a power they didn't have before. Anybody who knows how can travel back in time using a TEF. This, ah, autotemporal thing some of us do, it's a talent. Some have it, most don't."

"You stalled my car with that 'talent,' " Lucas pointed out. "If it's just brainpower, how did it do that?"

"Don't underestimate the human synapse," Wilson said, still busy with his computer. Then he looked up at Adam. "Get in the car."

"What?"

"In the car. Get in now. How much fuel do you have, Lucas?"

"About three quarters of a tank. Where are we going?"

"Away from here. Turn south when you can. Head for Tulsa or Oklahoma City. Someplace below caprock, where there's a good commercial airport."

Limmer opened the rear door and Adam crawled in beside him. His big, holstered Colt nudged Limmer, and he laid his Winchester behind the seat. "Are those things loaded?" Limmer asked.

"Of course they are. I just came from Emiliano Zapata's war. Empty guns would have got a man killed back then."

Outside the Explorer, evening dusk had set in again. The car started without a trace of complaint. Lucas Hawthorn put his own gun away and drove. They had gone less than a mile when an old, blue pickup passed them, going the other way. The old man at the wheel touched his straw hat in passing. At the Derby road, Lucas turned left and headed south.

"That 'trace' effect has to be latent harmonics, triggered by the conversion of gravity to light or vice versa," George Wilson explained. "It sets up a sympathetic resonance in the matter around it. In stone, it might sing for years, maybe even leave echoes in the crustal sphere. But in air, it should dissipate in moments. I want to go to Magda, Adam. We'll get a fair distance away from your last resonance, then go airborne. Ah, does anybody here know how to fly an airplane?"

"I can," Lucas said. "We'll rent a Cessna or something. Do you really think this will work? I mean, a time-jump from a plane? What if you pop out ten thousand feet up somewhen?"

"It will work," Adam said. "Timing doesn't take preset coordinates. I just . . . well, I sort of decide when and where I want to go, and I go there."

"You still didn't tell me when and where she is," Wilson said.

"And he won't, either," Limmer commanded. "It's best if we don't know."

It was well past midnight when Lucas Hawthorn inspected and paid for a sleek 172 at a little airport outside Cushing, Oklahoma. The air service attendant was sleepy-eyed and wore pajamas, but the 172's records were in good order and the plane had been well cared for. Lucas paid in cash.

As they boarded the four-seater, Edwin Limmer squinted at Adam in the light from the hangar. "I know you from before," he said. "I'd swear I do."

"Sure you do." Adam's grin flared the big mustache he wore—a shy, humorous grin like that of the boy he had been. "I found you a place to live once. Of course, I was a lot younger then. And you were a lot older."

"The same Adam!" Limmer's eyes widened. "So that *was* you!"

"Yes." His look said, Now that you know, forget it.

Limmer understood the look.

At 1:21 A.M., somewhere over Drumright, Oklahoma, a Cessna with starlight on its wings lurched slightly as the bright night around it dimmed, seeming to hesitate for a heartbeat. Lucas Hawthorn and Edwin Limmer both turned, knowing what they would see. The rear seats were empty. They were alone in the little plane.

The Cessna rode the night sky like a serene, dark bird, and Lucas smiled happily as he banked left, heading back to Cushing. "I like this," he said.

"I like it too," Limmer agreed. "George Wilson is a good man. He deserves a peaceful life, after what he's been through."

"I mean this airplane," Lucas said. "I like it. I think I'll take it home."

"What about your car?" Limmer frowned.

"You can drive a car. You drive it home. Then we'll see about sorting out tourists. Then I think we'll suspend our private use of the TEF for a while. I don't like the idea of sending anybody out there with a killer watching."

With runway lights coming to meet them, a twin rank of little beacons on the rolling, quilted dark landscape, Lucas lowered the Cessna's flaps for landing. "They look alike," he mused.

"Who?"

"Adam. He and George Wilson look alike. It's in their eyes, I guess. Shapes of their faces, color of hair . . ."

Limmer thought about it. Lucas was right. Despite the flowing mustache and archaic clothing Adam had worn, the two men did bear a resemblance. Wilson was fortyish and gaunt, Adam thirtyish, a bit taller and more robust. But they were alike. They could have been brothers.

Or possibly father and son. Aging progresses with duration, not with time. For a person who moves about in time, the two are not the same.

Who better to understand anachronisms than an anomaly? Limmer thought. As the lights of Cushing Airport's runway 225 raced to meet them, an ironic grin tugged at his cheeks.

The Stowaway Journal

September 3, 1999
I have been in real time, more or less all the time, for forty-seven years now. That means that I have endured the phenomenon of being alive for ninety-eight plus forty-seven years, or a total of one

hundred and forty-five years. It also means I am physiologically ninety-eight minus forty-seven years of age, or fifty-one.

And, surprisingly, I *feel* fifty-one. I am in good health, as might be expected of a person afflicted by progressive rejuvenation, and my mental state seems that of a reasonably content fifty-one-year-old man. This feeling of contentment is not surprising, in view of the fact that—unlike most people of any age—I know exactly what lies ahead. Barring the truly unimaginable, I will live another fifty-one years, growing younger with each passing year.

I have developed a sort of discretion regarding my condition. Until the inception of the first booster waystop, at the home of Lucas Hawthorn, I simply didn't tell anybody about it. It was easier that way. The least complicated situation I can project—should it become generally known without advantage of context that I am living the second half of a nearly two-century life span in reverse—is to be considered hopelessly delusional by those around me.

The emergence of Anywhen, Inc., changed that to some extent. Secrecy seems less vital when surrounded by confusion. But for all those previous years, the price of my secret was that I must, periodically, disappear and reappear in some other surroundings to start all over again the business of day-to-day life. About ten years was as long an interval as I ever allowed myself. Beyond that limit, it would become painfully obvious that I am becoming younger while everyone I know grows older.

Thus I lived a half-dozen separate, fragmented careers following my reentry from retrosync, always in small towns and always within a few hundred miles of where I first emerged in that wheat field in western Kansas.

For a time I did not know why I stayed within this region, except that the Whispers suggested it. I believe now that I have reasons. One is technical, though I do not know its nature or its significance: It is in this vicinity that something called the Deep Hole Event will occur. The other, and this one I well understand, is that this is the area in which the Institute for Temporal Research will be based, from which will emerge Arthur's Camelot.

I will be here then, fifty-one years from now. I have to be here then. It is where I will be born. Given the global events that lie ahead, I am reluctant to stray too far in the interim.

Another fifty-one years of waiting, to discover the reason I am here. A long time. Time is malleable, but duration is not. So even when people have mastered the past, they still must wait for the future.

I dwell now and then on something Adam said. Anybody who knows how can travel back in time using a TEF. *Back* in time, not forward. The past is cast. It's there to see, if we can get there. But to see the future, as Beejum has, one must travel with someone who has been there—someone who knows the way.

Maybe the only way a person can visit the future alone is the way all of us do—a day at a time.

Still, for people like Adam, I suspect there are no such limits. They have a talent, and they learn to use it. It sets them apart from everybody else.

I wonder sometimes why the world isn't more different than it is, considering all the potential alterations that George Wilson's little conversion cone—using the principle of a simple lamp invented by a man named Frank—offers.

I begin to understand why the Whispers are puzzled about their own future. It just seems like there should be more feedback than there is.

∞

We all see the past, but only time travelers can change it. We all change the future, but only timers can see it.

—EDWIN LIMMER, *The Stowaway Journal*

∞

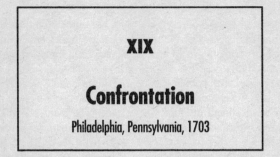

XIX

Confrontation

Philadelphia, Pennsylvania, 1703

"Do thee need assistance?" the cloaked figure inquired, bending to squint at the unlikely pair on the cobblestones. "Why, child, thy locks are full shorn."

Squatting there in silhouette, wide collars turned up against the rain that dripped from his tricorn hat, the man appeared grotesque and dwarfish, a bent greatcoat perched on two stockinged ankles and a walking stick. Lamp-lit runnels rippled around his buckled shoes.

Jack Higgins strove to sit upright, but KT-Pi's little hand pressed hard against his belly. A tingling warmth seemed to spread from her palm, through her fingers, and into the violated flesh of his abdomen. The intense pain of the bullet wound there seemed driven back by gentle waves of comfort. "Be still!" she urged him.

He had felt the bleeding stop—first inside, then outward until now he knew even the surface bleeding had ceased. Dripping rain and rivulets where he lay scoured away its traces, leaving only somber stains around the holes in his buckskin shirt.

A few feet away a carriage rattled past, its oil lamps highlighting the tableau. The man in the greatcoat touched his hat brim toward its occupants, then crouched lower, peering from the shadows beneath his brim. "This man is injured," he said. Then, as the receding glow lighted KT-Pi's face, he added, "Why, bless me, thou art no child at all! Be thee an angel, small one? Or perchance one of those 'little people' the heathen speak of?"

"My name is KT-Pi, sir," she said, her voice taking on the rhythm and accents of the man's speech. "And I am neither angel nor heathen. We are travelers here, beset by woes not of our making."

"Higgins," her patient groaned, lifting a hand. "Jack Higgins, sir. Of Kentucky. Where are we?"

"Thee reclineth in Quincy Road, sir." The man shifted his walking stick to clasp the extended hand. "Benjamin Hurley," he said. "May I perchance be of service to thee? There are medical doctors nearby, and a goodly inn. Do thee require bleeding, or a poultice?"

"He's bled quite enough already, thank you," KT-Pi assured him. The warmth of the little petal-shaped mender in her palm receded and she put it away. "I think you will mend now," she told Higgins. "But you must rest."

"He needs a bed." Benjamin Hurley nodded, his tricorn hat cascading rivulets of rain. "Have thee commerce for the inn?"

"None but in kind," Higgins growled. "Lost me pennies to a man at Harrodsburg over three nutshells and a pea."

"As rude soldiers rolled dice for our Savior's cloak," Hurley intoned. "So was it then, so be it now. Well, thee cannot lie here in the street. I have a house just yonder, on Elfreth's Alley, and I needs do atonement for the fine profit I turned this day at the wharfs. Perchance the Lord will take note that I open my door to the poor wayfarer." He stood, seeming to unfold within his greatcoat. "Come along, then."

Not offering to help further, Hurley turned and walked away, his stick tapping the paving stones. With KT-Pi's assistance, Higgins got to his feet and they followed. Higgins moved slowly, supporting himself on his long rifle.

In Elfreth's Alley, narrow redbrick houses stood shoulder to shoulder, facing ranks of high walls with a tiny street between. Here and there a lantern or sconced lamp shone, little haloed lights in the rainy murk. Somewhere in the distance a crier was making his rounds, his voice hollow echoes in the emptying streets.

"Sir, can you tell me the date?" KT-Pi asked.

Hurley glanced around. "Why, 'tis the second day of April, miss," he said. "A Thursday, I believe, since the proprietor governor's vessel sails at morning tide."

Limping along beside the little person, Jack Higgins noticed a faint glow coming from her cupped hands.

"And the year?" she asked. "What year is this?"

"The year of our Lord 1703," Hurley intoned.

Her fingers moved and the slight glow within her hands seemed to shift this way and that. Looking down past her bald head, Jack Higgins gasped. Little numbers flickered in her hands, like summer lightning bugs dancing. "What is that thing ye have?" he whispered.

"Comlink," she said. "But these vectors are all wrong. Something isn't right here."

"Amen to that," he said fervently. "But moments ago we were in the Green River wilderness . . . weren't we?"

"I think so." KT-Pi nodded, still concentrating on her comlink.

"An' isn't the year 1779?"

"That was," the little Whisper agreed. "But this isn't. Now we're in Philadelphia—I think—and the year is 1703."

They walked several steps in silence. Then Higgins asked, "How do you account for that?"

"We've traveled in time," KT-Pi said. "I'm a time traveler. I'm from the . . . well, from *your* future. And now you're traveling with me, it seems. We were—we call it 'shunted'—out of my conduit of travel, but something isn't right. These coordinates are wrong." She tapped at her comlink, entering various codes.

"That, I'd say, is a fact." The frontiersman nodded.

Ahead of them, Benjamin Hurley angled across the narrow pavement and rapped his cane on a wrought-iron gate. "This is my home," he said pointing past it. The tiny courtyard was barely two paces across, mostly occupied by stone steps leading up to a lamplit doorway deeply inset in the brick wall. "I make thee welcome here, strangers." He opened the gate, stepped through, and turned. "Well, must thee tarry so? Come in. Come in!"

Benjamin Hurley's house might have been gracious, had thought been given to the interior decor. And it might have been spacious but for the clutter. Aside from a sort of clearing before the great hearth, where one comfortable chair and a reading table were placed, the rest of the great room resembled a warehouse. Everywhere along the walls and in the corners were stacks and dumps of shadowy things of all variety—kegs and casks, wooden chests, piles of books, bolts of woolen fabric, turns of silk, plowshares and tubs and augers and various crafted metal devices.

Without his greatcoat and tricorn hat, which he left in the entryway, Benjamin Hurley himself was a motley man, spindly of limb but round-bellied and cheerful. He was older than he had seemed. Thin wisps of silver hair haloed a benign pink face with shrewd eyes. Carrying a lamp and stopping here and there to light tallow candles, he waved vaguely around at the assembled clutter.

"Miscellany," he said. "I dabble in proprietary cargoes among the Indee traders." He found a passable Quaker chair and a three-legged stool and set them before the crackling hearth, then picked up a hand bell and rang it energetically. "Mott will bring us some'at to warm our bones," he said. "Sit and rest thyselves." Without waiting, he took the comfortable chair and settled himself into it. "Now, what's this thee said—in such covert whisperings—about *time travel*?"

"I am a time traveler," KT-Pi said matter-of-factly, perching on the low stool. "I entered retrosynchronic conduit in the year 3007, at a place in eastern Pacifica—what you call the Pacific Ocean. Mr. Higgins is from your more immediate future. He was—or will be—injured by accidental discharge of a weapon in the year 1779, in what I believe is presently considered New Spain. I brought him with me inadvertently when I was shunted out of conduit. But we are not when or where we should be. I suspect a strong lateral event interfered with our transit. We encountered a tide in time." She looked at her useless comlink, tapped its pads a few more times, and shook her head. "You see, anywhere in conduit, there would be immediate response to this. Even in a lateral shunt, the vectors should have followed us. But I get nothing."

Higgins gaped at her. "How's all that again?"

Benjamin Hurley sat hunkered in his stuffed chair. His shrewd eyes seemed to penetrate the exquisite little person on the stool, examining her huge, dark eyes, her hairless head, her very soul. "Do thee speak truly?" he asked after a long pause. "Could it be? Are these things indeed possible?"

"I speak truly, sir," KT-Pi assured him.

Hurley considered it, then rang his hand bell again vigorously. "Mott!" he called. "Mott, awaken yourself and serve us! And no blasted tea, if you please! I, for one, am in need of a stout rum toddy!"

Mott was young and tousled, a bound boy, an indentured servant paying off his debt of passage as Hurley's butler and helper. He was just mixing toddy at the hearth—and stealing curious glances at KT-Pi and Higgins—when the front door knocker echoed through the entryway.

"A strange hour for visitors," Hurley muttered, then waved a hand. "See who 'tis, Mott."

The boy padded out of the room. His muted voice came from the entry, rising in protest, then he was back, tagging after a tall, dark-haired man with a flared greatcoat and no hat.

"He pushed right past me, sir," Mott told Hurley.

The intruder looked quickly around the room, then his gaze rested on KT-Pi. "So it *was* a Whisper." He tilted his head. "Which one are you?"

"KT-Pi," she said.

"Hello." He nodded. "I'm Adam. I picked up your signals. What are you doing so far from your conduit?"

"Adam? Are you? . . ."

"Yes, probably. I'm sure there are research notes about my presence. Why are you here?"

"Not by choice," she assured him. "Something happened. I was shunted out of conduit with Mr. Higgins here. But we—we encountered a cross-boost of some kind. Something very strong. I'm afraid we drifted."

"Obviously you did. This cross-boost, when did you encounter it? Reverse duration from present."

"Not more than an hour," she estimated. "You are a 'timer,' they say. Did you cause it?"

"No, but I know who did. A renegade timer named Quinton Arkland. A history-changer. I traced his back-path to a vessel moored in the Schuylkill Ways. A crown vessel called *Serenity*. Do you know of it?"

KT-Pi shook her head, but Benjamin Hurley nodded. "I know the ship," he said. "She saileth on the morrow tide for England. She is the proprietor governor's own vessel."

"Proprietor . . . do you mean Penn? William Penn?"

"The very same." Hurley shrugged.

"And do you know William Penn?"

"That I do, sir, but I do not know you, though you standeth uninvited in my private home."

Adam hesitated, then bowed slightly. "My apologies to my unwitting host," he said formally. "I am called Adam. And whose hospitality have I abused, sir?"

"Benjamin Hurley." Hurley stood and returned the bow. "It seems I have made a career this night of harboring time's journey-folk. What might thy business be with Governor Penn?"

"To save his life," Adam said. "Quinton Arkland does not intend for *Serenity* to reach the sea tomorrow, sir. I don't expect you to know what a pound of C4 can do to the hull of a wooden sailing ship, but a great deal of history will be altered if William Penn is aboard when it happens. I will try to stop Arkland, if I can find him. But if I can't . . . ." He shrugged eloquently. "Boom."

"I see," Hurley said.

"Then tell me, can you reach Penn? Can you keep him from boarding *Serenity*?"

"One hardly counseleth the proprietor governor as to his voyages," Hurley pointed out. "Some say that even King Charles and his brother, the Duke of York, are more like to ask than to tell where the Quaker baron is concerned."

"Then who does have Penn's ear?" Adam pressed.

"Only two, I reckon," Hurley smiled. "Chief Tamenend and King Profit."

"Tamenend . . . of the Delaware tribe?"

"The Leni-Lenape, yes. Governor Penn believes that Christianized red gentleman does magic. But Tamenend is far away at the moment."

"Then what of profit?"

Hurley considered in silence as long moments passed. Then he said, "It might be that the governor would be interested in recovering a certain chest of chinaware, considering that it once belonged to his mother."

"And what price might be put on this chinaware?"

"A gift carries no price." Hurley frowned. "Only were the governor to tarry in his collection of it, and thus be spared his life, and *know* of this circumstance . . ." He trailed off, deep in thought.

"Yes?" Adam prompted.

"Oh, 'tis nothing really," Hurley mused. "I was just thinking of how unsettled the civilities be between the crown and France. And Governor Penn *does* have it in his power as colonial proprietor to grant certain letters of marque. There are fine profits to be made these days in privateering."

"But that's—that's *piracy!*" KT-Pi chirped, realizing what they were talking about.

"No such thing." Adam grinned. "Just politics and business." With a searching look at Hurley, he asked, "Will you help me, then, sir? Will you detain Governor Penn, if you can?"

"Thy story's no stranger than most else I've heard this evening." Hurley shrugged. "Perchance one might assist, from simple curiosity."

"Good." Adam turned again to the Whisper and the frowning backwoods man. "I'll help you both to get home," he said. "But first I have a man to find, if I can."

With a parting nod, he turned and strode from the great room, Mott scampering after him. When the boy returned, Hurley arose from his good chair and went to the hearth. He leaned there, savoring the spicy aroma of rum toddy beginning to heat. Then he straightened. "Mott, what is the time?"

"Half-past ten, sir," the boy said.

"And time for thy writing lesson." Hurley nodded. "Fetch paper, ink, and your best quills, lad. I'll have you write a message to Governor William Penn. And when it is done, you may deliver it to Penn Manor."

"Yes, sir," Mott said.

Dogwatch was lax aboard *Serenity* on this night. The vessel was no man-of-war, but simply a commercial four-master snug among its harbor escort squadron—a fine frigate and twin brigs trimmed out for racing staysails. *Serenity* rested deep within the Schuylkill Ways within cover of gunboats and shore batteries, and her cargo was mostly personal effects of persons of the peerage. Nor was her primary custom—Governor William Penn and the forty-odd members of his retinue on this his second visit to his proprietary colony in America—yet aboard.

Thus the man who slipped from a dinghy to *Serenity*'s spring anchor line and from there to her dark, wet deck went unobserved. Barely a shadow among the shadowed cable tiers alongside her port rail, Adam crept from stem to stern, his eyes searching, then crossed beneath the helmshed and completed his circuit. Canvas tarps covered slung hammocks where sailors slept, their snores a muted symphony with the creaks and groans of a riding hull, the sporadic sounds of night bells across broad waters, and the steady drip and trickle of spring rain.

His deck search completed, Adam slipped into a forward hold just aft of the chain lockers and began working his way back toward the main holds, galley, and stern cabins. It was past midnight when he found what he was looking for—a little parcel of waxed linen tacked to the midships hull timbers at waterline. Carefully he removed the packet, clipped the wires thrust into its bulk, and removed the tiny digital clock from its wrap. He studied the dismantled bomb and frowned. This would have holed the vessel, certainly, but would hardly have destroyed it. The package was too small, the location not critical. A vessel so damaged might survive with fothering on its outer hull. It might even sink, but not quickly. And here in Philadelphia harbor, with boats and rescue at hand, there might be few casualties.

Serenity herself was not the changer's target, he knew. The target could only be Governor Penn. He looked again at the digital timer. It was live but not activated. The setting was for 10 A.M. Time enough to board passengers and stow gear, time enough to clear the ways by tow-launch and make sail with the outbound tide in Chesapeake Bay. Time enough for a series of blasts to blow the ship to splinters out in the open channel.

A series of blasts—that was how it was described in the official reports in London. A series of blasts and no survivors. The assassin was taking his time now, making sure. Whoever had placed this bomb was still aboard *Serenity*, and would return. Other bombs were being placed on the sleeping vessel.

Adam searched silently and methodically, and found the second one after a few minutes. It was swathed in rough sacking and taped to the keelson amidships. This alone would have broken the ship's back on detonation. He began dismantling the device.

But for a rough plank, he would not have heard the attacker. The man came from shadows, behind him, wielding a cleaving ax. At sound of his scuffing footstep Adam lunged aside, and the heavy ax bit a gouge in the oaken rib where he had been.

"A timer," the man breathed, raising his ax again. "You should have minded your own business, timer."

Again the ax slashed in the gloom, and again Adam dodged it. "Quinton Arkland?" he purred. "Why are you doing this?"

"Because I can," the man growled. Advancing, he raised the ax a third time. "Who's to stop me?"

Adam ducked low and lunged, going in under the ax. His shoulder caught Arkland in the midriff and threw him back against the inner hull. The ax flew away, clattering into the bilges. "I am." He planted a boot in the man's ribs. "My name is Adam. I'm here to stop you. I already have. Governor Penn won't be aboard this ship when it sails."

The growl of rage that came from Arkland was more animal than human. He rolled aside, got to his knees, and tensed himself. Moon-blond hair caught the dim lamplight, which illuminated the little triangle mark on his brow. His fingers toyed with a signal disc at his belt. "I'll have to answer to Kaffer for this," he muttered. "You've messed up a sweet deal for me. But you'll pay for it."

Adam held back, studying the man in the gloom. "Who is Kaffer?" he asked.

"Oh, no!" Arkland sneered. "I'm not telling you anything, except he isn't who you think. And this"—he indicated the little triangle on his brow—"this isn't what you think, either. I'm not one of his Deltas. I'm a timer!"

Kaffer? Deltas? The words were a puzzle, but Adam knew he wouldn't learn more from this man. He crouched, spreading his arms. But there was a flicker, and Arkland was no longer in front of him. Instead he stood in shadows, twelve feet to one side. Again he touched the signal disc, but hesitated. "I'll find you, Adam," he warned. "You're too late to save this ship, and I'll kill you for interfering. But not just yet. You just watch for me, Adam. Me, Quark! I'll find you when I'm ready, no matter where in time you are!"

Adam felt, more than saw, the dimming—the slowing of the light. Quark was timing! He rushed at the man. The murky, foul air of the hold seemed to shimmer.

Quark feinted aside, then struck. A roundhouse blow glanced off Adam's forearm, another caught him like a hammer in the midriff. He crouched and backed away. Quark was bull strong and furious, a maniac thwarted.

Adam braced himself, but again Quark backed away. Pale eyes gleamed with rage. The tiny light on the signal disc at his belt changed from blue-green to red, and this time his finger touched it. "If I don't find you, I'll make you come to me," he growled. Then the air shimmered again.

In the murky depths belowdecks, time seemed to dim and falter, but only for an instant. In the blink of an eye, the man who now called himself Quark was gone.

"Well, now I know," Adam muttered. "Quinton Arkland. Quark." I know him, he thought. But there *is* someone else. Who is Kaffer? And who are the Deltas?

The ruckus belowdecks had aroused crewmen, and now they swarmed the ship, searching for the source. Adam shouldered a hatch cover open and shouted, "Abandon ship! There's bombs aboard! All hands abandon!" Then he vaulted to the open deck, raced to the starboard rail, and jumped, willing transit as he went.

There were conflicting reports about the explosion in Schuylkill Ways in the rainy predawn of April 3, 1703. The word "bomb" was in survivor reports, but that could mean many things. It was concluded, eventually, that some spark had found its way into the magazines of the barque *Serenity*. The resulting explosions were heard as far away as Chester Town, and only splintered wreckage was recovered from *Serenity*.

A week later Governor William Penn, proprietor of Pennsylvania, sailed for London aboard a crown flagship with full escort. With his personal luggage, he carried a teakwood chest containing Dresden chinaware that had once belonged to his mother.

In September of that year, Charles II of England granted letters of marque to one Benjamin Hurley, entitling him to equip vessels at Philadelphia to patrol the Ocean Sea in defense of the crown.

∞

Infinity is all and infinity is nothing. Light and darkness, the truth and the lie, good and evil, heaven and hell . . . the shrouded past rolls out behind us while the future extends ahead, beyond horizons. From here and now, all roads lead to infinity.

—THE REVEREND JACOB ROSS

∞

XX

Timer

Wichita, Kansas, The Present

Amanda Santee Brink took a final tour of the house where she had resided for the past three years—the house that should have been home but never had been, really. She was a little surprised at how easy it had been to collect and pack all that was hers. Two closets and a little upstairs room—the room that had become her getaway place when she needed private moments—were empty now, their contents packed in boxes in the entry hall, with her luggage. Except for those, the rest of the house was virtually untouched. "It's like I was never here," she told herself, wandering through the cold opulence of the place. "Maybe I never really was, except in my own mind."

Absently she straightened a curtain and smoothed the edge of an Oriental rug. Expensive, she reminded herself. An *expensive* Oriental rug. That was a major criterion for Ray Brink. If something wasn't expensive, it wasn't worth having. The house was a showplace—a place where Ray Brink could impress people with his good taste in furnishing. Even the decorator who chose it all had been expensive. And there wasn't a trace of Mandy's presence in the place. All the little touches she had tried to add, Ray had systematically erased.

"Ray," Mandy muttered, resetting the security system, "you really are a twit."

She didn't enter an exit interval into the system. She wouldn't be leaving by the door, any more than she had entered by the door. The TEF in Maude's house was connected now to a programmed timer. When she was ready for retrieval, she would simply telephone the Hawthorns' computer and punch in a numeric code. Five minutes later she would be back in the steel-floored TEF chamber, luggage and all.

She glanced at her watch. She would wait another hour, to be safe. She didn't want to arrive while she was still there. The Whispers were vague as to the effects of self-encounters, but Mandy had no desire to meet herself in transit. It didn't seem like the thing to do.

She searched her conscience for feelings of regret and found none. She had done her best. For three years she had given everything she had to being a wife to Ray Brink and—at least—a decent influence on Leslie and Leland. Through it all, Ray had abused her, and the boys had ignored her. Leaving now, she only wondered why she had waited so long.

After returning to the spacious entry hall, she gathered her belongings into a compact cluster around the only piece of furniture she was taking—a battered old rocking chair—and placed the telephone beside it. Then she sat down to wait.

She closed her eyes, daydreaming of places—and times—she would visit. Around her, the house sat stale and still, the only sounds the hollow echoes of little house noises barely heard.

Then a harsh voice said, "Well, well! Who have we here?"

Mandy jerked awake. The man stood just feet away, towering over her. A big man, with a livid scab just above the bridge of his nose—a fresh scar, as if an inch of flesh had been cut away there. Like a removed tattoo. Untamed hair like spun moonlight framed a cruel, sneering face with wide-set, piercing eyes as cold as ice. She came to her feet and reached for the telephone, but he slapped it from her hand. In the same motion he pushed her, sprawling, back into the rocker. "Aren't you a pretty thing!" he drawled. "Where is Adam?"

"How should I know?" She struggled to stand again, and he raised a threatening open hand. The movement parted the long, stained coat he wore, revealing the array of weapons beneath it. There were at least two large guns and various other things.

"That answers my question," he purred. "You do know *who* Adam is. That means he knows who you are, too. You're no timer, or you wouldn't have used TEF to jump here. So who are you?"

"Am—Amanda," she managed.

"Well, you're no Whisper, Amanda. But you know them. So you're one of their station team. You're . . ." His eyes narrowed in recognition. "I know you! You're the one he followed to 1938 Hollywood! Well, now. I *have* caught live bait, haven't I?"

"What do you want with Adam?" she demanded.

"I'm going to kill him." The man smiled coldly. "Haven't you heard? I'm Quark."

"Well, you won't find him with me. I don't know where he is, and he doesn't know I'm here! That's the truth, I swear."

"Oh, I believe you." Quark nodded. "But he'll know soon enough, and he'll come looking for you. He isn't as good as me, but he senses retro-impulse. He's a timer. In the meantime, I might as well amuse myself."

He stepped toward her and old instincts came into play. Her foot lashed out, catching him in the groin. As he doubled over, gasping and cursing, she sprang from the rocker and kicked him again, this time from behind. Then she bolted and ran. Behind her the man shrieked, "Bitch!" and a gun roared. A huge, gilt-framed mirror in the formal room ahead of her exploded. At the corner she dodged to the right, skidding on Ray Brink's expensive teak-mosaic floor. A second bullet screamed over her head and gouged splinters from the antique armoire beside the fireplace. The whole house seemed to thunder with echoes. She crouched and headed for the great staircase, weaving this way and that. Behind her she heard Quark's heavy, faltering footsteps, and another gunshot.

"Adam," she breathed, her mind racing. "Adam, be careful. There's a madman here. He means to kill you." She concentrated on the words, wishing she could somehow will the message to Adam, wherever he was.

Quark! There had been comlink from L-383. Someone called Quark had penetrated the loop—as easily and puzzlingly, they said, as Adam had. And that someone was here now, shooting at her! Fear that bordered on blind panic drove her as she flew up the stairs, barely aware of bullets hammering into the risers, gouging the banister, shattering the brick fascia beyond. But even through the fear she knew, with a sick certainty, that Adam would somehow come to her aid and that the madman pursuing her would kill him when he came.

At the top of the staircase she dodged to the left and darted around a corner, into the long, elegant center hallway. She thought of the back staircase but rejected it. It was boarded up halfway down. A loose railing had necessitated repair, and the work had not been completed. It was in the back of the house, and it didn't detract from the elegance visitors would see.

The man behind her had stopped firing, but she could hear him coming, sweeping aside finery, destroying things as he came—Ray Brink's expensive things.

At a doorway she ducked to the right, into a large linen closet. After closing the door, she climbed onto a shelf and stretched upward, pushing aside the attic trap in the ceiling. As quietly as she could, she clambered upward, ignoring the swing ladder in its sockets. With a push, she lifted herself through the entry, edged aside, and lowered the hatch back into place. She lay there then, trying to stifle the sound of her own labored breathing. Below she heard doors slam back, glass break, and furniture topple as Quark searched for her.

The sounds came nearer, then ceased. In the sudden silence Mandy could hear her own heart beating. "Please, God," she whispered without sound. "Please . . ." But the prayer that came was not the prayer she expected. "Please don't let Adam come now." Her lips formed the words silently. "Quark will kill him if he does."

Not a prayer for herself. A prayer for Adam.

Quark's taunting voice came then, from nearby—so very close! He must be directly below, she realized. Right at the closet door . . . or maybe *in* the closet. "You can't hide from me, you know!" he called. "Nobody can elude a timer!"

She held her breath, waiting. A moment, then she heard his heavy footsteps receding. Somewhere down the hall a door crashed open and a window shattered. Then there were other sounds, farther still.

If she could only reach a telephone . . . Mandy eased the attic hatch up an inch, then another. Making no sound, she opened it and let herself down into the closet. The door was wide open, but the hall beyond was empty. Peering both ways, she scampered across to the master bedroom and ducked inside. There was a telephone by the bed. She could activate the TEF retrieval from here. With another glance up and down the hallway she turned—and froze. Directly before her, Quark stood relaxed and arrogant, the broken telephone in one casual fist.

"I told you, you can't elude a timer," he sneered. "You thought I was gone when I went down the hall. But I wasn't, you see. I was here all along. I saw myself go by. Then I waited for you."

He had jumped himself back in time, to trap her. With sick certainty she knew he would trap Adam the same way. And there was nothing she could do about it.

As if reading her mind, he grinned—a cruel grin. "Yes, I'll kill your friend," he purred. "In a way, I've already killed him. He just doesn't know it yet."

A faint sound came then, from somewhere outside the room—quick, padded footsteps on the stairs. Mandy whirled to the door. "Adam!" she shouted. "No! It's a trap!"

But it was too late. In the hallway, Adam topped the stairs, then dodged aside as a bullet whined past him. Mandy saw him, then turned and saw Quark standing in the middle of the hall, aligning a gun with both hands for another shot.

Adam dropped to the floor and rolled, and now there was a gun in his hand, too, spitting thunder. But at nothing. Quark had disappeared from the hallway, as if he had never been there.

Mandy turned, her eyes frantic as she scanned the empty bedroom where, a moment before, Quark had been standing . . . even while he—a moments-earlier he—was in the hallway, firing at Adam. Now he was gone. She stepped out into the hall, and Adam saw her. A happy smile began on his face, then froze in place as a bullet tore through him from behind.

Quark was there, at the head of the stairs. Again he fired, shot after shot at point-blank range. Adam's body twitched this way and that, spraying blood as the bullets ripped through him.

"No!" Mandy screamed. Beyond the now-still body, at the top of the stairs, Quark looked up at her and grinned. Casually he leveled his gun again and fired another round into Adam's corpse. The roar echoed through the house, punctuated by the little clatter of the ejected shell bouncing off the wall and rolling lazily down the steps. The big automatic remained open this time, its slide back and locked, empty. Quark threw it aside and drew another gun. He raised this one, thumbed the safety off, and pointed it at Mandy. "Bye-bye, bitch." He chuckled.

Outrage and shock shrilled in Amanda's mind. Staring into the bore of the gun, she felt no fear, no dread—only a screaming rage that drowned all other consciousness. For the first time in her life, Mandy Santee knew real hatred. All of her senses cleared and came into focus, and she rode the blinding tide of them.

In Quark's hand, the gun bucked and thundered, and Mandy saw its projectile splinter the door frame where she had been an instant before. She saw it from behind Quark, past his shoulder. "You missed," she chided. "I'm here, behind you."

He stiffened, started to turn, and she whirled, kicking him in the knee with all her strength. His pivot leg went out from under him, and he pitched aside, stumbling over Adam's body to thump into the wall.

"Good trick, huh, *timer*?" she taunted him, advancing. "You're not really very good at this, after all, are you?"

His pale eyes gaping, he raised his gun and fired at her point-blank. But she wasn't there. He gasped, and a small, hard-toed shoe came from aside, catching him full in the face. He felt his nose break, felt his lips mashed back against his teeth. Almost blinded, he lurched around. The woman was standing over him, holding Adam's bloody gun in her hand.

"You're just no good at all," she said, shaking her head in mock pity. "You should have taken up some other line of work." She raised the gun, pointing it at his face, then lowered it. "Oh, come on, *timer*," she said. "You could at least make this interesting. Use your pitiful talent, you worthless bag of trash! Do what I did! Leap downstream and aft, a heartbeat and six paces. Then you'd be behind me! Maybe you can shoot me in the back, the way you shot Adam."

She sneered at him, taunting, daring him. With a muted cry of fury, Quark focused his senses and leapt—and was behind her! Blindly he raised the gun and fired.

Yet as the roar filled the hallway, he saw what she had done. She wasn't there . . . just himself, slumped against a wall, struggling to rise. The shot took him—himself of a moment before—directly through the left temple. Beyond, the wall was splattered with blood, brains, and bits of shattered skull.

"I've already killed him," Quark said. "He just doesn't know it yet."

Somewhere outside the bedroom, quick footsteps padded on the stairs, coming up. Mandy whirled to the door. "Adam!" she shouted. "No! It's a trap!"

But it was too late. Adam had topped the stairs. Now he stood over the inert body of the man called Quark. "What a mess," he said. Then he turned to Amanda with a smile like morning sun. "Fantastic," he said with a nod. "And I never knew you were a timer."

"I didn't know it, either." She shrugged. "You saw it all? How could you? . . ."

"It was a probability," he said. "Yes, I saw it. I experience probabilities. We all do, with practice. I saw him shooting at me, and I felt myself die. And then I saw what you did. Lordy, girl, you're good! Better than I've ever been. A pure natural!"

"Probabilities?" She looked up into his eyes.

"Probabilities," he said gently. "That's all the future is. Just probabilities. That's how I knew to come here. I experienced the probability that he would find you here. It's more than foreseeing what might happen. It's almost . . . or actually, *living* it.

It's how I trace people like him. I see how things are if I don't go somewhen and do something, so I go."

"Then this—all this—it didn't really happen?"

"Oh, it happened, all right. Quark set a trap for me, and he killed me, just as you saw. But now, thanks to you, even though it actually happened, now it didn't and it never will."

"Like Scarlett O'Hara's red dress," she murmured. Lost in the deep warmth of his eyes, she stepped closer. "Do you see other probabilities now, Adam?"

"I certainly do." He looked down at her with gentle eyes. "Some interesting ones. And some not so nice. There was someone behind Quark before. Someone called Kaffer, using him. Kaffer and the Deltas. They'll have to be found now."

As first witnesses on the scene, when they escorted Ray Brink home from El Dorado, Detectives Soames and Myers were included in the police investigation of the dead intruder they found in his house.

The man would be identified as one Quinton Arkland, a missing person from Hannibal, Missouri. What he was doing alone in the home of a prominent Wichita attorney, armed to the teeth and dead from a .45-caliber bullet wound to the head, would remain a mystery, along with how he got in through a functioning security system and why he had run amuck there, wrecking expensive furnishings before shooting himself in the head at the top of the main staircase.

Some such mysteries are never resolved, and this one was only made more interesting by the fact that his self-inflicted mortal wound, delivered by the very gun he held in his hand, had been fired from at least fifteen feet away.

The owner of the house, Raymond Brink, threw up all over his expensive red-oak banister at sight of the body, then went to his room and stayed there. A month later, when his divorce was finalized, he sold his house and property to the Limmer Trust Company and moved away, to set up practice in California.

There was only sporadic media coverage of the strange death of Quinton Arkland. In a culture suffused with the illogic of drug-related incidents, the bizarre had become the norm and worthy of only limited notice. An exception was a fifty-two-second exposé on the local segment of network news by Chad Ryan, whose credibility had already been shredded because of an unbelievable story about volcanic eruptions, sailing vessels, and locally instigated subversive advances in the field of special effects.

Ryan and his station were sued by two well-known business-people for slander by implication, and when his contract expired Ryan moved to California to work for a documentary film company sponsored by environmental awareness groups.

Ray Brink's sons, Leland and Leslie, remained in Wichita until their father's affairs were settled, then they also left. As one of them commented to their mother, Mrs. Flosilda Brink Johnson, "We owe Mr. Flagg some horses and some time. We've decided to go work out our obligations."

The remark was never adequately explained.

∞

Our senses are not limited. The eye sees what is there, the ear hears every sound. It is the mind, shielding itself from the unthinkable, that picks and chooses.

—MARY GOLD, *Reminiscences*

∞

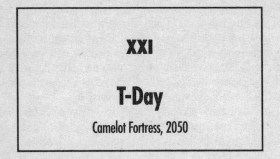

XXI

T-Day

Camelot Fortress, 2050

The walled avenues and great halls were empty now except for nervous porters here and there, moving luggage and personal effects to the debarkation centers at the main gates, a few members of the peerage supervising the relocations, and the grim, uniformed guardsmen of Arthur's personal legion who shadowed them, watching their every move.

High in the central tower of Camelot, just below the loft where the focalizer and generator waited, Arthur Rex stood at a wide, shielded window, watching the activity below. He was alone, and being alone now suited him. Within hours he would no longer be a mortal man. No other person on Earth held the power that was now at his command. No one had ever possessed such power, and no one else ever would.

The great room, now completed, occupied the second-highest level of the mighty tower. Big windows of shielded, blastproof plex faced all directions. The big chamber was unfurnished except in its center, where steel-reinforced arches soared high above a tall dais with a steel floor. Upon the dais rested a single artifact—a tall, high-backed chair of bright stainless steel. In its arms were the circuits controlling the generator in the loft overhead and the temporal effect focalizer directly above. Beneath the steel throne a crystal lens of superb craftsmanship glistened darkly, distorting the inky depths beneath it. Below, nearly ten miles straight down, rested the source of Arthur's secret power.

Antimatter, the early scientists had called it—a tiny globe of an inconceivable substance discovered quite by accident nearly a hundred years earlier. Those who found the thing had been drilling for depth, part of a study of the earth's crust and the underlying mantle. They had hoped for new data on tectonic shift. Some of them might have harbored hopes of tapping the planet's living heartbeat, the motive force that was the catalyst between pressure and vulcanism.

But what they actually found was beyond their understanding. They drilled for data and they discovered hell. Nothing had been left on the site of the Deep Hole drilling operation—not even bits of debris large enough to study. And the investigations that came later had resulted in the most absolute security cover ever devised by a habitually paranoid bureaucracy. Instituted by the military, the impenetrable blanket of hush had tightened with each puzzling new development until even the military was effectively excluded. The engineer of this masterful secrecy was Arthur Meeks— a meticulous and ruthless young diplomat with both USMI and Special Forces background.

The Deep Hole disaster had been the beginning of the Institute for Temporal Research. Among the most puzzling evidence extensive investigation uncovered was a series of anachronisms. There was a geologist's logbook, listed in the lost-and-found section of a Topeka shopping guide. The last entry in the book was dated and sealed the day before the implosion three hundred miles to the west. But the book had been found—in the parking lot of a Topeka supermarket— eight days earlier.

There were other such oddities, including a mysterious, fifty-year-old metallic badge turned in by a collector. It had been in his family for all that time—an oddity found in a ditch by his grandfather. The thing proved to be a driller's badge from Deep Hole. Its sealed, liquid-crystal pass code was still intact. A unique carborundum bore-bit found in a Pratt museum was traced to Deep Hole tool inventories. And, possibly the oddest of all, there was an old tintype photograph of a dead man found by buffalo hunters near Medicine Lodge in

1872. His clothing was unlike anything of the time. Now the dead man was positively identified as one of the Deep Hole engineers listed as missing more than a century later.

John Jacob Royce had believed the unbelievable. It was his trademark. With the backing of the Department of Interior, which since the Divestitures of 2007 had been central administrator of the Federated Free Zones, he founded ITR in 2020. One of his first draftees was the current genius-in-residence of actualist physics, Mateo Joaquin Goldman. Goldman, a protégé of Nicholas Tolafsson, later recruited the brilliant young physicist George Wilson, a leader in the field of particulate gravity.

It was Goldman who identified and isolated the element that had triggered the Deep Hole disaster. The substance was not a substance at all but a "black hole" phenomenon held in stasis by the earth's subcrust. Deep Hole had hit a pocket of retroforce. Under Goldman's direction, ITR reopened the devastated shaft and went looking for another one.

Wilson deduced from the known phenomena of Deep Hole that temporal manipulation is linked to gravity, and from the ubiquitous Frank lamp that gravity has a direct analog in magnetism. With these insights, he postulated from the "evidences" of Deep Hole that light and gravity are extremes of the same spectrum—a great circle of energies whose closing is the constant universal cataclysm. Following this theme, an ITR team demonstrated that both gravity and light can be slowed and manipulated, using each as a counterbalance to the other with magnetism and photoelectric radiance as the catalysts.

It was Wilson—with a select team of scientists—who actually built and tested three prototype temporal effect focalizers and the generator to activate them.

ITR had been Arthur's springboard. As head of security for the big project, Arthur Meeks had a kind of carte blanche unprecedented in world history since the days of the tyrant dictators. Meeks had set out methodically to build himself a power base using ITR. The Federated Free Zones were the perfect environment for him. By the time Mat Goldman's conjectures were expounded, Meeks had assumed absolute power over an area the size of the Roman Empire. The Panhandle FFZ extended from the Missouri River to the frontal range of the Rockies, and from the Republican River to the upper reaches of the Brazos.

And he had an arsenal. Control of a midcontinent's granaries gave him access to the manufacturing capacities of other FFZs. He stockpiled zen-guns and virtually controlled the production of John Jacob Royce's most notorious innovation, the Royce Armored ATV. From there it was only a technicality for Arthur to reduce the High Plains Free Zone to a personal kingdom and declare himself king. Even the Denver Guard's unexpected swarms of armed "Sparrow" ultralights and the Revivalists' valiant last-ditch stand at Long Mesa on the Cimarron had only slowed the Camelot victory.

Now Arthur had it all, and he was ready for the ultimate conquest—a victory over death itself. The focalizer could do more than pop objects back and forth in perceived time. It could, his scientists discovered, alter duration itself. For George Wilson and his team, this was esoteric science. But Arthur was a different kind of man.

For King Arthur, the T-effect focalizer was the means to live forever.

Now, watching the last evacuation convoys loading for departure, Arthur reviewed his plans. When finally the gates were closed, there would be no one left within the great walls except himself and the Trilate Council—the only three men who shared his rule. Three of a kind, they were—ruthless men, brilliant in their own ways, and useful to Arthur over the years. He had involved them in every detail of his reign, but always separately. And never for a moment had he trusted them.

This would be their first formal meeting as a king's council. He had declared them "chroniclers of the test," and he knew that each of them was sniffing out his secrets, seeking a means to overthrow him. It was this motivation, this energy, that had made them useful to him in his rise to power. But today their usefulness ended.

They and he would be alone in all of Camelot when he opened the great chamber to reveal the steel throne. It was what they all hungered to see. It would be the last thing any of them would ever see. The portal to the chamber was ringed with zen-guns set on full charge.

Arthur intended to share his ultimate victory with no one at all.

Tower by tower, quadrant by quadrant, the fortress was emptying itself. From every battlement, convoys of trucks and personal vehicles could be seen, little groups like caravans diminishing into the distance, each conveyance flying the colors of its house. For a mile or more, each outbound highway was flanked by the silhouettes of AATVs. The sleek rovers dominated the terrain with their guns. Here and there in the bright sky, fliers soared. With the consolidation of his realm, Arthur's arrogance had grown. His airborne gunships went where they would now, even scouting across treaty lines.

In the vast, rolling fields, where the grain harvest had begun, mighty harvesters worked their swaths unperturbed, though those operating them and those loading the grain for delivery to the elevators craned their necks to watch the spectacle of Camelot's occupants vacating the premises. It was a huge exodus. Arthur's fortress—built on what had been a fair-size high plains town in the days of nations—was huge.

Evacuation meant the removal of dozens of aristocratic houses in residence and many thousands of people. Some moved en masse to the railheads for passage to their own domains. A few trusted themselves to the winds with huge lighter-than-air craft. But most preferred the highways.

To the south, Lord Childress's household was a miles-long caravan on the horizon, heading for the realms beyond the Canadian. Not far behind them, a convoy of crawling vehicles bore the colors of Baron Hansford and his retinue. At the west gates, the final luggage was being loaded aboard the carriers of Lord Baca while a rank of eighteen-wheelers and passenger cars waited to receive the wares of Rupert Lord Graves, the Regent of Denver.

Lesser peers and their retinues already rolled the roads northward, toward the fiefdoms of Colby, Ashe, and Windom.

At the east gates the entourages of Lord Nash and Sir Hugo Winter had already gone, and final loading was being done for the entourage of Lord Sedgewick.

It was a complete evacuation. Arthur had decreed that Camelot was to be vacated no later than today, and Arthur's decree was law. By sundown, no one would remain inside the walls except Arthur himself and his chroniclers, the Trilate Council. Even the guards were to remove themselves beyond the gates.

It was whispered that Arthur's scientists had completed their work, that the theories developed by the old Institute for Temporal Research were now fact, and that Arthur was ready to fulfill his prophecy. He had the means at hand to live forever, and now he would use it.

It was a time of bustle and confusion, and for Lindy Rae Koch it was a time of disappointment. Once again she was attending to all the trappings, coordination, and administration of a removal without Ronnie's help. Lord Sedgewick was now commander of the Second Battalion, and as such it was his duty to secure all passages south and west, providing armed escort for the aristocrats evicted from Camelot and bound in those directions.

It would be good to return to Wichita for a time. The house there was pleasant. A stately manor built more than sixty years before, for someone named Hemingway, it still had traces of being lavish and opulent for its time. To Lindy, it seemed the house must have been home to a very pretentious person. But it was comfortable, incorporating the comforts and refinements of the late twentieth century, before the Paper Revolts and the ensuing collapse of federal and state functions . . . before the border mandates, the Divestiture, and the Fundamentalist Rebellions.

Sedgewick Manor had been an idle rich man's private home, converted and modified in 2012 by John J. Royce, one of the founders of the Institute for Temporal Research. The house had become headquarters of a fiefdom following Arthur's ascension in 2029.

The manor sat on a wide, low hill within the city of

Wichita—Lord Sedgewick's fiefdom. Its broad lawns had once been a country club golf course, and its drives had been municipal avenues.

It would be pleasant to rest there awhile, and Lindy Rae was assured that Ronnie would join her as soon as Arthur's latest work was complete. They would have a little time together then, maybe even time enough to begin a family. In her five years as Lady Sedgewick, Lindy Rae had known loneliness more than she had known love. Ronnie was seldom present, and the brief interludes they had been given had produced no issue. All around her, Lindy Rae saw young women with children. But she had none of her own.

Loneliness had become a way of life for Lindy Rae Koch these past several years. Ronnie was gone so much, and the constant intrigues of the great bastion that was Camelot made the growth of any real friendships impossible.

The last of the Sedgewick goods had been checked out at the gate, but it would be hours yet before everything was loaded and ready for travel. Transports were scarce in this time of harvest, and much of the kingdom's rolling stock was still out on the western perimeters. Less than a month had passed since the final capitulation of the diehard Revivalists in their strongholds along the Cimarron breaks and in the mountains beyond. It would be at least a year, the scouts said, before the situation on Camelot's western frontier could be normalized.

From the shade of a pavilion erected for her comfort, Lindy Rae watched the placement of bales and crates, the milling of servants and porters responding to the directions of household retainers and load bosses, the orchestrated chaos of the day. Then her eyes caught a flash of familiar color and she stood, shading her eyes. Beyond the crowds at the loading docks, her personal car was approaching.

Candy-apple red paint flashed in the sunlight, and bright chrome threw dazzles across the shadows.

The car was Ronnie's latest gift to her—a completely rebuilt, fifty-five-year-old Ford Explorer, modified for LPG fuel. It had already been loaded aboard a semi when Lady Sedgewick called for it.

There were still hours of waiting before the convoy could set out for Wichita. Her maidservant had suggested a way to pass the time. It would be evening before she was needed here. Plenty of time for a leisurely drive in the countryside. Without turning, she said, "Have you packed a lunch, Mitsu? We're going for a drive."

She heard Mitsu hurrying away to make ready. Her car pulled up beside the pavilion and its driver stepped out and bowed. He wasn't the usual driver, a friend of Mitsu's, but there were occasional replacements and Lindy didn't try to keep track of them. This one was a young man with the look of a rustic, as if he spent a great deal of time outdoors. But for the ill-fitting chauffeur livery he wore, he might have been a field hand or a tenant farmer on one of the king's steads. And he looked vaguely familiar. "Your automobile, Lady Sedgewick," he said.

Slippered feet scuffed on sand and old Shallet cleared his throat for attention. When Lindy glanced around, the retainer frowned, stepped forward, and bowed slightly.

"Pardon, my lady," he said, "but I believe the king's orders are that everyone go directly home."

"You're mistaken, Shallet," Lindy Rae said. "The king ordered Camelot evacuated. We are evacuated. We are outside the gates. His Majesty did not direct where or when we are to go from here."

"But, my lady . . ."

"I'm only going for a drive," Lindy Rae snapped. "The area is well patrolled and quite secure. Stay and see to the loading. I shall return presently."

"My lady, there are loiterers on the roads," Shallet persisted. "At least take guardsmen."

"Nonsense!" She waved dismissal. "Mitsu will be with me. And the driver . . . ah, what is your name?"

"I'm called Paddy, my lady." He bowed again.

"Are you armed, Paddy?"

"Of course not, my lady. But there is a weapon in the car, and I can use it. What is your pleasure?"

"Just drive, Paddy. I want to escape this clamor for a time."

"Very well, my lady. I suggest west then. The air is free of smoke out there."

Mitsu brought bundles and containers, and they boarded the car. Its engine purred to life, and Paddy negotiated the old streets around Camelot and turned on a road that was no more than a graded sand track arrowing between fields of wheat.

"This isn't the highway," Lindy noted.

"No, my lady. This is a farm road. The highway is a clamorous route, with the convoys outbound."

They had gone several miles—out of sight of all but the highest towers of Camelot—when Paddy pulled the Explorer over and stopped. Without a word he turned and handed Lindy Rae a folded, sealed paper. She opened it, read the message there, and read it again.

"Lindy," it said, and memories tugged at her. "I have thought of you so often over the years. Do you remember the little boys we found? I have seen another. An infant. There is so much I want to tell you. Paddy and I will soon have a child of our own. I wish you could be here when it comes. There are shadows in our house." It was signed "L."

Lucy.

She looked up from the letter, into the serious, troubled eyes of the driver.

"The child is due," he said. "There is no one to help her with it."

"How far?"

"Less than an hour." he said. "I couldn't get past the gates, so I waited. A man helped me. His name was Adam. He said I would drive for you and showed me your car."

Lindy Rae looked around at her maidservant. "You had a hand in this, Mitsu?"

Mitsu lowered her eyes. "They need you, Lady," she said.

"Well, let's don't just sit here," Lindy decided. "Drive."

An hour or so southwest of Camelot, by zigzagging farm roads, lay a valley through which a little stream wandered. Along this stream was a lonely little farmstead—rich, small fields too isolated to be worked efficiently by the massive machinery and mobile crews of Arthur's great wheatlands, but adequate for the efforts of a tenant family.

Just above the stream, at a place where three distinct bed-rock peaks jutted outward like ships' prows, was a rambling barn and a little cabin, and in the cabin a woman was in labor. Lucy had known that her husband had gone for help, and somehow she had withheld the birthing until that help arrived.

There had been no time for talk, though. Lindy Rae and Mitsu had gone to work almost before they had their coats off, and now the drama of new life was in progress while Paddy watched helplessly from the open doorway.

"Shadows in our house," Lucy's message had said. Now Lindy Rae knew what she meant. Though she knew who was present—three women and one man—it seemed somehow that a multitude had gathered in and around the little cabin. A dozen times Lindy Rae looked around at the suggestion of move-ment, only to see no one there. Yet if she closed her eyes for a moment, she would swear there were a dozen people in the room.

Shadows—shadows that moved and milled about busily but were never quite there. And every few moments she heard—or almost heard—voices that were silent but distinct, voices that spoke in quick, meaningless syllables.

Mitsu also sensed the presences, and her quick, dark eyes darted this way and that as the two of them did what they could to make Lucy comfortable and encourage her labor.

"The baby," Lucy gasped between spasms of contraction. "Did you see it?"

"Almost," Lindy Rae assured her. "It is coming nicely. Another push or two . . ."

"No, it's here!" Lucy raised slightly to point, and Lindy Rae glanced around. For an instant she imagined that she *did* see a baby—an infant cradled lovingly in the arms of a very small, large-eyed person with a bald head. But it was only an instant. The image was there, then it was gone, and shadows moved.

"That's my baby!" Lucy panted. "Did you see it, Lindy?"

"Hush, now," Lindy Rae urged. "You're contracting again. Push, Lucy! Push now."

* * *

Outside, the sun hung low over the horizon of the Cimarron breaks—the same sun that now gloried the west windows of the high tower of Camelot. Its rays filled the great chamber of the steel throne and cast bright reflections into the arch-dome above. The dome was open now, a vault from which hung the TEF unit, directly above the seat of power. Beneath the throne the grid had been rolled away, exposing black depths beneath. Deep Hole lay uncovered.

The throne itself cast a long, ominous shadow across the east quadrant of the chamber, shading the wide, staring eyes of the three men who sat propped against the closed portal . . . dead, staring eyes gaping from dead, astonished faces. "Regis," Arthur Rex proclaimed, pausing to look down at the three, "Malcolm. Emmett. Chief among my nobles, you three. The Trilate Council, balance of power for the eyes of my subjects." The king stood before his council, a smug smile tugging at his cheeks below eyes that had never smiled. "You truly believed, each of you, that you held power in my domain. In that way, you served your purpose. Such a shame, isn't it, that you could not live to see what power really is?"

He might have gloated more, but a shadow moved in the great room and he turned abruptly. From the corner of his eye, just for an instant, he thought he saw a person kneeling there, at the foot of his throne. A figure like a young child—a gaunt boy of ten or so, fair-haired and robed in rags—just straightening as if from the lip of the black shaft itself. Yet when he faced the vision, it was not there. He was alone in the great chamber. There was no one there but himself and three dead men.

Movement beyond the windows caught his eye, and he squinted against the slanting sunlight. Birds! Nothing but birds, a flock of pigeons spiraling upward around the tower. Their shadows must have been what he saw.

With an angry grunt, Arthur strode across to the throne and sat upon it. At the touch of his fingers on its steel arms, covers slid away and banked controls were exposed at his fingertips.

"It is time," he said to no one but himself.

A series of taps on twin keypads, and the screens in the arches above came to life, displaying diagrams and columns of figures. He glanced up at them, satisfying himself that everything was in order.

Time manipulation, his scientists had assured him. The technology was perfected. Now that cold smile played again on Arthur's face. It wasn't time he would manipulate now but its counterpart, duration. Where one went, so went the other, and the difference between altering one and altering the other was a simple shift of calculation. Arthur had never intended to change time. His purpose was to draw from it, to fuel a never-ending cycle of duration for himself. Time was endless. Only duration was limited. But those limitations could be removed.

Immortality, he thought. Now I shall live forever.

With a satisfaction as huge and pure as unallayed ego, Arthur activated the generator—the perpetuating series of lenses that focused all the gravitational and magnetic power of a captured black hole into the focalizer suspended above him . . . and into the duplicate focalizer just beneath his seat, which he did not know was there, until the instant of activation.

In that timeless instant, captured within the point of precise balance between gravity and light, the instant of perfect stasis, a man stood before the throne—a sardonic, dark-haired man with eyes the color of destiny. "Name's Adam," the specter said without sound. "Here's forever for you, with the compliments of Edwin Limmer. He's a friend of mine."

The twin focalizers hummed in perfect synchronization, and anachronism occurred.

And many miles away, in a small valley among the Cimarron breaks, anomaly occurred as a child was born. With a final, stifled shriek of effort, Lucy pushed her infant into separate existence and into the gentle hands of Lindy Rae Koch, Lady Sedgewick.

"A boy," Lindy Rae breathed. "A perfect little boy! Here, Mitsu, take him." She thrust the child into the waiting hands of her servant and turned toward the immaculate dresser top where sterile scissors awaited the cutting of the umbilical.

"A boy," Mitsu confirmed, beaming.

All around them, shadows moved quickly, and the cabin seemed full of soundless voices. For an instant, Lindy Rae felt dizzy. She turned to where Mitsu cradled the newborn child, and Mitsu glanced up at her, waiting. The girl held no child. Her ready hands were empty.

The child was in Lindy Rae's hands, and she blinked in confusion. Then the instant of oddity was gone. She was bending over Lucy's spread legs, holding a precious infant in her hands.

"A boy," she breathed. "A perfect little boy! Here, Mitsu, take him."

Mitsu took the child, beaming. "A boy," she confirmed.

"Edwin," Lucy panted. "His name is Edwin. Like the children we found. Do you remember the Edwins, Lindy Rae?"

"I remember. So this, too, is Edwin. And his family name, Lucy? I don't know your name now, yours and Paddy's."

"It's Rummel."

Like silent echoes, the shadows in the dim corners seemed to repeat, "Rummel." But the sound was no sound, and its components turned and wound, reversing themselves as the shadows shifted. It sounded—if there had been sound—like "Limmer."

"Rummel," Lindy Rae said. "Edwin Rummel, then. God give him long life."

From Camelot's old tower, they say, on frosty mornings and in the air of still nights, one can sometimes hear a scream of outrage. It resounds again and again, never changing, never quite ceasing—the once and always scream of a truly successful man.

"Around and around and around he goes," the children chant, "and where he stops, God only knows."

Twin temporal effect focalizers, one mounted and one planted, powered by the intense gravity of a trapped black hole, did their work. The anachronism is a perpetual knot in the fabric of the universe.

One and seven-tenths seconds—1.726480030, to be more precise—is time enough for a man to realize his fate. It is all the time in the world, when it's all one has—plenty of time to grasp and savor the agony and the irony of perfect retaliation, before it ends and starts all over again.

King Arthur is immortal now. He lives forever in his personal loop, one and seven-tenths seconds at a time—the same one and seven-tenths seconds, over and over again, forever. Every when there ever was still is, still frozen there in the multidimensional fabric of time. But a closed loop is not frozen. It happens over and over again, time after time for all time, perpetual and unchanging as heaven . . . remorseless as hell.

Around and around and around he goes . . .

The Stowaway Journal

August 4, 1998
Through all my span of retrosync, the Whispers were my companions. I learned from them, by observation. In many ways their philosophies became my ethic. Time, I believe, is the destiny of man. And history is his responsibility. The universe in all of its dimensions is ours to inherit as and when we can—but as stewards of a trust, not as conquerors.

It seems to me that those who journey back in time owe a measure of respect to history. We owe it to ourselves not to obscure the footprints of those whose journey forward beat the path that we now follow back. Observe, the Whispers say, but do not meddle. If we break it, we do our best to fix it.

But not everyone is as high-minded as the Whispers I have met. I have wondered, at times, if even all Whispers are. Being human—they no less than us—we are by nature intrusive, disruptive, and messy. No temporal device—no fixed code of conduct, no body of law, no warning flags—exist that can regulate against malignant anachronism, intentionally committed.

The Whispers evidenced little concern about temporal vandalism through my years in retrosync.

But then they had not yet encountered natural timers. Their only associations had been with their own kind, and the idea of intentional mischief by time travelers was foreign to their nature. Being a "primitive," though, I *did* think about such things. And in true primitive fashion, when I envision a problem, I am inclined to do something about it.

Throughout the pre-Arthurian history that I have observed, I find repeated again and again the phenomenon of civilization taking root in uncivilized surroundings. Often the means is simple and direct: If there are outlaws, get yourself a hired gun. A peacekeeper, a bouncer, a town marshal, an enforcer . . . a *constable*.

I have meddled with history more than once. It was at my suggestion that Lucas and Maude Hawthorn went into the time-travel tours business with Anywhen, Inc., which is rapidly becoming an avocation for them. At this point they have a corporate charter, business cards and letterheads, a catalog of more or less tested and debugged itineraries of famous events that they call their "Great Time" tours, and a computerized logistic program. They are discreetly but actively soliciting clients.

Teal Fordeen is a little nervous about all this, but I am convinced that Anywhen, Inc., would have happened whether we had been involved or not. With T1 transference now a reality in this era— thanks to the WHIS project—a time-travel agency is a travel agency whose time has arrived. I don't expect it will do much harm.

Being a primitive, though, I am less optimistic about human nature than the Whispers are. Those who have the inherent ability to manipulate dimensions are rare and remarkable people. But they are, first and always, *people*.

I have, therefore, taken action to provide a constable, and I am satisfied with the result. I saw him at work before I even began the process that may have secured his career. One of the common paradoxes of time manipulation is the "empty loop," or overloop—the future that affects the past that determines that same future.

The Limmer Trust and the Limmer Foundation were built on futures foreseen in the past. It seems only right that these institutions now and then return the favor.

I have made an overloop. Time will tell if I was right.

EPILOGUE

University of Kansas

Lawrence, Kansas, September 1964

Philo Embry, Ph.D., glanced up from his littered desk as firm knuckles rapped at his portal. The door opened and a young man looked in. "You sent for me, Dr. Embry?"

"I'd hardly call it that," Embry said with a frown, "since I had no better means of contacting you than to spread the word among my graduate students. But yes, Mr. Wills, I did request your presence in my office. So please do come in."

The young man who entered might have been a KU student, by age and demeanor, maybe an athlete by his physical appearance, and probably a GDI by his motley attire, but he was none of these things. To Embry he was a face in a lecture room, a name on a monitor list. A tall, dark-haired, quiet young man of about twenty, he was one of those dozens who sat in on a lecture now and then but never as part of the enrolled class.

"You're not a student here, are you, Mr. Wills?" Embry asked, waving absently toward the single chair facing his desk.

"No, sir, I'm not," the youth said. "I've monitored some of your lectures, though."

"Yes, I know." Embry put on his glasses, leaned forward, and directed a dissector's gaze at his visitor. "Do you have any idea why I sent for you?"

"No, sir, I don't."

"Mr. Wills, are you familiar with an organization called the Limmer Foundation?"

"Sure. It started with soybean futures. Edwin Limmer lived

a few blocks from where I grew up for a while." The young man's expression was careless, innocent, but abruptly Embry noticed his eyes. Direct, inquisitive eyes . . . wise eyes, Embry thought. Eyes that looked beyond the limits. "What's this all about, Dr. Embry?"

Embry sat back. "I've been contacted by the Limmer Foundation," he said. "I've been offered a retainer to teach you."

"Teach me what? Archaeology?"

"Whatever you desire to learn that I can assist with," Embry said. "With particular emphasis in certain fields, one being the study of history. It seems you have been selected as a beneficiary of the foundation, Mr. Wills. Somebody wants you to have a mentor . . . or at least a tutor. You know nothing about this?"

Wills shrugged. "Nothing at all. It's the first I've heard."

"Then you must have friends in high places," Embry said, nodding. "Or possibly some special skills. Do you have special skills, Mr. Wills?"

In the youth's hesitation, Embry had his answer. "You do, then. No, don't worry. I'm not asking what they are. Can you think of any reason why I should decline this retainer, Mr. Wills?"

"I guess not," the youth said. "Special emphasis on history? What's the rest of it?"

"That's what's odd." Embry leaned forward again, peering. "Ethics, they said. Basic, fundamental ethics. Not morality, mind you. Not etiquette, civility, legality, or any of those other behavioral facsimiles. I am to teach you about history. And I am to instruct you, literally, in the difference between right and wrong."

Wills looked as puzzled as Embry was, but he shrugged and nodded. "Okay," he agreed. "I guess you're my mentor. When do we start?"

"We already have," Embry said. "There are some things I want you to read. I'll give you a list. Also, I was asked to give this to you when I located you." He handed a sealed manila envelope across to Wills.

The youth opened it, puzzled. Inside was an old, time-worn

wallet, scuffed and frayed, split at the seams from years of use. It was empty, except for a pair of old, faded pictures—tinted halftone prints. They were studio portraits of Deanna Durbin and Buster Crabbe.

Embry stood, extended a hand, and said, "I have a class to assemble, Mr. Wills. I suggest we meet here tomorrow at nine to investigate what we have agreed to."

The young man shook his hand and started for the door, and Embry asked, "By the way, Mr. Wills, what *is* your first name?"

"Adam," the young man answered. "I'm Adam. See you in the morning, then."

Embry assured himself on the way to his first class that, with time, he would learn more about this puzzle. Right now he had other things to think about.

In room E-223 Philo Embry, professor of humanities, adjusted his glasses on the bridge of his nose and glanced at the clock above the classroom door. He scanned again the pencil-smudged chart before him, memorizing names and seat numbers. He removed his glasses and looked at the disorderly rank of young faces before him.

There were twenty-three of them. Young studs in rut and full-bloomed little disasters in glitter-eyed search of picket fences. Of these twenty-three, God willing, half a dozen would one day be graduate somethings.

Nowhere in the room did he see eyes that held the purpose, the intensity, the "knowing" of those he had just seen in Adam Wills. But then, he did not expect to.

Again he surveyed his flock, connecting names and faces. "Mr. Grimes?" he said. Near the back, a shaggy head turned to face him. "Mr. Grimes, there is a compelling reason why that seat you are occupying faces in this direction. The reason is that you are a student and I am a teacher. The placement of seats in a classroom is intended to focus your attention upon me. Please go along with us on this."

There were a few stifled chuckles and the scuffing of a chair being turned. Embry lowered his gaze to the front row. A miniskirt seated, he had long since determined, is no skirt at all.

"Miss . . . ah, Purcell, is it? Miss Purcell, would you please cross your legs?"

The little dumpling blushed and did as she was told. Embry sighed and turned to point a casual finger at the blackboard behind him. Someone had tucked a little envelope into the frame at its corner, but for the moment he ignored it. "Now that the gates of hell are closed," he said, "we can proceed. This is Humanities 101, according to your catalog of courses. What we will cover here are the principles of archaeology, the discipline by which we sometimes—rarely, but sometimes—unravel the mysteries of antiquity."

Having captured as much of their attention as he was going to get, Embry turned on his overhead projector and launched into his prepared text. "For example, the Pyramids at Giza." He placed a transparency, and the ancient pyramids appeared on the screen beside the blackboard. "These structures and others like them, erected at least three thousand years ago— apparently as funerary edifices—remain a mystery to this day. We know everything about the pyramids of Egypt except how they were built, *why* were they built, and exactly what is inside them."

He changed slides. "This is an aerial photograph of a 'snake' mound in Illinois, obviously a man-made construct dating from antiquity. Among the mysteries of such sites is: Why would ancient, primitive people have created emblems so large that their actual shape can be seen only from airplanes?"

His next slide change was interrupted by a rude sound from the back of the room. Embry looked up. "Mr. Grimes, may I suggest you alter your breakfast menu in the future? Thank you." He placed the next slide.

"These," he said, "are stone carvings found in the Yucatan region of Mexico. Many of them obviously are representations of either animals or gods or both, but the stylized nature of the depiction leaves much to the imagination. This, for example, might conceivably be a hummingbird or a highly stylized representation of some phenomenon such as a comet. Yet in the eye of the artist, it might have been the god Quetzalcoatl in earthly form.

"Here we have what might be a jaguar. Then again, its form could conceivably be that of a cubical serpent. And this, a trinity device, appears to be of two men—the radiants surrounding them indicate they were considered gods of some sort—standing beside a fanciful creature with extended fangs and long, upright ears—"

He paused at a mutter from the back of the room. "Yes. Mr. Grimes?"

"I said," the student repeated, "it looks like a forklift."

Embry glanced around at the screen. "Yes, it does, doesn't it! But, then, that is most unlikely. What would the pre-Aztecan civilization of Chichén Itzá—a civilization that did not even use wheels—know of forklifts?"

It was some time later when Philo Embry returned to the envelope left on his blackboard. It contained two business cards and a check from the Limmer Foundation. Five thousand dollars!

The foundation card stapled to the check had no name on it, only a brief handwritten note: "Initial retainer, A. Wills open acct.: per E. Limmer."

The second business card, unattached, had a logo like two parentheses connected by an X and the business name, ANY-WHEN, INC. There were two number codes, one labeled "phone" and one "fax." Each code had ten digits, with hyphens after the third and sixth. In tiny print at the bottom were the words "established 1998" and in the center of the card was a slogan.

"Have a nice time," it said.

Chronology

1996	Theory of bichronism proposed
1997	Invention of inertial energy lamp
1998	First booster, Waystop I; Anywhen, Inc.; First Whisper encounters with natural "timers"
2000	Tolafsson theory of variable constants—light-gravity relativity proposed
2002	Paper Revolts and the Trust Collapse
2003	Deep Hole incident; Tempus Rampant; major tectonic shifts; breakdown of orbital "comweb" systems due to wave redundancies
2003–4	Verification of Asian Abyss; global power realignments; PACT created; in America, border mandates, regional wars
2006	Latin Nations Convergence
2007	The Divestitures
2009	Fundamentalist mobilization, dissolution of interior states
2010–13	First substantial evidence of relationship between Tunguska (1910) and Deep Hole (2003); gravitic singularity theories gain acceptance
2012	Federated Free Zones
2029	Arthur's takeover of ITR
2037–38	Camelot; campaigns against Revivalists; temporal effect focalizer (TEF) perfected
2040	The Cimarron Siege; George Wilson retrieved
2044	Consolidation of power by Arthur Rex
2046	First recalled Limmer reentry
2050	Arthur's Anachronism; birth of Edwin Limmer in retrosync (reverse T2)
2410	Trans-polar Rift
2450–2600	Era of origin of Pacificans
2712	Opum suggests Timel conduit, upstream penetration of Time2
2744	Universal Experience Bank of Pacifica sponsors WHIS; Time1 (T1) conduit to the past begun
2910	Whisper expeditions encounter Arthurian Anachronism
2999	The "Lost Loop"

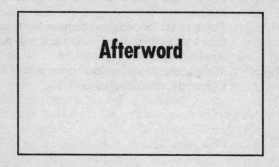

Afterword

Selected excerpts from *The Quest for When*, an overview of historical roots of bichronic time travel, compiled by Teal Fordeen (elscan 0-991-06ht. sm 103.11, trilev archives):

THE BICHRONIST VIEW

Ikebata's Thesis, popularly known as the Theory of Bichronism or Double Time, originated as a footnote in the controversial *Alternate Views on Where and When* authored by Hideo Ikebata (1969–2042). A proponent of the Actualist school of physics, Ikebata suggested that time be viewed as two separate phenomena:

- Time1 or T1 (experienced duration)
- Time2 or T2 (elapsed sequential duration or "real" time)

Although his basic premise was challenged, Ikebata did demonstrate mathematically in 1996 that Time1 is a product of wave phenomena, while Time2 is a matrix continuum.

THE TOLAFSSON EFFECT

In a leap of temporal theory four years after publication by Ikebata, another Actualist, Nicholas Tolafsson (1951–2018), a pioneer in the field of particulate gravity, proposed—based on Ikebata's findings—that an alternate view be taken toward Einsteinian limitations. Tolafsson argued that the continuum of elapsed time is altered by relative velocity rather than being a constant within which physical dimensions change.

Objects in motion, Tolafsson suggested, compress the time through which they pass. His initial theory, he quipped on numerous occasions, gave new meaning to the conundrum "Time flies when you're having fun."

In effect, Tolafsson proposed that an object moving at high speed has the same physical dimensions as when it is at rest. Einstein's oversight, according to Tolafsson, was in assuming that the speed of light is a constant and therefore a reliable anchor for the calibration of velocity. Tolafsson presented evidence that the particulate characteristics of photons are in fact evidences of gravitational origin and that the speed of light, like all wave phenomena, is variable and relative. The bullet from the gun, he argued, only *seems* shorter in flight because it goes faster than it actually does.

Some scholars contended that Tolafsson's view of duplicate continuums—real and perceived—bordered on being whimsical and was accepted by his peers for no better reason than that it was less confusing than the examples he offered. But the fact remains that Nicholas Tolafsson (who sometimes dubbed himself "The Nick of Time") is considered the father of temporal physics. His theories fostered extensive research into the effects of gravity and magnetism within a compressed continuum.

The discovery that gravity and light are two ends of the same spectrum resulted from research into Tolafsson's suggestions regarding the nature of electromagnetism.

A practical outgrowth of these researches was the development of selective gravitation, the principle behind all temporal generators, including the T-effect focalizer.

It is ironic that Tolafsson himself, in his later years, belittled all such force-generated temporal inducement as artificial. Though he offered no evidence to support his contention, he insisted that the human mind itself is all the hardware required for temporal displacement. His only recorded reason for this conclusion was the statement "Adam told me."

THE T-EFFECT FOCALIZER

Though clouded by legend, it is generally agreed that the temporal effect focalizer was perfected by George Wilson, a specialist in temporal displacement, between 2035 and 2039. Wilson, one of the technicians recruited by the Institute for Temporal Research (ITR), was a leader in the field of particulate gravity generation. He resigned from ITR in 2039 to join the Revivalist movement and was thought to have died in the Cimarron Siege in 2040. His body was never recovered, but his ITR records and an account of his discovery were later published by a protégée, Mariel Royce Alexander.

The first practical application of the T-effect focalizer probably was by Arthur Rex, in the year 2050. Though obscured by subsequent events, the legends of "King Arthur" and his infamous attempt to live forever are consistent enough to be accepted as historical fact.

An example of such legend is this excerpt from *Arthur Rex*, spool 19:

> Then did Arthur send them out from Camelot, all except the three who must bear witness. And when all were gone the king, himself and alone, entered the chamber and sat upon his throne of 440-C steel with the panels at his fingertips. All control he gathered there to himself so that none might be tempted to intercede.
>
> And when he was ready, he hit the switch.

THE BIRTH OF PRACTICAL TIME TRAVEL

Following the Arthur Rex incident in 2050, experiments in retrosynchronization languished through the Ages of Chaos and Rediscovery until bioimpulse discoveries in the twenty-eighth century shed new light on the old theories. It was Herr Magnus Opum who first suggested the possibility of biotic transfer in T2, in a treatise dated in the year A.D. 2712. Prior to that, partially because of the disappearance of King Arthur, T2 had been viewed more as a theoretical conduit than as an actual place.

Opum went so far as to claim that he had been visited by someone from another time, though no clear record remains of what, if anything, he might have learned from the mysterious "Adam," beyond the revelation that the legendary Nicholas Tolafsson was plagued by recurrent migraines.

A significant implication of Opum's theories was that T1— or experienced duration—might be regarded not simply as a sensory delusion but as a directional device and possibly even a vehicle with which T2 could be explored.

Early experiments, using selective gravity as a motive source, showed the past to be a better field for study and exploration than the future. Past events in a present-based continuum are fact, while future events are only potential and, as such, shift constantly.

"If they had known then what we know now," Opum explained, "they could have traveled forward. But what we know now is only what they knew then . . . that is, where we are so far. Thus the future we could have opened for them is our past, and we can only wait for revelation of the future that is ours by those who come after."

Despite his insistence on such limitations, though, Opum maintained a fascination with Nicholas Tolafsson's mysterious "Adam," whom he claimed to have met, as well. Throughout his career, Opum maintained that Tolafsson's legendary mentor was a real person and had not been limited by dimensionality. Adam, he suggested, was a singularity and an exception to the accepted laws of dimensional limitation. Moreover, Opum argued that Adam still existed. Any true time traveler, he reasoned, is still where he always was—anywhen.

His numerous attempts to locate "Adam," though, proved fruitless.

Herr Magnus Opum died by his own hand in 2736, a victim of frustration. In his final journal he wrote: "Each day I see the future and each day it isn't here." Still, his works shed new light on several old subjects. Within a few years it was proven that the T2 dimension is itself dimensional, though the question of sideways movement remained elusive.

WHIS

In the year 2744 a secular group associated with the Universal Experience Bank organized the World History Investigative Society, which was given full support by Sundome Central, including access to the MGMUA archives and a grant from Angeleana's unconsigned resources. The goal of WHIS was an expedition to the beginning of time.

Technologies of the Arthurian Age were replicated, with modifications to address bioduplication in the retrosynchronic state. The first expedition was delayed until 2910 by discovery of a violent anachronism in the 2050 range, apparently caused by Arthur Rex. Subsequent research revealed that the anachronism *was* Arthur Rex.

With the perfection of means to bypass the "time storm," the first of many generations of Whispers entered retrosync in the equinox of 2910.

Those early expeditions became a wholesale migration following the discovery of so-called bridges and gates in the earliest quadrants of the continuum, the "time when time began." To accommodate their growing numbers, the Whispers undertook the placement of booster stations at intervals along retrosync in those ranges farther back than Arthur. These were necessary to regain the momentum lost in negotiating past the Arthurian Anachronism.

Ironically, the ideal sites for base waystops proved to be those sites impacted by the temporal waves created by the anachronism itself. The likelihood of probability variation at each such locus was markedly lower than normal because the improbable had already occurred there. As pointed out by Ayem Fyve, who charted the booster system, the preferred acceleration sites were those impact points where King Arthur bounced.

Turn the page for a sneak preview of

FACES OF INFINITY

**Book Two
of
The Gates of Time**

He stood at the very lip of the maintenance sconce, seven feet beyond the observation deck railing and more than three hundred feet above the tiny strip of halogen-lighted pavement that was a city street at night.

Defeated, destitute, and sick at heart, he was beyond desperation. He had reached the end of his rope. A man bereft of hope, he had come here to make an end of humiliation, an end of the disappointments of a world where only cynicism could thrive.

Cold, erratic wind shoved at him, pushing him this way and that. It pasted his stained, torn tuxedo pants around his trembling legs and toyed with his thinning gray hair. He had lost his glasses, but he didn't need them. He knew where he was going, and he wouldn't be reading again. Nothingness . . . perpetual sleep . . . was a simple step ahead. Not even a step. All he had to do was lean into the wind.

They said I'd be a smash on Wall Street, he thought with bitter irony. My formulas. My theories. My wonderful little discovery . . . God! What an innocent I've been! Let my guard down. Hell, I never even had it up. Everybody's looking for a new idea, they said. Invention is the magic wand that makes it rain money. Sure, it rains money! But only for the swindlers and the cheats. Invention? Innovation? That isn't what business is about nowadays. It's about packaging and marketing and delayed option clauses. Used to be about building a better mousetrap . . . didn't it? Now it's the bottom line and nothing else. Sharks in a feeding frenzy, scavengers feasting on the scraps.

Who the hell are these people? he asked himself, as astonished as when he had first asked it. I don't know these creatures. If this is their world, then *where is my world*?

Management will love this, they said. A lamp that lights itself! Dynamism from gravity! How wonderful! Perpetual energy. A breakthrough. The classic better mousetrap! Commerce will beat a path to your door. Just wait till management sees this!

What management? There's nobody out there but accountants and lawyers and beady-eyed MBAs. There aren't any *managers* anymore! Just the terrible triad. Don't buy it, just take it . . . Just sell it, don't make it . . . If it isn't broke, break it!

They beat a path, all right, he thought. But it wasn't commerce at the door. It was slicksters and thieves. Sharks.

In the uncaring wind, his face contorted with the pain of lost ideals. Tears of frustration and defeat glistened in his eyes. There was nothing left. They had it all now. Well, not quite all. They had left him his IRS audits . . . and his mounting debts.

Slowly he rocked back and forth, feeling the shift of his own inertia each time he teetered toward the distant street below. But he didn't look down now, at the almost-deserted depths. Instead he raised his anguished eyes heavenward, where low clouds hung dull and somber, pierced by the taller buildings beneath them.

Somewhere below, within secure walls, deals had been closed . . . like doors slammed in his face. Innocent and enthusiastic, he had come to the party, only to find his life's work already dissected and parceled out, with no share left for him.

"Sorry, David," they had said through their plastic smiles. "But that's business."

"This is what it comes to, Irene," he muttered, his voice thin against the cold, playful wind. "A whole life's work, a life spent believing that if you do the right thing, everything will be all right. At least you don't have to be here to see this, now.

"I'll be a smash on Wall Street, they said. I'll bet not one of those bean-counters would know how to calculate the exact impact down there. But then, why should they care about the force generated by 150 pounds of spun-off profit potential falling 323 feet? Inertia conversion doesn't matter to anybody. Hopes and dreams and ideas don't matter. Only money matters."

Direct conversion of gravity to photoelectric energy—a simple reversal of the direction of kinetic flow. This was his life's work. But did they want to see its results? No, only to control the investment potential it would generate. Three hundred and twenty-three feet of free fall, and he wouldn't even light up when he hit.

"Good night, Irene," he breathed.

He closed his eyes tightly and rocked forward, giving himself to the wind. Just for a moment, he told himself bleakly, he could lose himself again in pretense. This time he would pretend he was flying.

He leaned, felt his weight shift to his toes at the edge of the glass-and-steel precipice, and his dinner jacket snugged sharply around his shoulders.

"Very messy," a high, reedy voice behind him said. He almost lost his footing, swiveling around to look.

The person holding his coattail was tiny—not much more than four feet tall. She—somehow he knew it was a she, though her head was as hairless as a fresh, pink egg—had both feet braced against the little wall of the sconce and was gripping his coat with both hands. The little garment that covered her from neck to feet, like a pilot's jumpsuit, revealed no particular contours. But it was her eyes that held his attention. They were the biggest, darkest eyes he had ever seen.

"You might want to reconsider this," she urged, struggling to hold him against his own inertia. "You'll almost certainly change your mind on the way down, and just imagine how you'll feel. At that point it will be too late."

"It's already too late," he shouted, angry at the interruption. "It's all over! Everything! Let go!"

"I can't," she piped. "My hands are cramped. I'm stuck. Do you want to kill me, too?"

A gust of wind staggered him and he reeled, his arms wind-milling for balance. "Will you turn me loose?" he demanded.

"I'd like to," she assured him. "Just give me a minute. You might not mind splattering yourself all over that paving down there, but I'd just as soon not. Have you ever actually seen what surface impact does to a human body? It's disgusting!"

"It's your own fault! You grabbed me!" He wrenched at his lapels, trying to free himself of the restraining jacket, and felt her tug falter.

"My feet are slipping!" she shrilled. "Help me!"

The wind and the height caressed him, inviting him to peaceful oblivion. But if he went, she would go, too. With a thin cry of frustration he threw himself back, and down. His right knee collided painfully with a scaffold anchor, his hand skidded on wet metal, and his face scraped against rough, tar-bedded pea gravel. He lay stunned for a moment, then groaned as protesting pain coursed down him—first his bleeding face, then the deeper, throbbing traumas in his wrist and his knee.

Beneath his bulk, something small squirmed and protested, then pulled itself free. Little feet scuffed on the pea gravel, and a little face not quite like most faces leaned close to study him.

"You're a mess," she decided. "But you'll live."

"Get away from me!" he whimpered, abruptly aware of his pathetic position. He lay bruised and bleeding on a cold, damp rooftop, with all the grim determination of moments before—the agonizing resolve to just once, just one last time, take his fate into his own hands and do something right—fading away. He had been ready. Now he was uncertain.

"I can't even jump off a stupid building!" he moaned. "Simple thing like that, and I can't get it done!"

"You're a pretty sorry specimen, all right," the little person agreed. "I think you should reconsider your whole life, if you're that unhappy with it."

"That's what I've been doing!" he grated. "What right did you have to interfere?"

"None, I suppose." She shrugged. "But after traveling far-ther than you can imagine just to see you, then chasing you all the way up here, I didn't want to lose you before I at least give you my card."

"Your . . . your card?"

"Yes." She produced a little white business card from somewhere and handed it to him. Unbelieving, he squinted at it in the light of a rooftop sign, and she held out a pair of glasses to him—his own glasses.

"You dropped these in the elevator," she said.

With his glasses in place, he peered at her. "Who . . . who or *what* are you?"

"I'm just a Whisper," she said casually. "But you don't know about Whispers, of course. We haven't happened yet. Just read the card."

Beneath an odd little logo—like two parentheses joined by an elongated X—were the words:

ANYWHEN, INC.
—Excursions, Tours, Sightseeing—
Adventures in Extratemporization
KT-Pi, rep.
—HAVE A NICE TIME—

Sitting on the cold, damp roof, thirty floors above city streets, blood dripping from his cheeks, his violated knee aching, his bruises throbbing fiercely, he stared at the innocuous little card.

"What?" he said finally.

"It's another option." The strange little person beside him gave another shrug. "You might want to look into it. Have you ever been to Kansas?"

DEL REY® ONLINE!

The Del Rey Internet Newsletter...
A monthly electronic publication, posted on the Internet, GEnie, CompuServe, BIX, various BBSs, and the Panix gopher (gopher.panix.com). It features hype-free descriptions of books that are new in the stores, a list of our upcoming books, special announcements, a signing/reading/convention-attendance schedule for Del Rey authors, "In Depth" essays in which professionals in the field (authors, artists, designers, sales people, etc.) talk about their jobs in science fiction, a question-and-answer section, behind-the-scenes looks at sf publishing, and more!

Internet information source!
A lot of Del Rey material is available to the Internet on our Web site and on a gopher server: all back issues and the current issue of the Del Rey Internet Newsletter, sample chapters of upcoming or current books (readable or downloadable for free), submission requirements, mail-order information, and much more. We will be adding more items of all sorts (mostly new DRINs and sample chapters) regularly. The Web site is http://www.randomhouse.com/delrey/ and the address of the gopher is gopher.panix.com

Why?
We at Del Rey realize that the networks are the medium of the future. That's where you'll find us promoting our books, socializing with others in the sf field, and—most importantly—making contact and sharing information with sf readers.

Online editorial presence:
Many of the Del Rey editors are online, on the Internet, GEnie, CompuServe, America Online, and Delphi. There is a Del Rey topic on GEnie and a Del Rey folder on America Online.

The official e-mail address
for Del Rey Books is delrey@randomhouse.com (though it sometimes takes us a while to answer).